NIGHTTIME
SURPRISE

Thad Morgan was only five feet away from his quarry when the man heard him and suddenly turned in the saddle. Thad leaped for his left leg, jerked it from the stirrup, and pulled hard at the man's body. Off balance, and with a muffled cry, the man tipped from the saddle and thumped heavily to the ground, where he attempted to scramble to his feet.

"Now!" Thad said in a voice that brooked no denial. "Call off your men, or I'll kill you!"

THE CONDOR

Jordan Allen

TOWER BOOKS NEW YORK CITY

A BELMONT TOWER BOOK

Published by

Tower Publications, Inc.
Two Park Avenue
New York, N.Y. 10016

Copyright © 1980 by Jordan Allen

1

Panama City, 1849.

A hot, steamy, breathless night. Streets muddy from the last tropical shower crowded with hurrying people. More vessels in the harbor than it had ever seen before, the nearby shore dotted with clamoring knots of shouting, would-be passengers, bidding for berths to California, flickering their torchlight on anxious, sweaty faces. Over all, a hum of murmuring humanity, with the occasional plinking of a guitar as the natives undisturbed by the flurry, try without success to maintain their indolent ways.

Inside the earth-floored hut it was stifling, but it was shelter, a makeshift inn that had housed 40 people the previous night. Now 37 of them were down on the beach, trying to book passage on crowded vessels, and only three were left.

A candle guttered on the floor. The woman held the baby and rocked it in her arms. The child moaned and uttered faint, hoarse cries.

"She's dying, Thad," the woman said. "She's dying. Can't we do anything?"

The man, tall, square-shouldered in a light-colored knee-length coat, rose desperately and paced the floor. "The only doctor I can think of is that red-nosed old character on the boat. What was his name? Hester? And he disappeared right after we landed from the canoes.

5

The city offices are closed, and I can't make any of these people understand what I want."

The woman sobbed. "She's dying! I don't want her to die."

He did not finish the sentence, but ran out of the door of the hut. The hut's owner, a dark-skinned Panamanian in ragged white ducks, slumped on a log outside the hut and grinned foolishly up at Thad as he emerged. He had made his hut into an inn to meet the rush of business, and the sudden wealth he had accumulated had enabled him to remain drunk on palm wine 23 hours out of 24.

Thad shook him by the shoulder. "Doctor!" he demanded. "Where is a doctor? Doctor! Medico!"

The man continued to grin, exposing broken teeth. "*No hay*," he mumbled. "*No hay medico*."

Angrily, Thad strode away from him and plunged into the muddy street. There were people hurrying along it, even at this late hour. The rush to California had filled the town with hopeful argonauts. Most of them were heading toward the beach, and all of them were anxious. When word of a new vessel's arrival came, there was an immediate rush to book passage, though there were not nearly enough shops to accommodate the throngs who had crossed the isthmus from Chagres and now wanted, above all else, to get to California before the gold was gone.

Thad Morgan splashed down a muddy alley and emerged on the shore, where a ramshackle jetty probed into the dark waters of the bay. At its end, the silhouette of the masts and spars of a sailing vessel stood out against the starlit sky. Shouting people clustered around the shore end of the jetty, calling out bids for passage. "Three hundred!" "Four hundred fifty for two!" Some waved paper money clutched in sweaty fists.

Morgan elbowed his way through the crowd, peering right and left into shadowy faces. He pushed through to the forefront, then elbowed his way back again, still searching. Men cursed him impatiently, then resumed their struggle to reach the passenger agent who stood on the jetty, harassed and troubled, his voice drowned out by the shouting bidders.

Someone clutched him by the elbow. "Thad! What's your hurry? All the berths are booked on this one."

Morgan looked around. The man was tall, expensively dressed in black, seemingly unaffected by the heat. His eyebrows were peaked like Satan's, and there was a constant half-smile on his handsome mouth, as if he found the world both amusing and contemptible.

"I'm looking for a doctor, Clay. The baby's terribly sick, and Jo is frantic. I wouldn't know where to look for a native doctor, and I wouldn't trust one if I could find him. I was looking for Hester, that drunk we met on the boat. He said he was a doctor."

Clay Moreau took Thad's arm and pushed him forward. "I just saw him! He's down front. Come on."

They wrestled their way through the crowd, and Clay gave a shout that could be heard over the crowd's noise. "Hester! Hester! Over here!"

Morgan saw him, thick-set, round-shouldered man in a wrinkled linen coat and a broad-brimmed white Panama. He reached his side. "Hester! You're a doctor, aren't you?"

The man turned a raddled, puffy, red-nosed face toward Thad, "Yes, sir. Certainly I'm a doctor! Degree from Harvard. What's wrong, sir?"

"Our baby's sick! Can you come right away?"

Hester's eyes narrowed. "I just made a bid for passage, and I think I've got a chance on this packet. I can't leave here now."

Thad was desperate. "I think she's dying, Doctor."

The crowd roared and jostled them. The passenger agent shouted, "No more bids! Berths are gone! Ticket sale is closed!"

Hester grunted. "Now he'll let those of us whose bids he took come up and bid against each other so he can fill his own pockets. I've got to get on this boat, Morgan. And I've got a chance here. I can't give it up!"

Morgan clutched him by his flabby arms. "Doctor!

7

You're the only one who can help! You've *got* to come!'' Hester pulled back and looked toward the wharf. ''You took an oath when you got your degree, didn't you?'' Thad was desperate, and the desperation sounded in his voice.

Hester grimaced. ''How far is it?''

''Only a few hundred yards, the third street up. Doctor, we'll be eternally grateful.''

But Hester refused to budge. He turned to Morgan, and his eyes narrowed. ''I'm giving up a chance on this packet, and there may not be another one for weeks. I'll come, but it'll have to be worth my while.''

''What do you mean?'' Thad's heart sank to his boot-soles.

''A thousand dollars. Cash on the barrelhead. Pay now, or I don't go!''

Thad stood there, frozen. Every instinct urged him to pull back his fist and plunge it into that swollen, beady-eyed face, netted with red veins. But the vision of Jo and the baby loomed.

He swallowed hard. ''Come on!'' he said. ''Be reasonable! I won't have enough left to get me and my family to California.''

''Maybe you're keeping me from getting there, too.'' Hester shook his head. ''It's a thousand, and we're wasting time. That supercargo is taking bids, and I want to be there if you can't meet my fee.'' He pulled his arm away and turned to go.

''All right!'' Thad snapped. ''I didn't know there were doctors like you! Come on over here. I'm not going to pull off my money belt in this crowd. I'll be robbed, and so will you.''

They stepped out of the throng to a shadowy spot near some palmettos. Clay Moreau, an interested spectator, followed them. Hastily, Thad opened his vest and pulled coins—gold pieces, fifties—from the thick belt he wore next his hide. ''Don't count it now!'' Thad warned. ''If it's short, I'll make up the difference. Come on! We haven't a moment to lose!''

He grabbed the doctor by the elbow and half ran up

8

the mucky alley toward the hut where Jo was waiting.

The next few moments were burned into Morgan's mind, and the scence persisted, in every tragic detail, for the rest of his life.

The little, sweaty, steamy hut, crowded with five people—Clay Moreau was still with them—the candle dripping a puddle of yellow wax on the floor, Jo cradling the little girl in her arms, gazing fearfully up at the doctor.

Hester, in his rumpled whites, grunted as he bent over the child. He felt her pulse, folded back an eyelid, then rose, puffing.

"It's too late," he said cruelly. "The kid's dead."

Jo Morgan uttered a low moan and broke into sobs. Thad stood there, sick and dazed, but he jerked himself back to reality as he suddenly saw that Hester had left the hut.

He ran angrily into the street and saw the doctor's fat back rapidly disappearing into the gloom in the direction of the harbor. He caught up with him, grabbed his shoulder, and swung the man around.

"You're not going to take a thousand for *that*, are you? You didn't do anything!"

"I certainly am, sir. You've probably made me miss this packet!"

Thad held on to the man's shoulder as thoughts raced through his mind. There was no one near. He could force this despicable old thief to give him back his money. But every urging of his past life kept him from it. He had made a deal, as unfair as it might be. It was a deal. He would have to keep it or not live with himself.

Clay Moreau came up and decided it for him. He grinned. "Why don't you kill the old bastard?" he asked.

Thad let go of Hester's shoulder, and the man turned and ran heavily down the slushy alley, panting with panic.

Suddenly, Morgan realized that these were the first

words Clay Moreau had uttered since they had left the beach.

That night, with the distraught Jo in the steamy hut, was filled with grief, desperation, and recimination. After she had exhausted her paroxysm of grief, Jo blurted out many things. "You shouldn't have brought us! She didn't have a chance! You risked everything, even your own baby's life, to run to a place you've only heard about." She buried her face in her hands. When she looked up, Thad saw a glint of hate in the beautiful dark eyes that had so attracted him. "I should have known better than to follow you! I should have known!"

He did his best to comfort her, but she turned away and stopped talking to him.

At dawn, Morgan and Jo, with Clay Moreau, went into the jungle with the pitiful little figure wrapped in a white blanket, and Thad Morgan buried his daughter. He put up a cross and carefully carved the baby's name "Priscilla Morgan, 1849," even though he knew the jungle rot and the insects would destroy it within weeks, leaving his daughter to lie in an unmarked grave.

It was Clay who comforted Jo, his arm around her shoulders, as they walked back to town. She had said no word to Thad since midnight.

Thad talked to Clay about it in the morning. "She's turned against me," he said. "I suppose it was wrong to bring them, but I didn't want to come alone, and the diggings won't wait. Another year and it would have been too late."

Clay smiled comfortingly. "Don't worry," he advised. She's upset. It's natural. She'll come to accept it."

"I don't know," Thad frowned. "I don't know. I've never heard that hardness in her voice. She blames me so. I think she hates me."

Clay put a friendly hand on his shoulder. He did not seem to be worried.

As for Thad, the leaden feeling in his stomach grew more and more oppressive. Jo had always been a trifle cantankerous. She flared easily and had occasional tantrums, but never before had he doubted her love. As doubt grew and the sick feeling inside him twisted his spirit, Thad realized for the first time how much Jo meant to him, how barren life would be without her, and how fearful he was of losing her.

His thoughts were interrupted by the sound of a man running down the street, his boots splashing in the mud.

"What's up?" Clay shouted as he passed.

The man turned a bearded face over his shoulder. "New packet's in. I hear they got passage to Frisco!"

"Come on!" Clay grabbed Thad's arm, and the two ran to the harbor.

The man was right. A sidewheel packet with auxiliary sailing rig was at that moment dropping anchor, and already the throng was gathering on the beach.

"I've *got* to get on this one!" Thad exclaimed. "I've got to get Jo out of here!"

"You go that way, and I'll go this!" Clay ordered. "Whichever one of us gets to that supercargo first, let's book for all three."

Thad pushed and shoved, winding up at the end of a short line. He saw Clay waving from the other side of the crowd, father back.

The passenger agent had set up his office with a table and chair on the beach. He was narrow-faced, long-nosed, and officious.

"Passage is five hundred on way," he told the man in front of Thad. "No discounts." Thad's heart dropped, and the man groaned.

"I haven't got it," said the man. "Can I pay half now and half when I get to Frisco?"

"Cash down now. If you haven't got it, step out of line."

Morgan felt desperate. After the $1,000 he had paid Hester, he had less than $700 in gold left, not enough to pay for both him and Jo. He frantically waved at Clay, who was making his way toward him.

He was at the little table. The passenger agent looked up at him from under his peaked cap, his mouth pursed and his eyes hostile. Two burly seamen stood nearby, guarding the pile of gold coins and paper notes rapidly accumulating.

"Five hundred one way. How many?" the man demanded.

"Three," said Thad. He had no idea how he would pay for them, but he was bound not to be forced out of line and back into that milling mob.

The man carefully licked his thumb and peeled off a long and elaborately lithographed ticket that looked as if it had the entire corporation charter of the Panama Line printed on it. He licked his thumb again and peeled off a second; then, after the thumb-licking ceremony, a third. With some flair, he folded them up, placed them in a large envelope, and held them out to Thad.

"Fifteen-hundred dollars, sir. Gold preferred."

"Well," said Thad, "I'll give you seven hundred in gold, and—." He fumbled with his money belt.

"What's the rest? Bank notes? And on what bank?"

"Well, let me give you the gold first." Thad struggled with the money belt, despite impatient remarks from those behind him.

"Hurry up!"

"Get out of the way!"

"Wager he ain't got the cash!"

Deliberately, Thad counted out $750 in $50 gold pieces. The murmur of the mob behind him rose in volume. The supercargo grew impatient. "Come on, mister! I haven't got all day, and these other folks want to buy tickets too."

Thad refused to be hurried. He had no idea what he would do when he had laid the money on the table. Grab the tickets and run? Sheer, desperate idiocy. He was no longer thinking rationally, but he was determined to prolong this chance to get Jo out of Panama as long as possible. If worst came to worst, Jo could go and he'd follow when he could, although he had heard of argonauts marooned in Panama for

12

months before they could raise the money for passage.

One by one, he laid out the gold pieces, finally coming to the last. He took a deep breath.

"There's six-hundred and fifty."

"I thought you said seven hundred."

"There's six-hundred and fifty in gold."

"And where's the rest? You still owe me $850. And I still don't know what kind of bank notes you have."

Thad stood there numb, frozen with despair.

"There's six-fifty," he repeated. He knew he sounded foolish.

"Well, if you haven't got any more, you've bought one ticket!" Petulantly, the man opened the envelope and removed two of the elaborate documents.

A voice sounded at Thad's shoulder. "Here's the rest—in gold." Clay nudged Thad and smiled as he thudded a leather bag full of gold coins on the table.

"You're paying for him?" The passenger agent looked suspicious.

"I'm one of the three he was buying tickets for. Go ahead. Count it. There's a thousand there. You owe me some change, mister."

Sourly the agent counted out $150 in banknotes.

"I'll take gold, if you don't mind," said Clay.

The agent looked up at the smiling face with its hard eyes under peaked brows and sullenly slapped down the banknotes to reach for the pile of coins.

On the way back to the hut, Thad stopped Clay in the middle of the muddy lane and said, "You don't know how grateful I am. I hope I can return the favor in kind." He grasped Clay's hand and shook it, hard.

Clay smiled. "I'm sure you'll be able to return it." He clapped Thad on the back. "Come on. Let's get Jo and get aboard."

"I've got a couple of crates of stuff," Thad said. "I'll go take care of them."

It was not until they had almost reached the hut that Thad realized Clay was now calling Jo by her first name.

13

2

The steam packet *Darien* moved slowly through the water, with much splashing from the sidewheels, clanking of huge walking beams, and growling of boilers and engines. The vessel was built to hold 250 passengers, and there were 600 aboard, give or take a dozen.

Of all the times in his life when Thad wanted to be alone with Jo, this was the most crucial. And this was the time when, for days, there would be no privacy for them—or anyone—on the crowded vessel.

The deck was filled with clumps of passengers who were standing, because there was no place to sit. To get the feel of the ship, and to divert Jo's mind from their personal tragedy, Thad was eager to lead her about the *Darien*. To do this, it was necessary to weave a path among the passengers, and it soon became evident that a lot of eyes were turned in their direciton. The passenger list was heavy on the masculine side. As heads turned for a second look, Thad observed that his wife was attracting much attention. Her traveling clothes were wrinkled, but her perfect features, dark hair, and creamy skin more than made up for it. There was no smile on her lips, and her eyes were troubled and sad, but she was still beautiful. Thad could not help but feel a sense of pride that she was his!

With luck, he managed to find a corner of the

saloon where the nearest neighbor was eight feet away, and he clutched her cold hand.

"Jo, can't we got on as we were before that horrible nightmare?"

She sat silent for a moment, then withdrew her hand from his and turned her head away.

He told himself it would not last, that it was grief over the child's death and that she couldn't possibly let it ruin their relationship. But as the days passed, he was not so sure.

They met people. One was a wizened little hard-muscled oldster who grinned cheerfully through a grizzled chin-beard.

"Jackson's the name," he cackled, thrusting out a gnarled paw to Thad. "Avery Jackson. What's yourn?"

"Thad Morgan." The old man's cheeriness was pleasant and distracted him momentarily from his gloom.

"Hopin' to do some minin'?"

"I guess that's what everybody on this boat is hoping."

"Not me." The old man grinned and spat a brown stream of tobacco juice over the rail, carefully gaging the wind before doing it. "When everybody's doin' somethin ', then that's the time not to do it. They'll be fallin' over each other by the time we git to the mines, and the best stakes'll be gone."

"Well, then, why are you going to California?"

Jackson winked, contorting his face into an amazing network of wrinkles. "Whenever there's a lot of people doin' somethin', there's a lot of other businesses to git into. Miners have to eat; they have to have clothes; they have to sleep; they have to git around; they have to have tools to dig. The big money's not findin' the gold. The big money's takin' the gold away from the miners—after they find it. I was down in Orleans in a couple of land rushes along the river. Worked out that way every time!"

Thad was interested. "What are you going into?"

"I'll think of somethin'." Jackson chuckled. "Oh, I'll think of somethin'!"

As the *Darien* sailed northwest and moved into the giant rollers of the open Pacific, it faced a quartering sea, which gave it an uncomfortable pitch and roll that bedded fully a third of the passengers. Jo was one of them. She lay miserably in her bunk in the crowded stateroom, increasing, if that were possible, Thad's feelings of guilt. He came to see her regularly, and when he did, she remained silent and turned her face to the wall.

After one of these visits, he made his way absently to the bow, where he had to hold his hat on against the strong, chill sea wind and brace himself against the plunging of the ship. For a long time he stood there, ignoring the cold and discomfort, almost forgetting where he was.

He had to make it up to Jo somehow. Of course, her blaming him was not entirely fair. They had both decided to come. She had been fearful, and he had persuaded her, true. But it had been a mutual decision.

The decision had been the result of Jo's discontent with their past lot. The hardware store on Charles Street in Baltimore had made them a living but not a large one. The work was hard, their house was small, and it was difficult to save up for the future. As far as he was concerned, he did not need riches. He liked running his own business. He was happy with Jo, and he had many friends.

Joe had come from a family of landowners near Annapolis. The scale of her life with Thad was not enough for her. She grew petulant and bitter, and Thad cast frantically about for a solution. He explored several business ventures, losing some money in one, and when news of the California gold strike reached Maryland, he seized upon it as the answer to their problems. Their baby was young but strong and healthy, and he held out to Jo the prospect of quick wealth.

But he would not go alone. She was willing to let him, but he would not. The prospect of being away from her for months in her discontent was something he could not contemplate. If there were blame to be assessed, it lay in Thad's determination not to leave Jo behind.

The wind seized Thad's hat, and he clutched it just in time as the *Darien* plunged into a huge roller. Cold spray showered him like ice pellets.

He drew a long breath. He *would* make it up to her. Arguing the responsibility out in his own mind was a futile exercise. He was, after all, the head of the family, and it was his decision that had brought tragedy upon them, whatever the reasons for it. He drew a long breath. He would go to California, and he would succeed. He would give Jo what she wanted, and maybe —after a time—she would forget the steamy little hut in Panama and the pitiful grave in the jungle.

With renewed confidence, Thad turned back from the bow and hastened to the main deck, where Jo lay in her bunk, seasick and distraught. He flung open the door of the cabin, prepared to talk cheerfully and confidently of the future, to bring her out of her depression.

Inside the room, he halted and slowly closed the door behind him. Clay Moreau was standing by Jo's side, and she was facing him. She was smiling.

Clay turned as Thad entered. "I was just leaving. Came down to cheer up your pretty little wife. She's feeling better."

He edged by Thad and exited into the corridor. When the door had closed behind him, Thad moved to the bunk. "I'm glad you're feeling better," he began, then stopped.

She had her back to him and was silent. He tried again, but she would not answer.

He had been going to tell her about his conversation with Jackson and how fortunate it was that he had thought to bring along some cases of picks and shovels from his hardware stock. From what Jackson said, selling things to the miners might be the best way to go.

But Thad's optimism and hope were chilled by Jo's silence. She had not forgiven him, and he began to wonder if she ever would.

Thad made up his mind to talk to Clay about her. He was troubled and uneasy, but he could not believe that Clay, to whom they owed so much, was anything but a friend.

He looked Clay up the next morning as they were nearing San Diego Bay.

Clay was talking to a person Thad had seen before and had carefully avoided, a plump, imposing matron of indeterminate years, steel-corseted to military erectness and clad in sweeping black with occasional feathers and glittering, ostentatious jewelry so large and gauche Thad felt it could not be real.

Thad turned away, but Clay saw him and beckoned. "This is Mrs. Emma Corson," said Clay. "Mr. Thad Morgan."

The two shook hands gravely, and Thad felt a firm, muscular grip in that plum bejeweled hand. The woman's dark eyes were intelligent, and they carefully searched Thad's face.

"Mrs. Corson is planning to go into business in San Francisco," Clay continued. He grinned. "A boarding house. The way people are flocking in, it ought to be a good time for boarding houses."

"It should be a good time for a lot of businesses," Thad said, thinking of Jackson's advice. "Are you going into business all by yourself, or with others?"

It was the wrong question. The woman looked at him sharply and drew herself up. "Two of my nieces are with me to help."

Clay was still smiling. "We're sharing what we've heard about San Francisco. It isn't much, but the more we know, the better off we'll be."

Mrs. Corson smiled with saccharine sweetness. "Mr. Moreau and I," she said in her deep baritone, "are con-

18

sidering a joint business venture. Are we not, sir?"

Clay nodded easily. "Yes, but not the boarding house." He winked at Thad. "Mrs. Corson has a little capital, and so have I. There are a good many things a few dollars, put together, can accomplish." He turned to Thad. "By the way, did you want to speak to me? We do have some things to discuss, now that we're nearing our destination."

Thad hesitated. "Yes, I guess we do."

Clay turned to the woman. "We'll continue our conversation later, Madam, if you'll excuse me. Mr. Morgan and I are already in partnership, of a sort."

He took Thad's elbow and steered him to the shelter of a lifeboat. "Her nieces are mighty goodlooking," he said, chuckling. "One's blonde and the other's brunette. Strange, there'd be such contrasting complexions in the same family."

Thad faced him. "Clay, I owe you some money."

"Yes, but there's no hurry."

"I want to get it paid off."

"I understand that, but I say again, there's no hurry. I came pretty well heeled. Besides, it'll take you awhile to pay it back. You'll need equipment to get to the mines. You may need a little more cash, and if so, just ask."

"I don't think I'll need any more, and I think I'll be able to pay you back shortly after we land."

"Oh?" The peaked brows rose with curiosity. "How?"

Thad had been intending to tell him about the shovels, but he remembered Jo's smile as Clay had leaned over her bunk, and he said nothing. "I think I have a way."

Clay gazed at him quizzically. "Well, I wish you the best. But I say again, there's no hurry. By the way, you *are* planning to go to the diggings, aren't you? Considering the way Jo feels, you'd better leave her in Frisco. I'll keep an eye on her. It'll be pretty rough in the mines."

19

Thad hesitated. "Thanks, Clay. I'm—I'm not sure what I'm going to go. You're very kind, and I appreciate it." He paused. "I'll remember what you said."

The *Darien* came fairly close to shore off Point Concepcion, and the passengers gathered by the starboard rail in such numbers that the boat heeled dangerously.

It was a sunny, warm day, and the sea, for a change, was smooth. The coastal mountains rose sharply from the sea. They looked dry and forbidding, the dark scrub chapparal covering most of the slopes, with here and there a dry ravine with boulders and signs of recent flooding.

Jackson was at Thad's side. "We're gittin' there," he said. "Ought to be outside the Golden Gate sometime tomorrow evenin'."

"I hope this isn't the way all of California looks," Thad said. "Doesn't appear to be enough water to get a good drink."

"Looks dry, all right," Jackson admitted. "But it's kinda pretty at that." He gripped Thad's arm. "Looky there! No, up there! Up in the sky! That big bird, floatin' around like a sailboat without movin' his wings."

Thad followed his gaze. High above the crags of the coastal sierra glided an unbelievably huge dark bird. It hovered slowly, descended with dignity, then found an updraft and rose again into the blue, all without moving its tremendous wings. Thad watched it, fascinated. It seemed dignified, serene, fearless, above all threat and danger.

"That there," said Jackson, "is a bird I've heerd about. It ain't a hawk or a vulture, even though it looks somethin' like a buzzard form a distance."

"Looks more like an eagle," said Thad. "That's a handsome bird. He's no buzzard."

"You're right," said the old man. "That there's a condor, the biggest bird in the world. There's only a few

20

of 'em, and they only live in California. Some of 'em spread their wings to twenty feet. They're scared of nothin', and they fly above all the storms. There are a lot o' stories about 'em I heerd from a couple of fellers who'd been here durin' the war.''

Thad took a deep breath and watched as the giant bird sailed silently above the crags toward the interior. "Afraid of nothing. And they fly above the storms.''

"Right,'' said Jackson. " 'Course, to do that, you got to have big enough wings. That's the secret. Big enough wings to hold you up.''

"Big enough wings,'' Thad repeated. His hand fell on his now empty money belt. *THERE are my wings!* he thought. *There are the wings that enable you to fly above the storms. Golden wings. Without them you struggle in the dryness and the heat and the chapparal. With them you could soar.*

He cast one more look at the giant bird as it floated, almost motionless, high above the coastal cliffs. Then he hastened down to the hold to check on the boxes of hardware he hoped had not been stored in a damp place.

3

San Francisco.

A city of tents, muddy, dusty streets, and bustling humans. Everyone in a hurry, pushing, jostling, speculating, gambling. Thad could see the activity from the bow of the *Darien* as the vessel came in to the rickety wharf.

Jackson appeared at his side. "Hear rents are turrible," he said. "Hundred-thousand a year for a board-floored tent, twenty-foot wide."

"Yes," said Thad musingly. "I've heard that, too." He swung suddenly toward the old man. "Avery, you want to make a little money?"

Jackson crinkled his face into a grin. "Always want to make a little money."

"Pass the word around that if any passengers on this ship want mining tools—picks and shovels and pans— I've got 'em. And I'll sell 'em for five dollars apiece, less than the going price in town. Tell 'em I'll sell from the dock, but they'll have to hurry, because the sale's only good for two days." He clapped the old man on the shoulder. "I'll give you a dollar out of every ten I make."

Jackson cackled with glee. "They's three minin' companies on board. I'll tell the captains, and they'll git the word out."

"I'm going into town with my wife to check prices,

22

but I'll be back before they unload the cargo. By the way, pick up all the old newspapers on the boat. I have a feeling this town would like some up-to-date reading matter."

Jackson cackled again. "There's no flies on you, Mr. Morgan! I'd like to take up with you! Atween us, we'd make a fortune!"

Thad smiled. "We're partners now. Hurry up. We're about to pull in to the dock."

Thad descended to the main deck and found Jo finishing packing the small steamer trunk that had journeyed from Baltimore by Vanderbilt liner, then on panniers carried by mules across the jungly isthmus, and now was destined to find some hotel room. Jo was holding a dress, a baby's garment. She hastily rolled it up and thrust it into her carpetbag when Thad entered.

"We're here," said Thad kindly. "Are you glad?"

Jo shrugged. "I suppose so. Anything's better than being seasick."

"Come on. We'll find a place to stay."

At that moment, the *Darien* thudded against the wharf, and the engine stopped. The silence was almost palpable after the hissing of the boilers, the splashing of the paddle wheels, and the clanking of the walking beams. Footsteps thudded on the decks.

"We'd better hurry," said Thad, "before all the hotel rooms are gone."

Jo did not move. "You haven't got any money. How can we afford a hote?"

Thad took her arm. "Don't worry," he said. "We'll have a hotel room. And we'll have money."

"Did you borrow more from Clay?"

Thad halted and faced her. "You mean Mr. Moreau?"

Jo was defiant. "No. I mean Clay. He's our friend. Our only friend."

"No, I didn't borrow more from him. I intend to pay him back before the week's out."

"You? Pay him back?" Jo was scornful. "How? You

23

let that fake doctor rob you of practically everything we had!"

"I'll pay him back. Trust me, Jo." Thad controlled his temper with an effort. "Come. It's time to go. We'll leave our things here. I've tipped the steward. He'll watch them until we get back."

They disembarked amid a happy, shouting throng and walked up Montgomery Street. Even after that terrible journey of thousands of miles over water and through jungle, Jo managed, with her gray traveling dress and her perky hat tipped forward over her piles of dark brown hair, to look beautiful. But her eyes were sad, and her mouth was downturned and sullen.

Vendors of food in ramshackle little stands called out their wares as they passed. A Mexican cowboy, lariat looped over his high saddle horn, galloped by. The afternoon fog hurried in from the sea, close over their heads, and a cold ocean breeze blew up clouds of dust and made them duck their heads against it.

At the City Hotel on the plaza, Thad got a room for $25 a week. When he took Jo upstairs to look at it, his heart sank. The walls were rough boards and the beds were small cots, each with a single worn blanket. There was a crude table, a chair, a piece of mirror, and a candle.

"We'll get a washbasin," said Thad grimly. From outside the dirty window, the fog drifted in, faster and faster, and the world was bathed in twilight gloom. Thad looked at Jo. Her lip was trembling.

"I'll go get our things," said Thad gently. "You make a list of the things we'll need."

"You haven't got any money," she said despairingly.

"I'll get it," said Thad stubbornly. "Make a list."

Once out of the City Hotel, Thad almost ran back to the dock where the *Darien* was tied up. En route, he paused once before a tent-topped, board-floored hardware store to price shovels, picks, and pans. Half smiling, he resumed his hurried pace and reached the ship just as Jackson emerged from the deckhouse with a huge stack of folded newspapers in his arms.

"I put 'em together best I could," said the old man. "Some pages are missin'."

"Don't worry about that," Thad said. "How many have you got?"

"About sixty-four, all more'n a month old."

"Go downtown and sell 'em for not less than a dollar apiece. Maybe you can get two in the hotels. Then come back and help me set up shop here." He pointed at the stevedores, long-haired Mexicans for the most part. "By that time, they'll have my boxes unloaded. They're almost down to that part of the hold."

Jackson laughed. "In business already! I'm glad I struck up with you, Pardner!" He waddled off on gnarled legs, the paper stacked high in his arms. Before he was ten feet off the dock a man halted him.

"Papers? Off the boat? How much?"

"Three dollars each," Jackson said glibly.

"Fine. I'll take two. He fumbled in his pocket, pulling out coins and paper. Jackson carefully peeled off two copies from the top of the stack, pocketed the money, looked back over his shoulder at Thad, who was watching the whole transaction, and winked ostentatiously.

Thad laughed. For a moment, he forgot the gnawing discomfort deep within him, which returned whenever he thought of Jo. This, after all, was the solution to their problems. He must get to work, and he must convince Jo that, despite the tragedy, they had a future together.

On Montgomery, Street, Jackson ran into Clay Moreau.

"Well! Selling papers, I see."

"Yep. Want one? Three dollars each. It was Morgan's idee. I'm just workin' for him."

"Morgan?" Clay laughed. "No, I don't want one now. They're the same ones I memorized on the boat." He hesitated. "What other ideas does Morgan have?"

"He's got a load o' minin' tools, and he's plannin' to sell 'em on the dock. I already rounded up a block o' customers for him. You watch! He'll be a rich man afore next week!''

"You mean he brought the tools with him? Must have been in those crates he mentioned."

"Right. They're bein' unloaded now. Well, you'll have to let me git on about my business. This newspaper game is tirin', partic'larly when you have to carry your stock with you." He cackled again and hurried off toward the plaza.

Moreau stood silently for a moment, ignoring the streams of people rushing past him in the dusty street. Lights were going on inside the tent-roofed stores and dwellings. All around him, in the dusk, the city was taking on a Japanese-lantern aspect, with yellow spots of light shining through canvas, dotting the hills in which the town lay.

Moreau frowned slightly, then snapped his fingers as a thought struck him. Then he moved briskly toward one of the few wooden buildings in the area. "J. Hobart, Wharfinger," the sign above the door said.

Clay entered the building and moved up to the raw-wood counter where an eye-shaded clerk with armbands above his cuffs was scribbling in a ledger.

"You own the wharf where the *Darien* just docked?" Clay asked.

The clerk raised his eyes, gazed at Clay suspiciously. "Yes. What about it?"

"Do you let people set up shop on your wharf?"

The man's eyes narrowed. "What are you getting at?"

Clay shrugged. "One of the passengers on the *Darien* —the one that just docked—is planning to sell some hardware he brought with him right on your wharf." He smiled. "So he won't have to pay rent for a place of business."

"Well!" the clerk immediately became indignant. "We'll see about that!" He bustled to the rear of the office, where a ponderous man in gartered shirtsleeves lopped over a desk chair so generously that the chair could not be seen. The clerk talked animatedly, and the ponderous man finally rose with an effort and lumbered

26

toward the counter, where he faced Clay.

"You say somebody's settin' up shop on our wharf?"

Clay nodded. "And set to make a killing."

The big man's tiny eyes reflected the clerk's suspicion. "And just why are you concernin' yourself? You got any objections to good business?"

Clay laughed. "None whatsoever. I believe in it. I'm here to make you a business proposition. Why don't you charge rent for the use of your wharf—and give me ten per cent for thinking of it?"

The fat man's face cleared. A tight smile appeared on his chubby mouth. "Not a bad idea." He turned to the clerk. "Why didn't one of us think of that—and save the ten percent?" He laughed rumblingly and turned back to Clay. "I haven't been keepin' up with rents around here except for our own. We're payin' thirty thousand a year." He scratched his head.

"I'd charge him a thousad," Clay said evenly.

"He won't pay that! He'll go somewheres else."

Clay leaned forward. "He'll pay it if you don't tell him you're going to charge him until after he's made his sales."

The three men looked at each other and all smiled. The big man said, "You're a right smart business man." He turned to the clerk. "Go out and watch the feller set up shop. After he's got most of his goods sold, come back and tell me how it's goin'." He tapped him on the shoulder. "Don't tell him who you are."

"And my ten percent?" Clay asked.

"You'll get it."

Thad impatiently watched the stevedores unload the cargo from the *Darien*. Every time they stopped to mop their beaded brows, his impatience grew. A small group of men had gathered at the wharf's end. One of them came up to Thad.

"Heard tell there was picks and shovels for sale here."

"There will be in a few minutes," Thad assured him.

27

"They're my picks and shovels, and I'm here to sell 'em as soon as they're unloaded."

The man nodded, and the group grew larger.

The man in charge of cargo handling approached Thad. "You've got a dozen cases of goods," he said, consulting his list. "We can get the first half-dozen out now, but the last will have to wait until tomorrow. No lights on this wharf for night work."

"Damn!" Thad felt anger well up in him. The delay wouldn't kill sales. In fact, once the news spread from the first buyers, it might improve them. But the thought of Jo in that depressing, rough little hotel room made him intolerant of time.

The man shrugged. "Sorry, but that's that."

The six boxes were unloaded a few feet away from the rest of the piled cargo. Thad found a crowbar and pried them open. He was immediately surrounded by a jostling, noisy crowd of eager purchasers.

"How much for the shovels?"

"How much for both a pick and shovel?"

"Got any gold pans?"

"What else is in them boxes, mister?"

Thad had thought through his sales program. "Everything here is ten dollars each!" he shouted. "Gold preferred!"

Jackson joined him in receiving the money. More than once, they had to swear at an overeager customer who reached into a box and was in such a hurry to get to the diggings he forgot to pay. When the price was announced, a part of the crowd grumbled and departed, but there were more than enough remaining to buy every last item Thad had unpacked.

He and the old man counted the gold pieces and hefted the sacks of dust. Jackson straightened up, grunting. "Must be more than six thousand dollars here, pard," he said. "Congratulations!"

Thad smiled. It was good, once more, to have the big wings. Now he'd pay off Clay, and he and Jo would go to Sacramento and the mines and start afresh. He thought to himself of Jackson's advice when they had

28

first met. "Don't do what everybody else is doin'." Maybe he wouldn't mine after all. He hefted a heavy sack of dust. Maybe there was more money in *not* mining.

An officious little person with paper sleeves and ink-stained fingers tapped him on the arm. "What's your name, mister?"

Thad looked at him. "Morgan. Why?"

"Well, Mr. Morgan, I represent the owners of this wharf. You've set up shop here, and we've got a rental charge."

Thad felt suddenly cold all over. "A rental charge? What do you mean? How much is it?"

"Don't pay him no 'tention!" Jackson advised. " 'Sides, you don't know who he is, anyhow."

"Oh, I represent the owners," the clerk said. "In fact, here comes Mr. Murphy, the manager, now." He jerked a thumb smugly over his shoulder. Thad glanced up. An elephantine individual in a floppy vest and sleeve garters was ambling toward them with a gorilla-like rolling gait.

Thad waited for him. "Is this your employee?" He indicated the clerk.

"He is that," Murphy nodded.

The clerk stepped officiously forward. "This man's name is Morgan, and he sold six boxes of hardware to customers on this wharf. I told him," he smiled maliciously, "that there's a rental charge."

Murphy stood spread-legged before Thad and Jackson. "How much did you clear here, mister Morgan? If it was picks and shovels you was sellin', you must have cleaned up. There's a shortage of hardware in town." He hesitated. "You must have made about ten thousand dollars."

Thad looked into the shrewd little blue eyes and recognized the trap.

"What I've made is my business," he said. "But I can tell you it wasn't anywhere near ten thousand. What's your rental charge?"

Murphy was trying to find out what the traffic would

bear. "If you didn't make ten thousand, you didn't make a very good deal."

"Tell me your charge," Thad demanded, tight-lipped. "And give me some proof that you represent the owners."

Murphy opened his mouth to speak again but saw in Thad's gaze that it would be futile.

The little clerk sidled up and, gazing meanly at Thad, said, "He was selling tools at ten dollars each, and he had six cases of 'em!"

Murphy was silent for a moment more, then said, "The rental charge is twenty-five hundred. And you can come over to the wharf office and pay me there."

Thad swallowed. "Do the other wharfs charge rental for this kind of thing?"

"Never heerd of it!" Jackson was hopping mad. He shook a gnarled finger under Murphy's fat nose. "I seen your little snipe here loiterin' around when the sale was goin' on! Why didn't you warn us earlier? We'd a gone somewheres else. Or maybe that's what you didn't want!"

Murphy shrugged and ignored him. "Twenty-five hundred," he said harshly, "or I tell the U.S. marshall about you. "He's busy, but his biggest job is protectin' us honest businessmen from sharpers like you. Now, come on to the office and pay up, or there'll be trouble."

Jackson danced around them, incoherent with rage. For a long moment, Thad hesitated. Several alternative courses were running through his mind. Then he thought of the other six cases in the hold of the *Darien* and the possibility of his going into business in this town. Starting with a row would improve neither his prospects nor his profits.

He took a long breath, swallowed his anger, and said, "All right. Come on."

Jackson followed, pleading, as he accompanied Murphy and the triumphant little paper-sleeved clerk to the wharf office.

A dark-clad, slim figure that had been standing at the

corner and watching slipped around the corner and out of sight as the four approached. Still excited, Jackson cast a quick glance in his direction as he vanished. Not recognizing him, he resumed his tirade.

That evening, Todd told Jo about his business deal. He found her lying disconsolately in the dark little room on the lumpy little cot. Only when he admitted the $2,500-dollar rental charge did she rouse herself.

She faced him angrily. "And you never thought to inquire before you started to use the wharf?" she demanded. "Thad, you're stupid! If you do have a stroke of luck, you'll wreck it by not thinking of something or by doing something idiotic! I've heard enough! I don't want to hear any more!" She flung herself down on the bed, with her back to him.

"I'm going to get you out of this hotel, Jo, into a better place."

"You'd better! If you don't, I'll leave anyway! This place is full of fleas!" She did not bother to face him as she spoke.

She was silent the rest of the night and would not bit him goodbye when he left early in the morning to unload the rest of his tools.

Once out of the hotel room, though he was unshaven and flea-bitten, Thad found Jackson waiting for him. His spirits rose unaccountably.

"I found a good place for us to set up shop," Jackson panted, hurrying along with Thad's longer stride. "City-owned beach south o' Rincon Point. I don't think anybody'll stop us there. And I been spreadin' the word."

He was interrupted by bells, bells of all kinds, shrill, deep, harsh, hoarse, tinkling, starting at different times but sounding from all over the city.

"Breakfast at the boardin' houses." Jackson answered Thad's inquiring glance. "They all start to ring about six-thirty. This here's an early-risin' town."

"We'll need to cart these crates down to the place you

said we could use." Thad turned to Jackson as they reached the pier. The hull of the *Darien* loomed above them.

"I already got that fixed," Jackson said triumphantly. "Hired a feller with two mules and a wagon fer fifty dollars. Thought you wouldn't mind."

Thad grinned. "You're a good partner." He halted as they reached the gangway. People were already moving about, all of them in a hurry. Kanakas, red-shirted miners, high-collared, hard-hatted businessmen—all were picking their way through the dust of the street leading to the wharf. They were going to other wharves and the other buildings and tents that cluttered the waterfront. A cowboy on a horse galloped by, powdering everybody with dust, which nobody seemed to mind. All were pressed and preoccupied by their own business.

The unloading chief was already on deck as Thad gained the dockside. "What about my cases?" Thad shouted.

"You'll have 'em in half an hour!"

"Where's our man with the mules and wagon?" Thad demanded of Jackson.

"He's comin' now," Jackson said. "See there, halfway up the block?"

It was a black man, nattily dressed and obviously quite prosperous, who helped them load the crates. He invited them to sit with him on the wagon's seat as they plodded through the increasing crowds of people toward Rincon Point and the public beach. Jackson improved the situation by advertising their wares in a loud voice. Thad was pleased at how many listened and turned to follow them. By the time they reached the beach and Thad had paid the wagoner, they were surrounded by almost as large a crowd as had met the *Darien* the day before.

"Fifteen dollars each!" Jackson shouted. "All tools fifteen each!"

Thad looked at him, puzzled. "Fifteen! But yesterday—"

"We had to rent space on that wharf, and we hadda pay this wagoner," Jackson explained, his whiskery face split in a wide grin. "You notice, nobody's leavin'."

Nobody left, and within two hours the crates were empty. With satisfaction, Thad counted the coins and bags of carefully weighed dust that he had accumulated.

"Nine thousand," he said, finally looking up. "And," to Jackson, "three thousand's yours."

"That's more'n we agreed," the little man said, happily. "But I ain't objectin'."

They were interrupted. A bearded man in boots and open shirt came up and gestured at the empty crates. "What'll you sell 'em for? I'm buildin' a tent store, and I can use that lumber."

"Twenty dollars each," said Jackson promptly, before Thad had an opportunity to be more modest. The man promptly counted out gold pieces for that amount and handed them to Thad.

"You *are* a good partner," Thad said again as they left the now empty beach.

"I may be better'n you think," Jackson said. "You got to keep your eye peeled for good deals and bargains in this here town. I pick up all the information I kin. Some is useful, some ain't. Fer instance, I heerd there's a cargo o' b'iled shirts an' collars out in the bay. What flat-topped son of a gun would think this town could use a whole shipload o' b'iled shirts for is way beyond my understandin'. But it's there. I cain't figger no earthly use fer it. Kin you? If you kin, we could get 'em pretty cheap, cuz there ain't no buyers."

Thad was about to respond, but fell silent. Jackson looked up at him.

"You're thinkin'," he said. "Mebbe you *can* find a way to use b'iled shirts in a town like this—"

"Maybe I can," said Thad thoughtfully. "Come on. Let's go to Portsmouth Square and look at the posters and announcements. I saw some yesterday I want to see again."

4

Jo was still lying on the bed in the darkened little room at the City Hotel, trying to sleep and blot out both her memory of the recent past and the uncomfortable irritating present.

A knock sounded at the door.

Wearily, she struggled to her feet, made a gesture at straightening her mussed hair, and opened it.

A tall man stood there, a man with upturned brows and a half smile, dressed all in black.

"Clay!" she exclaimed. Her hand immediatley went to her hair, and she pulled her robe around her. She was uncomfortably conscious of her sleep-flushed face and mussed appearance. "I'm not . . . really ready to receive callers."

He smiled. "You'll receive *me*, Jo. May I come in?" He swept off his hat in a courtly gesture and stepped confidently forward.

Holding her robe around her with one hand, Jo gestured toward the single straight chair in the room. Clay took it, his manner easy and amiable. She hesitantly sat on the edge of the bed.

"This is hardly proper," she began, but he cut her off.

"There's nothing improper about this," he assured her. "A friend calling to see how you are. And especially in San Francisco. This town doesn't worry about the proprieties." He leaned forward, his mouth still smiling, but his eyes were filled with concern. "How are you, Jo? Are you feeling better?"

"I—I suppose so. But I don't know if I'll ever feel really good again. My baby, in that horrible jungle. And—" She waved a hand around the shabby, bare little room. "Now this."

"I can't help what happened in the jungle," said Clay. "But I can help this. I don't know what Thad's planning to do, but I presume he's figuring on going to the diggings. If he does, he can't leave you here in this place."

"I wouldn't stay *here*!" she shuddered.

He quenched the smile that started at her response and assumed an air of sober sympathy. "Of course you can't stay here. What I wanted to tell you, Jo, was that, if you want a place to stay while Thad's at the diggings, well, I'm starting a boarding house and restaurant with that woman I met on the *Darien*. Mrs. Corson, her name is. And you're welcome to help us there, if you want. We're putting up a new building near the plaza. I'd be able to look after you. Thad wouldn't have to worry."

"Oh, Thad!" she grimaced. "He shouldn't have brought us! He should have left us home."

"Well, I know he's trying to set himself up in business here."

"We still owe you money—a lot of it."

He reached for her hand, and she hesitantly let him have it. "That," he said, "is the least of my worries. And I don't want you to think about it for a minute. I have perfect confidence in both Thad and you, and I know he'll pay me back when he can and as soon as he can. So forget that part of it. But do think about what I've said. *You* shouldn't go to the diggings. It's a rough life, and you've had more than your share of rough times recently. Our boarding house will be ready in a couple of weeks. It doesn't take long to build things here in San Francisco, and we've already got a tent stall with a foundation. You should stay there. You're most welcome.''

"But I couldn't stay without paying, and Thad doesn't have much money."

"You could help us get started. We'll need help. Mrs. Corson has two nieces with her, but we'll need more people than that to run the kind of restaurant we have in mind. You could help, and you could take part of your pay in food in lodging. We'd also pay you something additional.'' He saw he had said enough. She was thinking deeply.

Clay rose, his slim, dark-clad form tall in the tiny room. "I'm glad you're feeling better, Jo. I must go now.''

At the door, he took her hand again. He could feel her clutch it, unwilling to let him depart, but the dictates of propriety were too strong. She said nothing, although her lip trembled.

He smied in a friendly fashion. "You'll think about what I said, won't you?''

Her hand tightened on his. "Oh, Clay, you know I will! I look a fright, but I'm glad you came!''

His smile disappeared. His gaze went from her soft brown hair past the creamy complexion, the dark eyes, the sultry mouth, and what he suspected was a perfect figure under the bulky robe.

"You don't look a fright, Jo,'' he said quietly. "You'll never look a fright. You're beautiful. And I'm glad I came, too.''

With that he departed, smiling to himself, knowing he had timed his invitation, his compliment, and his departure exactly right to make the greatest impression. He could imagine her now, seated on the bed, thinking about what he had said, how he had looked, and how he had taken her hand.

He was right. Jo was seated on the edge of the bed, and she was thinking.

Thad and Jackson were out on the windy deck of the

Ginny Belle, a two-masted topsail schooner, arguing with the captain, who had black muttonchop whiskers, a irascible disposition, and a sense of his own importance.

"You've got ten gross of still shirts and wing collars and a supply of silver cufflinks and collar buttons. What are you going to do with 'em?" Thad asked, laughing.

The captain bridled. "Sell 'em, of course! There's been nothing like that out here since the rush started."

Jackson chipped in with a mocking cackle. "Anybody ever tell y' why there ain't been anything like that out here since the rush started? It's cause everybody wears red shirts and bandanas. That's why! Nobody dresses formal out here."

"Well, this is a growing community, and it won't be long until it desires some of the refinements."

"How long are you victualed to sit in the harbor?" Jackson chuckled gleefully. "A year? Two years? This plce sprung up like a toadstool, and it ain't wearin' b'iled shirts. Not yet!"

The captain swung on Thad. "Well, if this cargo can't be sold, why are you here asking about it? You seem to think you can sell it. You're certainly not willing to take it off my hands because you feel sorry for me."

Thad nodded. "That's right, Captain. But we're in different circumstances. I'm here to stay. I'm a resident of California, and I've got time to do a few things. I'm not the captain of a ship that has to sail in a few days or a few weeks. I'm planning to go into business, maybe several businesses. I agree with you. Sooner or later, Californians will want stiff shirts and collars. That'll be when more women get here and when they begin acting civilized. But it'll be awhile. I'll make a deal with you, Captain. You can't sell those shirts now unless you give 'em away. I'll pay you something for 'em, not their full value, mind you, but something, on the chance that I can hold on to 'em until they're valuable. What do you say?"

The captain stiffened angrily. "Look, you're the first

one I've talked to. You came out here almost before I got my anchor down! How do I know what you're telling me is correct? I don't intend to do anything until I've looked into the matter further."

Thad turned decisively. "Then you won't do business with me. I either leave here with a deal in fifteen minutes, or you'll have to find another buyer. And you won't. There aren't many people in town right now who're planning for the long term. They're making a fast dollar wherever they can make it. And storing shirts for a year or two isn't in their minds."

"He's right!" Jackson nodded emphatically. "My pard's right! You'd better talk business, mister, or," and he cackled again, "you'll lose your shirts!" He roared with glee. "Get that, Thad? He'll lose his shirts!"

The captain was shaken but pretended not to be. Still stiff and unbending, he asked, "Not that I'm interested, but what kind of a deal are you talking about?"

Thad was ready for him. "Ten gross is fourteen-hundred-and-forty shirts. I'll pay you fifteen-hundred for the lot, including the cufflinks and collar buttons. Take it or leave it."

The captain reddened with anger. "But that's only a dollar a shirt! I paid more than that for 'em myself."

"Oh, this is your own cargo? If you can't sell 'em at all, the *whole* loss is right out of your own pocket. By the way, what are you planning to take back as return cargo?"

"Livestock. I've already got a deal at the south end of the bay."

"And if you carry back these shirts with a maindeck full of cows, what condition do you think they'll be in on your next trip? Because you'll still have 'em with you, I guarantee it."

Jackson laughed loudly. "After a couple of years, when you do sell 'em, feller's wife is goin' to say, 'Ever' time I go out with you to the opery, you smell like a barnyard. What in hell is the matter?' " He roared

38

again with laughter.

The captain was silent for a moment. "Let me go in and talk to my first officer," he said grudgingly. "He's a part investor in this cargo. Will you wait a minute?"

"Not long," Thad warned. "The longer I think about this deal, the worse it looks for me. You'll at least get most of your money out of it. I may be stuck with the whole laundry bag."

The captain moved rapidly toward his cabin. Out on the sunny, windswept deck, Jackson sidled closer to Thad. "You sure you know what you're doin?' Fifteen hundred for b'iled shirts, and you said yourself you can't sell 'em."

Thad smiled. "Nobody can sell 'em—in the present market," he agreed. "What I've got to do is change the market demand."

"Change the market?" Jackson scowled in puzzlement. "What do you mean?"

"Tell you later," said Thad. His dark eyes were confident. "Here comes our friend, the captain. And by golly, he looks like he's ready to talk business."

The captain approached and, followed by his hulking first mate, began a gambit that had clearly been quickly planned in the cabin. "We don't believe you," he said. "We don't think it's impossible to market stiff shirts in San Francisco."

Thad turned on his heel and moved toward the rail. "Fine, Captain. I'm sort of getting cold feet, anyhow, after listening to my own arguments."

"Now, wait, sir!" The captain quickly circled Thad and stood between him and the rail, where a rope ladder hung, leading to a bobbing rowboat below. "As I said, we don't believe you. We think we could sell this cargo and make a nice profit on it. But we think you may be right about the time factor. It may take awhile to sell shirts, and we've got other things aboard that we know will go fast—hardware, cooking utensils, heavy boots, and warm outdoor clothing. We don't want to be delayed. So we've decided to make you a counteroffer."

Thirty-five hundred for the shirts and jewelry."

Thad took him by the shoulders and set him firmly aside. He was smiling. "No hard feelings, Captain, but I'm not interested. When I persuaded you that this cargo would be hard to sell, I persuaded myself, too. I wouldn't pay a nickel more than fifteen hundred if you had twenty gross and gold jewelry, and I'm even talkin' myself out of that, the more I think about it!"

"Now, wait!" The captain was suddenly the supplicant. "How about three thousand? That's two dollars a shirt. You can't touch 'em for that, not shirts of this quality, even at home!"

Thad shook his head stubbornly and moved toward the rail. "Come on, Avery. More I think about it, more I think it's a bad deal all the way around. Sorry, Captain."

The captain inserted himself between Thad and the rail. "All right, then, you highwayman! Fifteen hundred!" His face was red with frustration, and his muttonchops were trembling with rage.

Thad looked at Jackson. "I'll pay the man. You go see the first officer and find out how quick they can jackass those boxes out on to the wharf."

He left Jackson in charge of the unloading, telling him to wait for his return, and he hastened off toward Portsmouth Square. He found another hotel, the Union, just off the square, and looked up the proprietor, who, to his relief, was not wearing a red shirt and corduroys, but rather a dark suit, a high wing-collar, and a carefully trimmed mustache.

"We are trying to bring the amenities of an eastern inn to this frontier," he man said in answer to Thad's question. "Accordingly, my prices are high. Forty dollars a week, meals extry." He cleared his throat pompously, lifted his heavy brows, and regarded Thad's disheveled appearance with some disdain. "A trifle high for you, perhaps?"

Thad was impatient. "No, the forty dollars is all right. I want a room for at least a month. It's for my wife. I'm going to the diggings, and I want a place for her to stay."

"You're going to the diggings, and you want it for your wife?" The man was suspicious. "In that case, it'll be in advance, and when the advance runs out, out she goes."

"Well, the room isn't the only thing I want," Thad said, ignoring the suspicion. "I want a place to store some boxes—an attic, preferably, where it's dry. I'll pay a little extra for that. Not much, but a little."

"What's in the boxes?" the proprietor insisted.

"Merchandise," said Thad glibly. "It's nothing that'll start a fire and nothing dangerous. It's dry goods. I'm planning to sell 'em when I get back from the diggings, which'll be in less than a month. I'm not planning to stay away long."

The proprietor's mien changed. Here, apparently, was a man of property. He cleared his throat pretentiously. "Well, sir, I'm sure we can oblige you. This here is a new building, as you can see, and our attic is empty. It gets warm up there, close to the roof."

"That won't hurt," Thad said. "But I don't want any dampness or mildew."

"Well, I'm sure we can do business. Can I show you the room?"

"I'm not sure yet. I need something else. I need a big room where a ball can be held, with music and dancing."

The proprietor melted completely and became an eager salesman. "This entire lobby can be turned over for that purpose."

"Not big enough," Thad objected. "Not nearly big enough. There'll be a lot of people at this ball."

The proprietor snapped his fingers and grinned. "I have it! You saw the saloon next door, Monihan's Bird Cage? Well, I'm part owner, and I'm sure we can arrange to hire out that place for you for a night. It's plenty big. You could get a couple hundred people in there."

"Let's look at it," said Thad.

Hastily, the man led the way out the front door and down the dusty street to the batwings of the flimsy building adjacent. Even at that early hour, strains of galloping piano music came from the interior, together with the murmur and occasional shout of a noisy throng. The air inside was thick with cigar smoke; the clink of bottles and glasses was incessant; the pianist thumped the keys without interruption and without style. Five tables of poker were being played, with hangers-on watching, and the long bar was crowded with thirsty men.

"This'll do," said Thad. "Five hundred for the night. Take it or leave it. Pay on my return from the diggings, but I want the night reserved."

"Which night'll that be?"

"Don't know yet, but I'll tell you as soon as I can. Is it a deal?"

"Well—" The man hesitated and rubbed his mustache nervously. "I'll have to consult my partner, but—well, yes. I think we can do business at that rate. Okay, friend, okay." He put out a hand and shook Thad's with enthusiasm. "Of course, if my partner objects—"

Thad stiffened, scowled, and looked as menacing as possible. "We just shook hands. That means something where I come from, even if it doesn't in California!"

"Oh, it's a deal! It's a deal! Never fear, I'll get my pard to agree." He led the way nervously back to the hotel. "Now I'd better register you and show you the room."

Thad hurried back to the wharf, where he found Jackson standing guard over the wooden shirt boxes and smoking a battered, blackened, and odorous corncob.

"Got 'em all off," the old man said cheerfully. "And here's the jewelry. I been watchin' that special." He indicated a small box atop one of the crates.

"Good!" Thad said. "I've got a place to store 'em for the time being. And we'll need another wagon."

5

Jouncing along on the wagon they hired, which was drawn by a single mule, at the corner of Jackson and Montgomery they encountered Clay Moreau. Thad pulled up the mule. Clay came to the boot and looked up at him. His peaked brows were quizzical, and the half-smile still on his face.

"You look as though you have a job. What'd you do. Hire out as a driver?"

Jackson spoke before Thad had a chance to speak. He leaned in front of Thad and said proudly, "This here is California's smartest businessman! He's goin' to be rich! He's not drivin' fer anybody! He's workin' fer himself!"

Thad laid a restraining hand on the old man's arm. He had been about to tell Clay what he was doing, but for no reason he could pinpoint, he suddenly decided not to. "I do have a little deal going, Clay. I'll be able to pay you back very soon now."

Clay made a deprecating gesture. "No hurry. No hurry at all. But I thought you were going to the diggings."

"I am," said Thad, "probably tomorrow. But I won't be gone very long, at least on this trip."

Thad clucked to the mule, which reluctantly resumed its stately pace. Clay stood there and watched the wagon as it rocked and swayed over the ruts and mudholes of

Montgomery Street. He rubbed his chin, and his intelligent eyes were thoughtful.

When the wagon rounded the corner and disappeared behind a row of tent structures, Clay turned around and walked quickly in the other direction, toward the harbor. At a wooden-floored tent with a crude hand-lettered sign in front, saying "Piccadilly Pub," he entered through the tentflap and found himself in a barroom no different from the dozen others springing up all over town. This was perhaps cruder than most, with planks laid on beer barrels to form the bar, the bottles and glasses set up on boxes two feet behind the planks.

He paused inside the entrance. The place was not crowded, but there were a half-dozen loungers plus a hulking, six-foot bartender with shaggy black hair and a two weeks' growth of black whiskers on his heavy jaws.

Clay nodded to the bartender and approached him. "Matt, I've got a little job for you even before you take over the running of our saloon. Are you game?"

"If it don't take me outa here durin' business hours. I got to keep this place goin' until yours opens up." His voice was deep and hoarse.

"Well, you'll have to work out the timing yourself. I don't care how you do it, just so it's done soon."

The big man gazed at Clay with cold blue eyes. "What's the job?"

Clay moved closer and glanced around to make sure he was not wihtin earshot of any of the loungers. "I want a man robbed."

The big man's expression did not change. "What's he got that you want?"

"Nothing that I want."

"Then what the hell do you want me to rob him for?"

"Money. But you can keep half of what you find."

The big man looked puzzled. "I don't quite get it," he said. "What's our end of it?"

"He owes me money, and I want him to keep on owing me. I don't want him to pay off. He's got some

44

cash now, and I want it taken away from him. You can keep half of it. I just want him not to have it."

Matt shrugged his bearlike shoulders. "Where do I find him?" His cold little eyes narrowed. "I might need an advance to hire somebody to tend bar while I'm out."

Clay smiled contemptuously, reached in his pocket, and tossed a twenty-dollar gold piece on the counter. "You can return that from your profits on the deal," he said.

"All right. Who is he?"

Clay leaned forward and spoke in low tones. The big man repeated the information in a rumbling undertone. Clay leaned back. "He's probably moved by now, but the clerk at the City Hotel will know where he's gone."

Clay left the Paccadilly Pub thoughtfully. As he walked back toward the center of the busy town, his expression relaxed into a humoriess smile. Thad had been swindled by the fat doctor in Panama; he had been outmaneuvered by Clay in connection with the wharfage charge; and now that he finally had a growing stake, he would lose it to a thief. Jo's respect for Thad was already thin, and he would see to it that it would completely vanish.

Clay's smile broadened. He was thinking of Jo, the way she looked, the way she spoke, and her dark eyes.

Thad walked quickly toward the City Hotel, hoping what he had to tell Jo would finally bring a smile to her face. The gold pieces were heavy in the rawhide bag with the drawstrings that made his coat pocket sag. He was reasonably satisfied with the Union Hotel and its proprietor. Jo would be safe there for two or three weeks. Although he had hoped that she would acocmpany him to the diggings, he did not delude himself. He was reasonably certain she would not want to rough it again. If she refused to go with him, it would shorten his trip, but that was not as important as it once had been. More and more, Thad was coming to the conviction that digging for gold was not what he was going to do.

Avery Jackson had had a considerable influence on his thinking, he reflected, as he sidestepped a lurching wagon heavily overloaded with wooden crates from a recently arrived vessel. Jackson said that those who made money in a rush were the ones who let others do the rushing and then provided them with the necessaries of life. That, Thad thought, was sensible. He had already proved the truth of it since landing in San Francisco.

He was not worried about making money. He could make it readily enough. He had proved that. Coming west had given him and Jo tragedy, but it could also give them success beyond anything they might have hoped for in Baltimore. San Francisco was a violet, excitable, unrestrained place, unhampered by precedent, full of men and women who were searching for quick fortune. Decisions were made quickly. He who hesitated was not only lost but had no chance at all. Life was mercurial.

Thad took a long breath as he hurried. If it were not for Jo and the little grave in the jungle, he would be enjoying this. It was, he thought, his kind of life, the kind he responded to.

But if he lost Jo in the process . . . . He resolutely put the thought out of his mind. She would come to her senses. She must. It was only natural. But Thad could not keep himself from feeling that the situation was rapidly becoming unnatural. Women flared in the face of personal tragedy and became bitter, but where there was love and regard between two people, those other feelings did not last long.

Yet Jo's bitterness was not lessening. Instead, she seemed to grow more bitter day by day.

Again Thad put the thought out of his mind and concentrated on th crowded street, the hurrying throngs, and the glass-blue sky overhead with the puff of fog just beginning to show over Twin Peaks. Another block and he would be at the City Hotel.

How should he begin with Jo? What words should he use? He frowned. This was the first time in their married life he did not know how to speak to her. He hoped she would be feeling better, or, if not better, at least less angry. It was hard to talk to an angry woman. Almost impossible, in fact.

As he passed a narrow aperture between two new buildings, whose raw lumber still smelled of the forest, a hulking, bearded figure stepped out behind him. Thad felt a hamlike hand on his shoulder and a pricking sensation in his back, just under the right shoulder-blade.

"Slow down," commanded a hoarse, rumbling voice from behind and above. "But don't stop walkin'. Just slow down. Bub, you got a knife ready to slice atween your ribs if you make a false move."

Thad felt, and smelled, a heavy alcoholic breath close to his ear. The acrid odor of a huge, sweaty body that had not seen a bathtub in days, assaulted his nostrils.

"Now don't turn around," the voice continued. "It don't make no difference to you what I look like. But don't do anything that'll make people around us think there's anything funny goin' on."

Thad slowed his pace, thinking rapidly. The knife pricked him again, this time more deeply, just to show it was still there, Thad felt. There were people all around, hurrying people, people who were paying no attention to anyone else but minding their own business with a vengeance. The man behind him, from all the unseen evidence Thad could gather, was huge. And the knife was sharp. If he turned to fight, the knife could disable him before he could get fairly started. If he flung himself forward, away from the knife, he would be on the ground and helpless before what was apparently a human gorilla.

He looked up. There, ahead, just a half-square away, was the unimpressive facade of the City Hotel. Jo was there—he hoped. So close—and yet so far away. Were

47

there any policemen in this town? He didn't suppose so. The place was too young. People took care of their own affairs.

The heavy voice behind him resumed its instructions. "Now we're goin' to turn around and go back to that place I was waitin' for you in. We can jest kinda stop and head back the way we came. But I'm goin' to stay behind you, and this knife is goin' to be in your ribs all the way."

Thad cast a desperate glance at the City Hotel. Jo was there and there were many things pulling them apart. But this hulking monster was not going to be one of them. Thad suddenly crouched and, from that position, launched himself at the huge, booted legs, aiming at the knees clad in khaki work pants above the scarred, dusty boots. One of the big knees bent backward, and the man uttered a howl of pain. At the same moment, Thad rolled desperately and threw himself away from the descending knife, which he felt rather than saw. As it clashed against the dusty street, the big man pounced on it, scrambled to his feet, and charged, growling.

People stopped to stare, but they were not of a mind to interfere. The two men were in the dusty street's center, both crouching. The bearded, unkempt attacker was holding his knife, a long hunting blade, flat in his hand, his finger and thumb on the base of the blade. He had fought with knives before, Thad concluded. As for Thad, he held his arms away from his sides, ready to leap from under the glittering blade when it slashed forward.

A circle of men stood around them, silent, waiting.

As he stood there, weaponless, wondering what his next move should be, Thad examined his assailant. The man was well over six feet tall and must have weighed 230 pounds. His black, shaggy, shoulder-length hair was uncombed and greasy, his beard untrimmed and black as night. The man wore a dirty gray hunting jacket that was almost too small for him. He was hatless. His cruel eyes gleamed in the black, hairy face.

Thad knew he had never seen him before.

The man was circling now, the knife gleaming in the sunlight. The ring of spectators gave when the man got too close to the line of people and closed in when he moved in the other direction. Thad swore at himself. Why hadn't he bought a gun? In this kind of country, you had to have some means of defending yourself. He was weaponless, helpless in the face of that long-bladed hunting knife and the thick, long, gray-clad arm wielding it. Weaponless! Was he to die on this dusty San Francisco street before he could reach Jo? Would Jo ever know what happened to him? He had failed her. He had taken their child to her death, had been swindled twice already, and now was about to be murdered before he had a chance to tell her of his recent success and take her to a more livable place.

He was suddenly terribly angry. He would not let it happen! Not before he saw Jo! Even if he had to grab that glittering blade with his hand and wrench it away from his attacker. He would probably lose the use of his hand. Therefore, it had better be his left hand.

If only he were not weaponless!

The rawhide bag of gold clinked against his hip. He was *not* weaponless!

The bit man was circling closer. Suddenly, Thad was coldly calm. He fumbled for the bag of gold in his pocket and withdrew it. It was big and heavy, a ready-made slingshot, bigger than most, and a little awkward. He must not let it be jerked from him by the man's arm. He must let the man attack, must let him get close, very close.

The crowd muttered happily. This was going to be a good fight after all. It was not as one-sided as it had first appeared.

The huge man charged. Thad gripped the bag of gold pieces and nuggest firmly, not too close to the draw-string, but not too close to the bulky contents, either, so that he would have leverage when he struck. The attacker put his massive left arm up in a defensive gesture, and Thad was fearful of striking the arm and having it pull the rawhide bag out of his grasp.

He retreated. The knife flashed, and Thad nimbly sidestepped. It flashed again before Thad was ready, and it ripped his coat. Thad felt a searing pain down his left side. The man had drawn blood, but the wound was not deep.

Again he charged, this time roaring like a bull, and again Thad leaped backward, as the line of spectators melted away to give the gladiators room. Again the knife flashed, this time in a downstroke. It ripped Thad's left sleeve and again drew blood. The spectators moaned and muttered with satisfaction and excitement.

Thad knew that another slash might disable him forever. Yet the big man was intelligent enough to keep his left arm up and in the way. Thad wondered about the thick hair. Was it thick enough to protect the skull?

Then, without waiting for another attack, Thad leaped forward as the man was circling for another assault. He surprised his opponent. The man had not thought he would be attacked. He had felt the knife was the only effective weapon in this combat. Thad lifted his arm, leaving his body undefended for the moment, swung the heavy gold bag down in a full-armed sweep, and—Thad knew luck played a large part in it—smashed the heavy rawhide bag down squarely on the top center of the man's black-thatched skull.

The man fell to his hands and knees. The knife was still under his right hand. He was dazed. Thad took advantage of the moment, moved deliberately close, and aimed carefully this time. He brought the bag down in another full-armed swing, this time on the base of the man's skull. The man collapsed, falling face forward on the dusty street. Thad took no chances. He stamped hard on his right hand, kicking the knife away from the broken fingers and picking it up.

"Kill him! Kill him!" Somebody in the crowd yelled excitedly.

Thad merely pocketed the knife. He turned to the

crowd. "He tried to rob me—of this." He indicated the rawhide bag. "What do we do with him?"

"Lynch him!" the cry went up. "String him up!" Two individuals, neatly dressed in contrast to the throng of miners around them, hurried to Thad's side. "If he tried to rob you," one of the men said, "he'll go before a vigilante court. We've just set one up." The man had sidewhiskers, a beaver hat, and a brown frock coat. "I'm Benson," he said. "Ezra Benson. Come on, you. Help tie this fellow up!" He raised his voice and directed it at the surrounding throng. "Come on, some of you. Bring a rope. He's due for a trial before the committee."

A short time later, Thad found himself in Ezra Benson's office, in the Bank of Mission Valley. It was a two-story false-fronted wooden structure like most of the more permanent buildings in the city, but it was located a little apart from the press of wood-floored tent structures and wall-to-wall wooden shacks that clustered around Portsmouth Square and the Plaza.

"Good reason for it," Benson answered Thad's question. "If anybody dropped a match in this town, it would go up like kindling. Here at least I've got a chance to survive." He whirled energetically toward the group of men who were dragging the huge bartender, who was struggling futilely with them. By now his hands were bound behind him, and his ankles were hobbled with heavy rope. He looked somewhat dazed, and a huge lump was rising on the left side of his head behind the ear.

"Bring him into my office," Benson ordered. "Somebody go get Clark and Studebaker. We'll try him right here. It takes five for a tribunal. I'm here, and you're here, Scott, and so are you, Weatherford. We'll have enough, and we'll get this over in jig time!" He rapidly circled his rolltop desk, which was open and covered with papers, and plunked himself down in the chair behind it, which he whirled to face the roomful of men.

Benson was well dressed, Thad saw. He had on a brown broadcloth frock coat and gray trousers that were kept from riding up by straps under the insteps of his polished boots. A large ruby ring, set in heavy gold mounting, was on his right hand, and a thick gold watchfob showed on his waistcoat. He had a square, honest face, intelligent blue eyes, a gray mustache, and a ready smile. When he took off his beaver hat, his thick gray hair was neatly groomed and wavy.

Thad was impressed, not with the ring and the evidences of wealth, but with the honesty and friendliness in his eyes. Benson kept up a rapid fire of conversation as he arranged the group in the room on chairs to present a semblance of order.

"You just got into town, I take it," he said, addressing Thad. "Some of us who've been here a little longer decided to do something about law and order. We're getting a U.S. marshal, and we'll have other peace officers shortly. But until we do, and until there are enough of them to maintain order, we must take matters into our own hands. Otherwise, this place will fall apart, and nobody will be safe."

Two other men stamped into the office, one tall and cadaverous, with drooping black mustache, baggy eyes, and loose storekeeper's clothing, the other in miner's red shirt, corduroy pants, and boots.

"This is Thad. What'd you say your name was? Morgan? Thad Morgan. Morgan, this is John Studebaker and Elmo Clark. Now let's get to work. The prisoner here—by the way, what's your name?"

Matt shook his black and hairy head stubbornly and refused to do more than growl. The men holding him shook him roughly and impatiently. "Speak up, Clod!" one of them barked. "Or we'll fix it so you're whistling into your own left ear!"

A glint of fear appeared in the big man's eyes. "Matt. Matt Barnes," he rumbled. "I keep a saloon over on Battery, and this feller attacked me. I didn't jump him."

A howl of disbelief arose from two of the men in the room. "I seen you!" one yelled. "I seen you come out'n that alley and jump this feller!" He indicated Thad by a wave of the hand. "I seen you! So don't pull none of that malarky!"

"Ah! We have a witness. And one who's willing to speak up!" Benson sounded pleased. "Now, Morgan, you tell us what happened."

Thad did so, without embellishment. "I've got some money. He must have heard about it somewhere." Thad suddenly turned to the big, hairy man. "Where *did* you hear about it?"

Again Matt mumbled hostilely, and again his captors shook him until his teeth rattled. "Speak up!" one mining type with beard and bowie knife ordered. "Or mebbe you talk better without yore front teeth!"

"A feller came into my saloon. Told me about you, where I could find you. Wanted to split." The deep voice rumbled loosely.

"Who was the man who told you about Morgan?" Benson asked. "Did you know him?"

Matt's eyes did not meet those of his captors. "Never seen him afore in my life. Said he'd be back later to see how I come out."

"I don't believe him," said Benson disgustedly. "But we're dealing with *him* now. We'll push him on the other in a few minutes. Anybody else see him attack Morgan?"

Another man nodded and said, "Yeah, I'll testify. I saw him, too. Morgan was walkin' along, and this feller jumped him. Clear case."

"All right," said Benson, and his eyes hardened. "There's two witnesses. Scott, you're a lawyer. You got any suggestions before we take a vote?"

"Hey, wait!" the big bartender was suddenly fearful. "don't I get a chance to defend myself? Don't I get a lawyer?"

"Why should you have a lawyer? Morgan doesn't have one." Benson was scornful.

Scott, a thin, spectacled man with precise features, shook his head. "The man's right, Ezra. He ought to have legal defense."

"Come on, Scott!" said Benson. "You know as well as I do that we can't go through the formalities. There are two kinds of law: justice, with a lot of red tape, and equity. We'll have to stick to equity until we get more civilized in San Francisco. We've got the victim and two witnesses who attest to certain facts. The only one who's denying 'em is the accused. I think we've got a clear case. Waiting around will only complicate it and obscure the facts we've got."

Scott shrugged his thin shoulders. "We must get judicial procedures started in this town. But, under the circumstances—" Benson dominated him, Thad saw, as he dominated the entire room. There was something about his personality that drew all eyes to him, that silenced voices when he spoke, that made him the center of attention without any overt action on his part.

Benson looked up. "Anybody else got any information for us before we make a decision?" His eyes ranged over the crowded little room. There was no response.

"Anybody think we haven't got a clear case?"

There was a murmur of agreement. "It's clear enough!"

"What more do you need? Two witnesses—"

"This fellers a thug. He needs a rope necktie!"

Benson said, "All right. We'll take our vote right out in the open. Scott, Clark, Studebaker, and Weatherford. Gather round." The four made their way through the crowd and came forward.

Thad looked around the crowded little room. The morning sun was beginning to heat it up. Benson sat at his desk, his back erect, his hands flat before him, his eyes hard and cold and determined. Clark, stocky, bearded, in his red miner's shirt, leaned over the desk, one fist on it. Studebaker, a thin man in brown clothing, looked soberly at the prisoner, aware of the seriousness of the moment. Weatherford, tall, gaunt, with dark

54

drooping mustache, a storekeeper's apron tied around his waist, slouched in the rear. Scott, slight, erect, a birdlike man with thinning gray hair and lines around his mouth, nervously polished his glasses.

Behind them shifted and maneuvered forty people, as many as could crowd into the little room. There were bearded miners, shaven gamblers with cold eyes, dark-skinned Kanakas, several Californians, who were brown-skinned and mustached, with sombreros, silver ornaments and open shirts. The room stank of unbathed humanity, now beginning to perspire, and the odor almost overwhelmed the huge, frightened man whose beady eyes in his shaggily bearded face flickered nervously to the faces of his judges.

Thad felt a heavy sense of oppressiveness, of looming tragedy.

"All right," said Benson. "How many think he's guilty? I'll hold my vote and cast a deciding one if it's needed."

He turned to the four. "Studebaker?"

"Guity."

"Weatherford?"

"Guilty."

"Clark?"

The man in the red miner's shirt exploded, "Guilty as hell!"

Benson, Thad saw, had saved Scott, the lawyer, for the last, so that he might be swayed by the unanimity of the vote. "Scott?"

The thin man hesitated, removed his glasses, polished them with his handkerchief, put them back on, and said, reluctantly, "He's guilty, in my opinion, but I'm worried about our procedure."

"Well, I'm not," said Benson. "We've got four guilty votes, and I'll add mine to them, so it's unanimous. Now," he regarded the prisoner balefully, "we've got to decide on the penalty." But he was not allowed to finish the sentence. There was a loud reaction from nearly everyone in the room.

"Hang him!"

"Give him a rope necktie!"

"We can't have thieves or killers around here!"

"No man'll be safe!"

"He's got to be an example!"

"Let's show the Sydney Ducks they can't run rough-shod over us!"

"Hang him!"

Benson nodded in satisfaction. "The feeling seems to be unanimous. We can either hang him or flog him out of town. Which'll it be? We'll vote again. What's your vote, Studebaker?"

"Hang him, and let's be quick about it. I've got to get back to work."

"Clark?"

"I agree. He's a no-good. He'll do it again unless he's put out of circulation."

"Weatherford?"

The tall man grimaced. "I don't like to kill people, but there's only one answer to what he done in a place like this."

Benson turned to the lawyer. Scott was uncomfortable, and showed it. Benson did not bother to voice the terrible question. He merely looked at Scott, and waited.

Scott hesitated. Thad knew what was running through his mind. There had to be quick, exemplary justice at this time, or criminals would overrun the community. Yet his lawyer's mind rebelled at this summary shortcutting of protocol.

Scott took a deep breath, removed his glasses, put them on again, and said, "Ezra, this procedure bothers me!"

Benson plunged into the breach. "It bothers all of us. But what's the alternative? We asked you to join this vigilante committee because we thought you were for law and order."

"I am! You know I am, but—."

"But what do we do to bring it about? Wish we had different procedures. We will have soon, but we haven't got 'em yet. So what do we do in the meantime?'' He moved closer to Scott and hovered over him, dominating the smaller man physically as well. "What's your answer, Scott? If we hang him, it's got to be a unanimous vote. That's agreed. How do you vote?''

Scott hesitated again, swallowing miserably. He said, "Oh, all right! I'll go along. But I don't think it's right! I don't think it's right!''

Benson smiled. It was not a cruel smile, just triumphant. "All right, boys. You know what to do next!''

Thad saw Matt's eyes open wide to satre as he suddenly realized what was to be done to him. They bshone with terror. For a moment he was speechless, then he cried out in an animal-like wail of panic. "Hey, wait! You can't do this!''

"Watch us!'' said one of the men holding him. "See if we can't! We're goin' to get rid of thieves like you.''

Thad saw perspiration spring out on the big man's forehead below his greasy black hair. The staring eyes rolled with terror. "Hey, wait!'' The hoarse, rumbling voice trembled.

Thad stepped forward. "Just a minute, Mr. Benson. I want to say something.''

Benson paused in his push toward the door. "Yes, what is it?''

"I was the one attacked by this man. He was trying to hold me up, and he didn't succeed. I agree with Mr. Scott. I don't think you should kill him.''

Benson frowned, and Thad again felt the power of his personality. It would be easy to give in to Benson. It was unpleasant to have him scowling at you.

"He tried to kill you,'' Benson said.

"But he didn't do it,'' Thad remonstrated. "And he didn't succeed in the holdup, either. I'm in favor of law and order, too, but a man's life is a man's life!''

"Well, his ain't worth much!'' the red-shirted Clark burst out. "He's a rapscallion and a no-good, if I ever seen one! Don't be chickenhearted, lad! This is a rough town, and we don't want it to get any rougher!''

"There ought to be something else besides hanging him!" Thad persisted. "Beat the hell out of him, kick him out of town. But he's a human being."

"He doesn't look very human to me," Benson said. "And he sure doesn't act very human. Come on, Morgan, let us get on with the business at hand!" He motioned the crowd, together with those who were hauling the big hobbled bartender with them, toward the door.

Thad quickly circled them and stood in the entrance. "I don't think you should kill a man for what this man did!" he said forcefully. "I don't want his blood on my conscience."

Benson moved forward to confront him, inches from his face. "It's out of your hands," he said firmly. "It's out of your hands! Now step aside."

The others were determined. Thad was pushed roughly aside. He followed the crowd, which grew quickly larger as it moved with its prisoner toward a livery stable with a block and tackle mounted on a protruding beam above its door. It was used for unloading hay, Thad knew, but now it was destined for a more sinister purpose.

Matt was pleading for his life. His cries and arguments sounded periodically above the crowd's noise, but there was no wavering. Benson led them on, moving quickly to forestall any further hesitation.

6

There was nothing more Thad could do. He felt utterly helpless as he assessed the size of the growing crowd and estimated its determination. He wondered whether, if he mounted a wagon and tried to harangue them, it would have any effect. He decided it would not. The men were no longer individuals, they were a mob. Their eyes shone with excitement. They laughed as they looked at one another for moral support, echoing one another's cries of accusation and profanity.

Thad had seen a mob like this once before, in back-country Maryland, when it had lynched a slave. Something happened to human beings, he concluded, when they acted in concert; it made them less than human. They were now uncontrolled and uncontrollable.

Every nerve in Thad's body cried out against what was happening. He had been a party to it. It was the man's crime against him that was leading to this killing. It was not his fault, but Thad knew he would have this on his mind for the rest of his life, unless . . . unless he did something about it. Something. Anything. Maybe it would be futile, but it had to be something.

He took a deep breath and plunged into the crowd. It did not wish to give way, and the men swore at him and elbowed him back.

"Let me through!" Thad panted. "Let me through! I've got to stop this!"

"Stop it? What do you mean, stop it?" A grizzled oldster glared in his face. "What's wrong with you? We're keepin' the peace, and this needs to be done."

Two strong hands gripped his elbows from behind. Thad tried to jerk away, but the hands held.

"Thad!" a familiar voice said in his ear. "Thad! It's me. Clay. Stop flailing around!"

Thad ceased his struggling to force his way through the crowd and turned to face Clay. Clay looked the same, the same black frock coat, black hat, peaked brows, the same engimatic, cynical half-smile.

"Quit trying to save the big lugger," Clay said. He rapidly got between Thad and the crowd and, steering him by one elbow, pushed him out into the street. "He's a crook and a killer. He's getting what's coming to him."

"Well, I don't want him killed for what he did to me!"

Clay's back was to the stable, where a knot of men under Benson's direction were preparing the big bartender for the noose that was being tied. He kept pushing Thad farther away. "What are you trying to do? Ruin your chances in this town? You're either on the side of law and order or you're not. They don't accept any halfway measures."

There was a sudden flurry of cries and a tidal movement of the crowd.

"He's makin' a break for it!"

"Don't let him get away!"

"Grab him!"

Clay swung swiftly, frowning, suddenly concerned. Then the noise quieted.

"They got him again," he said, the half-smile returning. "He mustn't get away. Bad for everybody."

Thad was puzzled. Clay had seemed almost personally troubled when it appeared for a brief moment that Matt might escape. Then the suspicion left him as the argument resumed.

"Come on," said Clay. "Let it happen. You can't stop it anyway. You tried, and you've seen you can't. If you try any more, you'll be under question in this town from here on out.''

Thad halted and gave in. Clay was right. He couldn't stop it. He'd tried. He knew he would wonder the rest of his life if he tried hard enough. He had tried. But Clay's argument was compelling. It mustn't be presumed Thad was on the side of criminals. The idea was repugnant to him. He tried to put it out of his mind, but it remained. The seed Clay had planted took root, despite Thad's revulsion at the thought of it.

Clay led him away. As they walked, the mob's muttering quieted. Matt's voice rose in screaming protest, and there was a *thump!* as Matt's cries ceased. The crowd's murmur returned, but in a lower, muffled key.

Thad did not look back. He knew Matt was dead, knew that the crowd, now suddenly doubtful and guilt-ridden, was dispersing. He felt sick, nauseated.

Clay, however, was unaffected by the tragedy. His mouth still smiled crookedly; his eyes still held the gint of amusement. He began to talk about Thad's trip to the mines.

"You figure on going pretty soon?" he asked, as they turned the corner into Montgomery Street.

Thad nodded. He opened his mouth to explain to Clay how his intentions had changed, how, on Jackson's advice, instead of mining he planned to perform some service for the miners. Suddenly, he decided not to divulge his plans. Why, he could not say. He looked at Clay searchingly. The cynical amusement, the smooth manners, the easy conversation—all were the same as they had been. This was the man who, at a moment of crisis, had lent him a sizable amount of money on pure faith. If Clay had not produced his gold on the steamy beach at Panama, he and Jo would doubtlessly still be in that godforsaken hell hole. Or he would have had to send Jo on alone. Or they would have been stricken by the fevers common to that place. Yes, Clay had done him a big favor. A big, big favor.

Thad opened his mouth again to speak, then closed it.

He would not tell Clay at this time. Maybe later.

"I want to pay you what I owe you," Thad announced, fumbling in the rawhide bag for gold coins, which he thrust at Clay. "That ought to take care of it."

Clay glanced at the coins in his hand. "More than enough. The amount, plus interest. But I wasn't in any hurry to get repaid. I don't mind having you as a debtor."

Thad shook Clay off at the entrance to the hotel where he had installed Jo. Clay gave signs of perfectly willing to accompany him to the room, but Thad bade him goodbye at the door.

"I plan to go to the northern mines tomorrow," Thad told him. "I'll look you up before I go."

"Do that," said Clay. "And don't worry about Jo. I'll keep an eye on her."

Thad felt an undefinable surge of resentment at that remark. He no longer was indebted to Clay, other than gratitude for a favor. The last thing he wanted was for Clay to think he had an option on Jo. It was one thing to have been befriended by Clay, but the price was far too high if it drove a wedge into his marriage. Nevertheless, the good news he was bringing Jo overwhelmed this momentary cloud in his thoughts, and he bounded up the stairs, after nodding to the obsequious, stiff-collared manager.

At the door to their room, Thad smiled to himself as, to test its weight, he hefted the bag of gold pieces and dust that had saved his life such a short time before. He entered the room and found Jo seated in a creaking rocker by the window, gazing morosely out at the bustling streets below. Her eyes were no longer red from weeping, but the grief had been replaced by a hardness that was even more dismaying.

"I'm back, Jo," he said hesitantly.

The rocker's weary rhythm was scarcely waltered. "I see you are. What foolish thing have you done now?"

It was hardly the welcome he had expected. Instead of being overjoyed, Jo had turned a cold shoulder to him.

62

What could be the trouble? If it was the death of the child, the loss had been his as well. Or was it something—or someone—else?

"Listen, Jo. I've made some money."

"You've *made* some! Instead of losing it! That's a big change."

Thad bridled at her outburst but, with effort, managed to swallow his anger. "Jo, don't act that way. I'd do anything for you. But with the way you're treating me, I feel like a stranger."

Jo continued to look away and remained sullenly silent.

Thad went on. "After a trip or two to the mines, I'll have saved enough to start a business of our own. In the meantime, you can stay in town comfortably. I've got a room for you at a better hotel, the Union." He seated himself in a chair and drew it close to her. "This town needs new ideas, and I've got some."

"So far, your ideas haven't been very good," Jo asserted.

He rose, frowning with disappointment. He had hoped to divert her by his plans, by describing the numerous alternatives open to them, by accounting for the success he had recently experienced.

"Don't you want to hear what I've done?" he asked quietly.

She stood up and faced him. "No, Thad, I don't. I don't want to hear anything about you. If only we hadn't met! You've brought me nothing but disaster. Go ahead and go to the mines. I may be here when you get back, and I may not."

Jo's hostility struck Thad like a physical blow. He knew she was despondent, wrenched by grief. But he was unable to fathom why that natural sorrow should turn to hate for him. She was being unfair, tremendously unfair to him. He had all he could do to prevent himself from slashing back with an angry rejoinder. They had not had that bad a life. She had always been restless, ambitious, and dissatisfied with the present.

That was the main reason, in fact, why they had come West. Until the death of the little girl, there had been no serious difficulty.

He suddenly thought of several things, including Clay's comforting Jo on board the crowded ship and Clay's concern for her when he heard of Thad's proposed journey to the mines. The only time he had seen Jo smile since the tragedy had been when he surprised her with Clay.

For the first time, Thad realized he was jealous—murderously jealous. It had been bad enough worrying about Jo's hostility and the possibility of losing her. Whenever that thought surged in Thad's brain, he resolutely put it away. He could not bear to contemplate it. The thought of life without Jo made him physically sick. But now, with it having thrust on him not only the possibility of losing her but the idea that she might be taken from him by another, the threat was too much to bear.

Thad faced Jo, looming grimly above her. "I think you'd better come with me to the mines." His voice was low but trembling with emotion.

She laughed harshly. There was no humor in it, only derision. "You must be crazy!" she snapped. "I'll take no more trips with you, Thad Morgan. I will *not* go to the mines! Don't say one more word about it!"

Thad gazed at his wife, searching for words. He did not have them. They had gone to plays in Baltimore, he remembered, where the men always said exactly the right thing, to their women, no matter what the problem or crisis, and Thad had silently yearned for that ability. But he did not have it. Words were not his forte. He had done things and told about them, briefly and in simple language. But it was now a complex matter he was facing, and he had not sublety of language.

What made it doubly frustrating was his inner feeling that Jo wanted to argue, that perhaps a violent argument, a trantrum in which both would let out the seething pressures that had accumulated for days, would solve their mutual problem. All he could think of to say was that she was wrong, that she was unfair, that the loss had been to both of them, not only to her. The words that came to his mind to say these things were simple and short and brusque, and he knew they would not bring about the necessary catharsis.

He had a temper too, and he was not sure how long he could contain it. Jo was so unfair.

She stood there, stiff and unyielding, her lips set in a stubborn line, anger glinting from her eyes. He confronted her for a long moment, then ran worthlessly out of the room. He went blindly down the stairs two at a time and plunged out onto the street. The sky was crystaline and the sun blinding. He stood for a moment on the street, trying to gather his thoughts.

Avery Jackson hurried up behind him.

"Hey, where you been? I been waitin' in the lobby fer ye. If we're headin' north tomorrow, we got to get in some supplies."

Thad turned toward him grimly. "We're going tonight! Whatever we need, we'll get now! Where's a stable? I'll buy us a couple of horses. You get the rest of the stuff."

"There's one down near North Beach. But what's eatin' you? We ain't in that much of a hurry."

"*I* am!" said Thad. "If you're coming with me, get moving. We've got to get those boiled shirts up in the attic before we go."

Jackson hobbled after him. "Now, listen. Don't go gettin' me a horse! Get me a mule! Durn sight more sure-footed on them mountain trails. And we got to git a pack animule."

"I'll get me a horse and you a mule. We don't need anything else. We'll travel light."

Jackson gave up trying to keep up with him. He halted, panting, and called after him, cupping his hands around his mouth. "Don't be in too much of a hurry about buyin' them animals! Be sure they ain't spavined."

Thad kept on, without looking back. He had to get

out of town, out of this place. He had to move and move fast. He had to find someplace away from the hurrying people, somewhere quiet where he could think through what to do next, what to do to bring Jo back to him.

At the corral, he halted, took a long breath, and shook his head as if to get the cobwebs out of it. Horse dealers were notoriously dishonest. Jo had already taunted him for allowing himself to be cheated. He would never be cheated again. Never. And definitely not by the horse dealer, who was already approaching him, a hairy-faced, snaggle-toothed, grinning huckster.

7

The next morning, Thad and Avery Jackson rode south along the shore of the bay toward San Jose. Away from the morning fog of San Francisco the day was bright and gave promise of being hot. As they rounded the hills south of the town and the plain leveled out, the trail wound through yellow fields of wild mustard that were dotted with gnarled and crouching oaks whose dry leaves rustled in the breeze.

"This here's a good mule," Jackson said. "And your hoss looks pretty good, too. You must've druv a fine bargain."

Thad grunted. "It wasn't easy. The fellow tried to skin me, and I told him I'd beat him to a pulp if he didn't give me a fair price. He argued a little, but he gave in."

Jackson chuckled. "I wish I'd seen it. You're gettin' more direct in your methods."

Thad didn't answer. The brightness of the day did not reflect his mood. He hadn't gone back to the hotel room that night, and his argument with Jo clouded his mind and gave him a sick, sinking feeling. The day grew hotter. Bluebottle flies buzzed in the air. The breeze died, and the sun became a blazing, burning furnace. The plodding of the horse under him grew to an obligato that drummed in his brain. He could think of nothing to help, no solution. Maybe he had been wrong to leave without another attempt to talk to her. Yet he remembered the hardness in her voice and eyes; he knew it would have made no difference.

Jackson regarded him somberly, guessing the reason for his despair. From time to time, he essayed conversation, but Thad was in no mood to talk. At noon, they rested their mounts by a tiny, muddy stream that ran down from the peninsula hills, and Jackson pulled out the strip of beef jerky from his knapsack.

"Hungry?" he asked.

Thad shrugged. "Not much."

"Have some anyways." Jackson sliced off a hunk of the leathery substance with his jackknife and thrust it at Thad. "It'll do y' good, and it don't do no good to starve yourself, even if you're worried about something'."

Thad took it wordlessly and chewed it in a preoccupied manner.

"You know, sometimes," Jackson said, "if y' got a problem, if y' stop thinkin' about it for awhile, it somehow seems to settle itself in your mind. Answers come up that y' ain't thought of before, because you've got so tired thinkin'. Why don't y' knock off on whatever it is that's botherin' y'. Mebbe tomorrow mornin' the answer 'll hit y' plain as day."

Thad looked up and forced a smile. "Thanks, Avery," he said. "Maybe you're right." He rose and examined his horse. "I think both of 'em are rested now. Let's get moving." They stopped at a ranch that night near San Jose and shared the hospitality of a Yankee rancher.

The rancher's garden crop had been carted off by Sonorans during his absence at the mines. His Mexican wife and half-Mexican child had almost been carried off with the produce, but their screams and struggles had convinced the thieves that they were not worth the trouble. The man, Bledsoe, shook his head at Thad's announced intention of heading across the San Joaquin.

"It's hotter'n the seven jaws of hell," he said. "You'll be parched afore you've gone two miles, and you're likely to die o' sunstroke. You better take an extry goatskin full o' water. You'll need it."

Thad was not sure how the water would taste after being overheated in a goatskin, but he accepted the gift with thanks, and he and Avery set out early the next morning before the heat of the sun was high.

Bledsoe had been right. Before midmorning, the temperature rose to what Thad thought must be at least a hundred degrees. No breath of air stirred to rustle the tired leaves on the occasional live oak they passed, whose shade they quickly sought. The fields of mustard gave way to brown grass that looked as if it had never seen a drop of water. The carcass of a rangy steer lay, half-rotted, at the edge of a damp spot in the ground that tried to be a slough; flies buzzed around it. Perspiration soaked Thad's shirt, soaked through his hatband and hat, and stained his corduroy trousers. Jackson was not much better off, although his dried-up little body seemed to tolerate the heat better than Thad's.

At noon, they found a scrubby live oak and threw themselves down in its shade to eat some more jerky. Jackson looked at Thad sidewise through bloodshot blue eyes. "Any answer occur to y' this mornin'?"

Thad sighed. "Not yet," he said. "But this morning I think an answer's possible. I didn't yesterday."

"I told y'!" Jackson chuckled. "Sometimes y' got to wait and let things simmer."

Thad rose and adjusted the cinch on his horse's saddle. "I think there's a way out of almost anything," he said. "If only you're smart enough to find it. The only problem is, you've got to have some leverage."

Jackson patted his mule, who looked away. "That's right," he said. "But findin' the leverage is part of the answer to the problem."

"Let's go!" said Thad. He mounted his horse and moved out of the shade into the blazing, blistering, burning sunlight. He shaded his eyes with his hand and looked back at the coastal range of mountains bhind them.

"Those hills look pretty good compared to what's ahead of us," he said.

"They do, at that," Jackson agreed. "But you got to remember, there's more hills, and bigger ones, beyond the San Joaquin. Mebbe they'll be even prettier."

Thad halted his horse and pointed. "Look at that!" he said. He indicated something in the sky over the coastal range.

"What are ye lookin' at?" Jackson demanded, squinting.

"That bird," Thad said. "That big bird, sailing around the crags. Looks as big as an elephant."

"That's the same bird we saw from the deck of the ship," Jackson said. "Remember? I told y' then. It's a bird that only lives in California. It's the biggest bird in the world. It ain't afraid of anything, and its wings are big enough, so it flies right over the storms. It's a condor."

Thad sat looking at the dark speck in the sky. It sailed smoothly, confidently soaring in the air currents without any motion of its huge wings.

"It's those big wings," Thad said, half to himself. "Those big wings keep it above the storms and let it sail wherever it wants to go without a fuss."

Jackson looked up curiously. "That's right," he said. "It's those big wings that let it fly right over trouble."

Thad's hand inadvertently sought the money belt around his waist. He said nothing, but— *here are my wings,* he thought. *Gold gives a man wings in this country, or anywhere. Gold enables you to fly above the storms.*

His eyes grew hard. *I'm going to have big wings,* he thought. *The biggest I can get. Right now, I don't see how they can keep Jo with me. But they'll help. They certainly won't hurt. And maybe they're the answer.*

Jackson was watching Thad as he sat and silently peered into the sky over the mountains, watching the big bird vanish into the clouds.

"Come one!" said Thad, urging his horse forward toward the hot lowlands. "We've got work to do!"

70

They rounded the southern end of the bay, avoiding the marshes whose edges gave off an odor of rank, steaming, rotting vegetation under the broiling heat of the sun. The pools at the edge of the bay were purplish-red with white sediment around the edges. Thad looked at them carefully.

"Nasty lookin', ain't they?" Jackson remarked.

"Not to me," Thad said shortly. "They look like salt beds to me. Everybody needs salt." He jumped off his horse, splashed into the shallows, dipped his fingers in the red pool, and tasted them.

"It's salt, all right," he said, remounting. "We'll keep this in mind. Got to find out who owns it. Maybe we can start a business right here."

They left the shores of the bay and began to wind through the rolling, brown, bald-looking hills that rimmed it. There were a lot of them. As shallow as the valleys were, they seemed to gather up the heat and focus it on any travelers who dared their trails. They traveled half a day through the baking, rolling, sun-browned range. Only as the sun was descending did they emerge upon a slope to look down upon a vast plain that shimmered in the heat; the wavery horizon dimly showed through the bluish haze as a distant range of snow-capped mountains.

They halted their horses and dismounted. Jackson removed his hat and mopped his wet brow with a blue bandana. "That there's the San Joaquin," he announced. "I heerd abut it. And beyond it's the Sierra. It's in that range that the Donners got stuck and began eatin' each other."

Thad sighed. "It's a big country."

"It sure is," Jackson agreed. "There's room enough for everybody here. Before long, everybody's goin' to be here, because it ain't a bad place, seems like."

"The flats look pretty good for farming," Thad mused, "if there's enough water."

Jackson pointed. "There's a row of bushes and trees. Must be a crick. And there's a house. See? Just beyond

71

the bend in the crick. Let's bed down there for the night, if we can.'' Thad nodded.

They mounted again and let their tired mounts descend the slope at their own pace. The headwaters of the creek, lined with live oaks and chapparal, appeared over a rise, and the two of them headed for it.

"Got to watch out fer snakes in that brush,'' Jackson said. ''I heerd there's plenty of rattlers in this country. And they're big ones.''

Thad pulled up his horse. "That's no rattler.'' He pointed.

Jackson followed his gaze. "By gollies, you're right! That's a woman!''

The woman wore a broad-brimmed hat and brown clothing. She was seated on a rock, peering out over the plain. Her horse stood nearby, grazing. She was not aware of their approach until they were within three hundred yards of her. Then she sprang to her feet and whirled as if frightened and angry. She had been pre-occupied, Thad felt, with a worry of her own; intruders were not welcome.

Sh awaited their coming without moving forward to meet them. She was dark-haired and dark-skinned and held herself proudly erect. She wore a leather-reinforced brown divided skirt and boots with spurs. She must ride a lot, Thad thought.

Thad took off his had, nodded toward her, then put it on again. "Ma'am, is that your place over there?'' He nodded at the distant, sprawling adobe in a clump of oaks by a small brush-clad stream.

She waited for a moment, then decided to answer. "*Si*,'' she said. "That is my home.'' She spoke with a Spanish accent, but seemed to have no difficulty with English.

"We'd like something to eat and a place to bed down for the night.''

Again she paused. "From where do you come?'' she inquired

"From San Francisco. We're heading for the diggings.''

She looked piercingly at Thad and then at Jackson. "You are not from—but no, you cannot be. *Bueno*. Come with me. We will talk to my father and see what can be arranged." She put one foot in the big, worked-leather Mexican stirrup and mounted her horse with the ease of long experience, uring it to a gallop. Then she set off down the gentle slope at a breakneck pace, paying no attention whatever to the two men behind her.

Thad and Jackson looked at each other, silently agreeing to follow at a slower pace. In a short time, they were splashing through the stream to gain the shade of the oaks, where they dismounted and looped the reins of their mounts around a hitchrail already occupied by the girl's palomino.

She was waiting for them on the pole-columned veranda. The house, Thad saw, was more elaborate than any of the structures they had seen thus far on their journey. It had several rooms, a tiled roof, two elderly rockers on the porch, a well with a sweep, and a corral. It looked lived in.

"Come in," she nodded her head, still unsmiling. "We will see *mi padre*."

It was cool and dark inside. The floor was clean-swept earth, with scattered Indian rugs. There was a spinning wheel plus two dark and hard-to-distinguish oil portraits of the family's ancestors. The furniture was heavy and clearly handmade, a lot of it. The signs of prosperity were the silver-framed mirror and tall silver candlesticks.

"Wait here. I will get him," she told them, moving quickly out of the room toward an inner chamber.

"She doesn't seem very friendly, but she's going to take us in," Thad remarked in a low voice.

"It's the law of hospitality in these parts," Jackson said in a whisper. "I've heerd these people never turn down anybody who wants lodgin' or a visit. There was a time when they had bowls o' coins out so guests could help themselves if they was a little short o' cash. But I don't see anything like that here. I guess those days are gone."

73

The girl returned in a moment with a white-haired man who walked slowly by her side. He had a silvery mustache and goatee, and his face was kind. "*Mi padre* says you can stay, and we will give you *cena* and *almuerzo*. We rise at dawn. There will be *carne y frijoles* in half an hour."

"*Sientese, sientese!*" the old man motioned to chairs and a chest with a rug over it that served as a settee.

Thad and Jackson introduced themselves. "We've only been in California a few days," Thad said, "but we're going up to get a look at the diggings before any more people get there."

The girl, still unsmiling, said, "There are many of you *yanquis* coming to our land. And you cause much trouble."

"No, no!" her father made shushing motions with his hand. He spoke in Spanish to the girl, and she translated.

"He says I must not make you feel unwelcome, that you are not responsible for our trouble. He says I must introduce us to you. He is Don Pedro Esteban Sarmiento y Lugo. He is the son of one of the soldiers who came with Portola nearly a hundred years ago. And this is our rancho, the Rancho Santa Elena. It was given to his father by the King of Spain." She hesitated, then said bitterly, "We have been able to keep it for nearly a hundred years."

Her father broke in with rapid Spanish, and she spoke again. "He says we will keep it for many more hundreds of years, for me and my children and grandchildren. But," she shrugged, "I know that is not the case, and so does he. By this time next year, it will not longer be ours."

Thad was interested. "What do you mean, it will no longer be yours? What is happening to it?"

She opened her mouth to speak then closed it again. "I do not think it is any of your concern," she said stiffly.

Thad nodded. "You're quite right," he said. "It isn't any of our business. Ah, this looks like our dinner. I want to tell you and your father how grateful we are for your hospitality. You are very kind."

The stout Mexican woman who entered, carrying a tray with steaming dishes on it, was barefoot, but she and her clothes were clean, and she smiled warmly at the visitors.

"That smells mighty good!" Jackson said, sniffing the air. "Didn't realize how hongry I was!"

The two were invited to gather around the heavy, handmade table and, by the light of another pair of huge silver candelabra, they confronted plates heaped with fried beans, tortillas, and a beef stew with the tough beef mercifully cut up into small chewable pieces and doused in a sauce so hot it had to be softened with a substance that was not too harsh, such as tomatoes, yellow summer squash, and a red wine.

The smiling Mexican woman leaned over the girl's shoulder as she served the last plate. "I hear *caballos*. Should I put *dos platas mas* on the table?"

Thad saw the girl stop eating and turn pale. "No, no, Maria," she said. "Do not trouble yourself." She stopped eating, excused herself, left the table, and went out the front door, where she stood for a long time peering toward the hills Thad and Jackson had just crossed. Finally she re-entered, and her face was shadowed. She sat down again at the table but made no move to eat.

Her father stopped talking to Thad and asked in English, "What is the matter, *Carita*?"

"Two riders approach," she said. "I think it is the two who were here before."

The old man stopped eating, too. His face reflected the same concern as the girl's. "I had hoped," he said gently, running trembling fingers through his white hair, "that they would give us at least another day of peace."

"But they will not. You know they will not." She rose and paced nervously to the window, ignoring the two visitors. "What answer do we have for them today, *padra mio*?"

75

The old man rose and went to his daughter's side. The meal was over for the two of them. "We must have faith in God," he said. "An answer will be provided." He put his arm around her shoulders, but she flung angrily away.

"We have had faith before," she retorted, "and things have become worse and worse!"

Thad and Jackson looked at each other with raised brows. Hoofbeats were clearly audible now, and they grew quickly louder.

The old ranchero suddenly remembered his duty as the host and hobbled back to the table. "You must excuse my daughter and me," he said in English. "We have forgotten our manners! We should not permit our worries to afflict our guests! Please, I beg you, continue your meal. Maria! Maria! More wine for the gentlemen, *por favor!*"

The two riders pulled up before the house. Their boots clumped on the veranda, and there was a heavy pounding on the door.

Don Pedro looked helplessly at his daughter as she opened the door and flung it wide. Thad watched with interest. Dusk was heavy outside; the fading glow of the setting sun over the distant hills placed the two visitors in silhouette. One was short and round and the other tall and stooped. The short, round one pulled off his flat-crowned sombrero and entered the room without ado. When the candlelight fell on his features, Thad saw that his hearty, red, smiling round face had blond eyebrows and was topped by straw-colored hair. The light was strong enough for Thad to see that his clothing was expensive and well kept. The tall, stooped man behind him was droop-mustached, clad in dark clothing, and wore two heavy pistols low on his hips in holsters attached to crossed cartridge belts. He was not smiling, but his eyes were watchful as he stood with his back against the wall next to the door.

The round-faced man chuckled happily. "Sure is nice to see you again, Miss Elena," he said, reaching out a pudgy hand, which the girl, after hesitating, took

76

timorously. Thad saw that his eyes did not reflect the smile of his mouth. "I see you have company, he said. "And who might they be, Miss Elena?" He made no effort to release her hand, holding it as if he intended to hold it the rest of the evening.

"They are two travelers who asked for food and lodging," she said, attempting to pull her hand away.

The man continued to smile and refused to release her. Instead, he moved closer and put a heavy arm around her shoulders, all the while holding her hand in his. He regarded Thad and Avery with interest while the girl attempted to slip out of his grasp.

"I'm Buck Bronson from San Jose," he said. "Now that I've greeted the little lady here, I'll come over and shake hands with you two." He released the girl, who moved quickly away from him in obvious relief, and stuck out his thick-fingered hand in Thad's direction.

Thad rose from the table and took it. It was warm and sweaty. "My name's Morgan," he said curtly, the dislike in his voice obvious. "And this is Mr. Jackson. We're on our way to the diggings, and these people kindly offered us hospitality for the night."

"Headin' for the diggings, hey?" Bronson said. "Well, that's sure where everybody's going nowadays. That is, everybody but those of us who have business around here." He turned, smiling happily, toward the old man. "Don Pedro!" he exclaimed. "Good to see you again! You certainly keep a fine house here!" He looked around appreciatively. "Kept it in good shape for me, I see!" He chuckled loudly. "I know our two visitors here won't mind if we excuse ourselves for a little business talk. Will they, now?" He looked hard at Thad as he spoke, then he moved again toward the girl, reaching out a fat hand for her arm.

She drew back angrily. "Señor, whatever you have to say can be said in the presence of our guests." Thad saw she was afraid to be alone with Bronson with only her father for protection.

Bronson's pale, freckled face stretched again in the most amiable of grins, but again his smile did not extend to his cold eyes. "Oh, come now, Señorita! You surely don't care to discuss personal business in front of strangers!"

She faced him squarely. "If there is anything to discuss, discuss it here!" Her father, his face drawn with concern, rung his wringkled hands in agitation.

Bronson tried again. "We could go in the next room, Señorita, and have a pleasant little chat. In fact, you and I could go there alone, without botherin' your father at all. You're pretty much in charge of things here, anyway."

The girl laughed in his face. "Señor, you must think I am a fool! I would not be in a room alone with you under any circumstances!"

Bronson's smile remained, but his face colored briefly with anger. "Oh, well, if that's the case, then we'll talk business right out in public." His face hardened, and the smile vanished. "I came here to tell you, Señorita, and your father, that you've got just thirty days left. But if you'll turn over this homestead to me today, you can still keep those grapelands up on the slopes, and you won't owe me any more money—which you will surely do if you wait thirty days!"

The girl regarded him thoughtfully. "So, if we bargain today, we have a better arrangement? We keep the grapelands, and we have no debt?"

Bronson nodded, and the smile returned. "Can't afford to turn it down, can you? You'd be a fool, otherwise."

The girl was still thoughtful. "Why are you in such a hurry, Mr. Bronson? Is there some special reason?" Her intelligent dark eyes probed his.

Bronson shrugged his shoulders. "Only to keep your debt from gettin' any bigger, Señorita. After all, twelve percent a month mounts up fast!"

Thad looked at Jackson unbelievingly. "Twelve percent a month!" he muttered. "How long ago was that loan made?"

Jackson shook his head. "Listen!" he whispered to Thad. "I think I know why that coyote's in a hurry. I

78

heerd in Frisco that the U.S. gov'ment was plannin' to pass a land law that would keep sharpers like this from stealin' the Mexicans blind. That's why he don't want to wait thirty days.''

Thad stood there, listening to the fat moneylender arguing with the girl. With every sentence Bronson edged closer to her, and she retreated. Although a smile still creased his features, his growing irritation showed in an angry flush. Finally, he gave up with her and turned to her father.

"Don Pedro," he said brusquely, "your daughter is a fool, but I hope you're not one. You borrowed twenty thousand; you already owe me a hundred and thirty. In thirty days, I will take your land and cattle for satisfaction of the hundred. But you'll still owe me the thirty plus interest for the next thirty days. You'll owe me forty-five thousand cash, which you don't have. In fact, you have nothing! If you deal with me now, you'll have the grapelands and no debt. I wish your daughter'd realize I'm here as a friend.''

The old man's face was wrenched with worry. He remained silent for a long moment. Then he said, "Perhaps you are right. It seems to be the only way.''

The girl rushed to his side and clutched his arm. "No! Papa! No!"

Her father turned toward her sorrowfully. "What else can we do? If we end by owing him a fortune, which we cannot pay, and no property with which to raise money to pay it, there is nothing left for me but prison.'' Then there was a silence, a long silence, in which the old man and his daughter regarded each other with hopelessness while Bronson stood spread-legged, trying to keep the smile from his face.

Finally, the girl turned. As she opened her mouth to speak, Thad pushed back his chair, scraping it loudly on the floor, and came to the side of his hosts. "Bronson," he said, "I couldn't help but overhear what's going on. You've made these people an offer, so the least you can do is give 'em time to think about it. Let 'em tell you tomorrow what they decide.''

79

Bronson allowed his smile develop but he shook his head meanly. "Nope! One of the terms of that offer is, it be taken up immediately. And immediately means now! I ain't disposed to wait. The offer's clear enough. If they accept now, I'll take the ranch and stock, and they'll have the grapelands and owe me a measly thirty thousand. If they sell the grapelands, that'll cover it. If they wait till the loan matures in thirty days, they'll owe me a bundle, and they'll have no grapelands and no means to pay it. I think I'm bein' right generous. But," and his face darkened threateningly, "I want a decision *now*! And I don't intend to wait another hour."

"All right," said Thad with an easiness he did not feel. "Give me five minutes to talk to these folks over in the corner. Maybe we can figure something out."

"I don't know why I should," Bronson grumbled. "They wouldn't talk to me private." He grudgingly acceded, and Thad jerked his head at Avery Jackson. The two of them talked in a low voice at the table as the old man and the girl stood helplessly by.

Thad kept his voice low. "Avery," he said, "don't these miners need meat?"

"They sure do!" The old man grinned up at Thad. "I begin to see what you're drivin' at. But it's a job to git cows crosscountry and up to the diggin's. It'll cost a bit of money."

"I've got money."

"But if it goes for that, and the deal don't work out good, you're back where you started."

"*We're* back where *we* started," Thad corrected. "You want to let this shyster," he nodded toward Bronson, "ruin these people?"

"Nope! I sure don't! Go ahead! I'm with y'!"

"What'll a cow bring at the mines?"

"One to five dollars a pound, dependin' on where it is, I'll bet—judgin' from Frisco prices. I'd say at least two hundred a head, even though they're these thin Mexican longhorn critters."

Thad gazed into space for a moment, musing. Then he turned to Don Estaeban. "How many head do you have on the ranch?''

The old man looked puzzled.

"Six hundred more or less. We have not counted in some time, and I have seen many calves in the spring.''

Thad nodded. "If I could sell five hundred head at the mines for you, and give you enough to pay off this leech,'' he said, indicating Bronson, "giving you and me both something besides. Would you let me try? It's a risk. I haven't been to the mines yet, but from what I've heard, they need meat.''

The man thought for a moment, his eyes searching Thad's. Then he turned to his daughter and spoke in a low voice in rapid Spanish.

"I am willing,'' Don Pedro said at last. "We would be no worse off—''

"Oh, yes you would be,'' Thad countered. "If you take the offer he's making today, you can clean up your debt—if you can get thirty thousand out of that grape-land, as I understand it. And if you work with me, we might both lose everything we've got. On the other hand, we might make quite a lot, and you could keep your ranch. It's a risk and a chance. I want you to make the decision, and I don't want to be blamed afterward. I'm not pushing you into anything.''

Again the girl and her father conversed. The old man's face brightened as they talked. Bronson saw it and strode forward.

"You've had your five minutes,'' he said. "What's the answer? I'm not waitin' any longer!''

Thad glanced at Avery. The latter bared his snaggled teeth in a quick grin. "Go!'' he said.

Don Pedro turned back to Thad. "We will accept your offer, Señor.''

"And if we fail,'' the girl added, "we will at least not have given in to this animal!'' She tossed her head at Bronson and sneered dramatically.

Bronson reddened with rage. He moved forward. "You better know what you're doin'!'' he threatened. "You're passin' up your only real chance!'' He jerked a thumb at Thad. "Do you know this *hombre*? Every seen him before? How do you know he ain't plannin' to run off with your cows?"

"I have not seen him before," said Don Pedro, "but I have seen you! And that is enough!"

"Well, you're not usin' very good sense." Bronson moved still closer.

Thad came between them, his face inches from Bronson's, which was a good head below his. "You have no claim on this family for another thirty days. They'd appreciate your leavin'."

Bronson glared, snapped a glance over his shoulder at his mustached gunman, who was still leaning against the wall, then swore, turned on his heel, and stamped out of the house. The tall, dark armed man followed him quietly, looking over his shoulder at Thad as he left the room, closing the door quietly behind him.

The girl's expression softened. She came close to Thad and looked up at him gratefully. 'Señor," she said feelingly, "I do not know how to thank you! This is the first hope we have had in weeks." There was a sultry note in her voice.

Thad drew back. "Don't thank me," he said shortly. "I expect to make money out of this deal, or I wouldn't have proposed it. Now let's get down to business. We've only got thirty days, and we've got a lot to do." He turned away toward Jackson. "We got to get a couple of hands to help us get these cows to the diggin's. See if you can do that. I'll work out some kind of contract with these people."

The girl stiffened and retreated. She was not used to her charms being ignored so openly. She regarded Thad with a puzzled gaze. Why had he helped, if—?

But Thad was asking her for pen and paper, and she went to get them.

8

The San Jose rancher had told them that the San Joaquin was hotter than the seven jaws of hell, and, Thad concluded, he was right. Furthermore, driving over two hundred head of cattle across dusty flats was much different from perspiring all by yourself on a horse whose pace you can control. The rangy Mexican longhorns were as fleet as antelope and churned up a choking cloud of dust. It made little difference which side of the herd he rode; the wind seemed to shift so that his lungs were always full of the tasty soil of the San Joaquin. Moreover, Thad and Jackson and the three *vaqueros* Jackson had hired were hardly enough manpower to round up strays and keep the herd moving at an effective fast walk.

At the end of the day they had made fewer miles than Thad had hoped, and the three *vaqueros* were muttering among themselves around their own campfire.

"God to watch them boys," said Jackson, gnawing off a hunk of jerky. "They ain't happy."

"Why?" Thad asked. "I thought they were Don Pedro's men."

"They are, and that's just the problem. They're so loyal to him and his ranch, they hate to see him sellin' off his stock. They don't understand the problem. Don Pedro tried to explain it to 'em, but they want to write off the debt by killin' Bronson. They may have the same attitude about us, because we're sellin' off the stock.''

"Well, for Pete's sake, let's try to explain it to 'em again. We've got to move fast with this herd. We can't afford any complications." He rose and made his way; to the other campfire. Squatting down he nodded amiably at the three dark-visaged, mustachioed cowboys, who regarded him balefully in the firelight.

"Any of you boys speak English?" Thad asked.

One of them, the younger of the men with fewer Indian features than his companions, nodded sullenly. "I do, a leetle."

Thad nodded. He waited a moment, then asked, "You like Don Pedro and the Señorita?"

"*Mucho*," the man said. "They are good to work for. They are good to us when we are seeck. They help our wives and our *niños*." He scowled. "We want nothing to hurt them!"

Thad nodded again. "I like them, too," he said. "I did not like Señor Bronson and the thing he was trying to make them do."

The man turned to his companions and jabbered in rapid Spanish. Then he turned back. "We did not like him either. But the Señorita would not let us do to him what we wished to do."

"I am helping Don Pedro and the Señorita," said Thad. "It was their wish that I do so."

The man shook his head stubbornly. "We do not believe you, Señor. We think you deceived Don Pedro and the Señorita, just as Bronson deceived them. Selling their cattle cannot be good for them. What will they have to live on?"

"Selling the cattle will let them pay their debt to Señor Bronson."

"Ah!" the man's eyes glittered with hatred. "Then you are working to help Señor Bronson."

"No, no!" Thad protested. "I do not like Señor Bronson. But they owe him money, and it must be paid, or he will always be able to harm them."

"Bah!" the cowboy shrugged. He pulled a long knife

from its sheath in his belt and ran his thumb along the blade. "This would take care of him and wipe out the debt! He need not be paid."

"Oh, yes! He must be paid," Thad insisted. "It is the way the *yanquis* do things. If a debt exists, it must be paid. The *alcaldes* will insist. And even if Bronson is a bad man, they will help him get the money Don Pedro owes him." The *vaquero* sat silent. "If we sell the cattle for a good price, Don Pedro can pay off the debt and buy more cattle. I am trying to help Don Pedro and the Señorita."

The *vaquero* explained the matter to his companions in Spanish, and they responded. He turned to Thad. "We are not certain of you, Señor. We think you lie."

Thad thought hard. If these suspicious *vaqueros* became hostile, they could decamp with most of the herd, and there would be little he and Jackson could do about it. Moreover, their long knives could be used against him as well as against Bronson, once the money was collected. He shrugged and smiled to himself. His risk was already high, and so were the stakes. He might as well increase the risk a little more.

"You," said Thad, pointing to the light-skinned cowboy, "will be with me when we collect the money, and you will take the money and carry it back to Don Pedro. I have a share of the money coming to me, but you shall carry my share as well. Now are you satisfied?"

The man made him repeat the proposal; he then entered into a lengthy and voluble conversation with his friends. Finally, he turned back to Thad and thrust out his hand, which Thad took.

"If you do this, Señor, and are not playing tricks on us, then we are *amigos*. We will help you do the thing you are doing, but we will not have the Señor and the Señorita hurt!"

"I have shown you that I am trying to help them," said Thad, "by trusting you. I do not want you to hurt them either." He assumed a fierce frown. "The money that you carry must get back to them. All of it!"

"Do not insult me, Señor," said the other quietly. "I am an honest man." His eyes were threatening.

"I too am an honest man," said Thad. "Let two honest men shake hands." He again thrust out his, which the other, after a moment's hesitation, took. With the second handshake, the man's suspicions seemed to vanish. He broke into a broad grin. "My name ees Fernando," he said. "I think we can be friends!"

From that time on, the herd moved more rapidy. The *vaqueros'* mood changed from sullen obedience to cheerful and noisy enthusiasm.

They circled Stockton, although Thad insisted they halt while he and Avery explored the cattle market there. The steers could be sold, they discovered, but at prices considerably below what Avery thought could be obtained in the diggings themselves.

"'Course," he said, rubbing his grizzled chin thoughtfully, "there's two sides to the question. Another hundred, hundred and fifty miles of this scorchin' heat'll take pounds off their weight."

"But there's a lot of difference between seventy-five dollars a head and the two hundred you think we might get."

"Yep. There is that."

"Then let's go ahead. How long do you think we'll be on the road?"

Four or five more days. Mebbe a week."

"We'll still have half a month left, even if we have to try more than one camp. You agree we should go on?"

Jackson grinned and his eyes twinkled. "As the feller says, there's a heap o' difference between two hundred and seventy-five!"

They pushed on. That told Fernando of the decision, and the reasons for it. The Mexican agreed vociferously.

"Señor, you can get more than two hundred a head in the mines!" he said. "It would be foolish to sell in Stockton. You are doing the right thing."

To Thad, the succeeding hours and days blended into

a heat-hazed picture of quick, pink dawns with much bustling and shouting around the campfire, the aroma of hot coffee and frying bacon, then hours with the glaring sun climbing in a brassy sky when the dust mingled with the sweat that ran from beneath his hatband, and his perspiration-soaked shirt stuck to his back and felt clammy in a spot of scarce shade beneath a dusty live oak. The rumbling thud of many hooves mingled with the constant shouts of the *vaqueros* as they cavorted around the herd tightly astride their horses as if they were one piece of flesh and muscle. Then, as the long, bone-weary day ended at sunday, there were the quick California dusk, again the campfire, and the constant, night-long patrols of the *vaqueros* circling the herd in turn.

At noon on the third day, Fernando, seeking some of the cattle in a thicket by the river, suddenly reared his horse and thundered away, shouting.

"Bear! Grizzly! Where ees gun!"

In a moment, Thad, who was only a hundred yards behind, saw the lumbering monster emerge from the thicket, rise easily to his hind feet, and paw the air angrily. It was a huge animal, towering more than seven feet on its hind legs.

"Do we have to shoot him?" Thad asked, remembering what he had heard about the danger posed by wounded animals.

Fernando was excited. His eyes were wide, and his hands trembled as he held the old Spanish gun.

Thad was not confident of the *vaquero's* markmanship. "Eef he comes for us, we must shoot!"

"If he doesn't, let's just fire to scare him away," Thad advised, bringing his horse up beside Fernando's.

The bear sank smoothly and gracefully to all fours and stood there swinging his huge head, glaring at his enemies. Jackson came up and joined them.

"Whooee!" he chortled. "What a beast! The behemoth o' Holy Writ! What do we do with him?"

"Scare him off," said Thad. "And try to keep him

from hurting any of the cows—or us."

The bear came forward slowly, still swinging its head angrily. Thad could imagine that mighty body crushing a foe.

Fernando raised his rifle, but Thad pushed the barrel up. "No, no! Just scare him! If you only hurt him, he'll be more dangerous than ever!"

"But Señor! I have only one bullet in the gun! It takes time to load! Eef he does not scare away—"

"We're on horseback," said Thad.

"But they move like a racehorse!"

There was a sharp report from Thad's left. Jackson had pulled a revolver from his pocket and fired it in the air. The bear paused. Fernando saw it hesitate and he suddenly decided to do as Thad has asked. He fired the rifle in the air. As it went off with a sullen roar and a cloud of acrid smoke, the bear reared up, whirled around, and bounded off into the brush. Thad glanced at Jackson, who grinned at him as he pocketed the smoking pistol.

They passed by Sacramento, a collection of huts on the riverbank, and the big fortress owned by the Swiss expatriate, John Sutter. It was crowded with people and lay close by Coloma, where, Fernando told them, Sutter's man first discovered the gold that had opened the country.

Then they were in the Sierra foothills. The heat grew even more intense. Each hour saw them climbing higher toward the distant range of blue mountains that, men said, contained the Mother Lode.

At last, they came to a town. Thad, Jackson, and Fernando left the herd and approached it. There had been occasional miners in the streams before that, squatting in the cold mountain water with pans or jiggling rockers. They had watched with awe as the herd rumbled dustily by and shouted questions, but here the streams were crowded with men, working almost shoulder to shoulder. Tents and flimsy shelters crowded the riverbank; clotheslines were hung with the red shirts of miners; and the mining equipment was more elaborate. Some miners had diverted the stream into sluices, with riffles of wood on the bottom to catch the gold as the water rushed past. Others had huge rockers that resembled baby's cradles, into which they shoveled the gold-bearing gravel and then energetically agitated it for the heavier metal to sink to the bottom.

Some patched and ragged miners, worked with simple jackknives in rock crevices. It was one of these who, as Thad passed on horseback, leaped to his feet, shouting with glee. The man looked around frantically. He had to show someone his find. He saw Thad and rushed up to his stirrup. "Look! Lookee there! I'm rich!" he yelled. He pushed a fist-size lump of dirty rock in Thad's face. "It's all gold!" he cried. "It's a nugget! Worth a fortune!" And he danced off, still shouting.

Jackson shrugged. "He'll spend it all in a week, gamblin' and buyin' our high-priced beef. Come on, let's find a store where they sell vittles."

They came upon a tent-covered, wood-floored shack with canned goods, some hams hanging from beams, and piles of oranges and lemons that had been carted up from the valley. The storekeeper was thin-faced, evil-eyed, and dour of expression.

Thad told him, "We've got cows outside town. You want beef?"

The man's eyes narrowed. "Cows? How many?"

"Two hundred head."

The storekeepers eyes flickered. "Two hundred head? Where you got 'em?"

Jackson shouldered his way forward. "Now just a minute, mister! We asked you a question, and you ain't answered it. You want beef?"

The man hesitated a moment longer, then shrugged elaborately and said, "I'd have to see 'em before I bought 'em. But nah; we don't need beef here. We got canned stuff and hams."

Thad was incredulous. "What do you mean, you don't need beef? With all these people here, you mean they're not interested in fresh meat?"

The man shrugged again. "Where would I store it? It won't keep in this heat."

"Oh the hoof, of course, until you're ready to sell it."

The man looked Thad up and down. "Where'd you say it was?"

"Outside o' town."

He turned away. "Not interested."

In the street, the three took counsel.

"Looks like we were wrong," said Thad. "We gambled and lost."

Fernando shook his head. "Ees hard to believe. Are there other *tiendas*?"

"That's the biggest," said Thad. "The others—you saw 'em—are pretty small. He'd be the one to do it, if anybody did."

Jackson rubbed his chin stubble. "I ain't so sure he's not interested."

"He certainly brushed us off," Thad said.

"Yeah, but he was awful interested in where the cows was. He asked twice. I think we better be real careful watchin' that herd tonight."

"Well," Thad said, "I'm not that suspicious. We'll watch, all right, but I think he meant what he said. I think he's not interested."

That night they watched. Thad told the Mexicans, "Stay with the cows. I'm going to look around."

He did so, trotting his horse up a hillock that overlooked the milling, lowing herd. He went even farther away, toward the town, and stationed himself in a clump of cottonwood where he could watch the main trail.

Sitting there in the darkness, Thad found he could not keep his thoughts under control. He was filled with an inexplicable melancholy that rapidly gave way to frustrated anger.

What does a man have to do to come out ahead?

He had worked hard, had not been too fond of the

bottle, had not chased other men's wives, had loved his family, had grasped for more when he really was not much interested in grasping for more because Jo had wanted him to. What more could he have done?

And yet everything had turned out wrong. Everything. Here in the darkness, with the stars of the San Joaquin blinking brightly overhead, he seemed to see reality more clearly. And reality meant that Jo was lost to him.

He should not be this far away from her. What was she doing now? He closed his eyes and swore under his breath. Was Clay with her? He had been too confident of Clay. And yet, something had held him back when the urge to confide had come upon him. He had been suspicious of Clay even on the boat, a suspicion he had not admitted to himself but that was present nonetheless.

He should go back. He should abandon this herd of someone else's cattle and the futile business of trying to make a fortune in the diggings when every other mother's son in the country was trying to do the same thing. He should turn his horse and go back to camp and tell Avery to finish this job for the darkeyed señorita at the rancho.

Thad suddenly became alert. Four horsemen thudded out of the dim halo of light that fogged the entrance to the town's main street. They were galloping and pulled up not a hundred yards from where Thad was sitting on his horse.

He heard muttered voices. Then three of the horsemen continued into the darkness while one retreated toward the same clump of cottonwoods that sheltered Thad.

Thad held himself silent and hoped against hope that his horse would not whinny or stamp. Before two minutes had passed, he had the lone rider identified. Without question, it was the storekeeper, the stooped, sour-visaged curious individual who had said he was not interested in the herd but did want to know where it was located.

This was what Jackson had suspected. Maybe some things did turn out all right. Thad dismounted, looped his horse's reins over a thick chaparral branch, and moved as quietly as he was able toward the man sitting stoop-shouldered on a bony nag whose hearing seemed, fortuitously, none to acute. He was only five feet from his quarry when the man heard him and suddenly turned in the saddle. Thad leaped for his left leg, jerked it from the stirrup, and pulled hard at the man's body. Off balance, and with a muffled cry, the man tipped from the saddle and thumped heavily to the ground, where he attempted to scramble to his feet.

Thad was there to prevent it. The man's scrawny body was out matched by Thad who pinned the man to the ground. Then Thad jerked the short-muzzled derringer from his pocket and held it to the man's head.

"Now!" Thad said in a voice that brooked no denial. "Call off your men, or I'll kill you!"

The man said nothing while trembling with fright. Thad yanked him to his feet, pulled him toward his own horse, and unlooped the reins from the chaparral branch. He took a lariat from his saddlehorn, tied the man's hands firmly behind him at wrist and elbow, and holding one end of the rope, urged him forward.

Remounting, Thad led his frightened prisoner like a dog on a leash. The man followed, half-trotting in the dust.

"When we get to the top of the hill," Thad said, "I'm going to fire my gun to get attention, and you call off your men. Or you'll get a bullet through your head!"

They made their way to the top of the hillock.

9

Joe was still angry when Thad left the hotel room. It required several hours for her anger to abate. When it did, she began to feel uncomfortable. The hotel, although better than the City Hotel with its raw wood interior and primitive furnishings, was still no house of luxury. It did have wallpaper, in a rather obnoxious flowery mulberry design, a washbasin and pitcher that were not cracked, battered mahogany furniture that had survived a trip around the Horn, and a brass bedstead that sagged only slightly in the middle. But it was mid-afternoon, and the San Francisco fog was coming in, casting a pall of gloom over the city. It was not dark enough to light a candle, but the room was dismay, and Jo sat by the window feeling more and more sorry for herself.

Maybe she had been too hard on Thad. Maybe, in her own best interest, she should have not angered him the way she did. He was gone now; although he promised to be back soon, she knew he was enraged at her lack of sympathy. She was not sure of his reactions would be on his return.

Maybe she should have gone with him. Though she was alone in the room, she bit her lip and shook her head vigorously. She would never go anywhere with him again, unless it was too civilized and comfortable, safe place! She still remembered their horrible stay in Panama, the sticky, sweaty, mosquito-laden discomfort of those hours; the terror that had gripped her as her little daughter became ill and would not respond; the rage she had felt at the puffy-faced doctor Thad had dredged up from the harbor; the sinking, leaden feeling as her baby died in her arms.

Jo rose from her rocking-chair and paced the floor of the little room. It was all Thad's fault! He had no business taking them, a woman and a child, on a journey filled with danger, disease, and death. True, she had been dissatisfied in Baltimore with the hardware store and their circle of friends, but there were other ways to make a fortune. Thad had chosen the worst and most difficult, and it had brought tragedy upon them all.

Deep within her she felt a small qualm at her having disposed of the problem as she had. A tiny, gnawing voice told her it was not all Thad's fault, that she had played a large part in it, and Thad's charge of unfairness had not been entirely wrong. She angrily resolutely to suppress such thoughts and resorted to the simpler solution.

It *was* Thad's fault. Thad had had no business bringing them to California. Their child was dead. He had no business leaving her alone in San Francisco. Everything he did was wrong. Everything.

She sat down again in the rocker by the window and looked out at the fog-gray city. A lump rose in her throat. She was the most miserable of women. She had been mistreated and misused. Life owed her more than this.

There was a knock at the door. It surprised her, and she sat for a moment before she responded. Then she hurried to the mirror over the bureau and adjusted her hair and dabbed at the tearstains on her face.

The knock was repeated. She went to the door and opened it.

Clay Moreau stood there, black hat in hand, his brows still peaked over amused eyes, his smile quizzical.

"I came to call. I thought you might be lonesome."

94

His voice was soothing, calming, and most welcome.

Joe was flustered, "Clay! I'm—I'm glad to see you! But it's hardly proper for me to invite you in."

He nodded smoothly. "I know that. I'd like to take you out to dinner. I promised Thad I'd look after you. I'll wait for you in the lobby. No hurry. Take your time."

He turned, smiled at her over his shoulder as if he knew she would not refuse, and headed for the stairs. She closed the door, filled with pleasurable excitement. Everything Clay had said and done was right.

Everything Thad had done was wrong . . .

They went to a place called the Golden Eagle on Montgomery Street. It was a simple board building with a false front and the image of a large eagle hanging over the door. The fog was drifting in now, very low. Jo could feel the mist on her face. She hoped it would not make her hair stringy, but Clay's constant smooth and soothing conversation diverted her attention, and she found it impossible to worry about such matters.

Inside the restaurant, all was bright lights and gaiety and thumping piano music and loud conversation. The place was crowded. Half of the room had dining tables with white cloths and crystal and silver plates; the other half had tables with poker and faro going on. Along the wall behind the gambling tables was a long bar backed by a magnificent mirror and hundreds of bottles. Two fat bartenders with waxed, upturned mustaches presided.

There were women there, too, women in bright red short skirts and decolleté necklines, young women with paint on their smiling countenances who bodly approached the men around the gambling tables and joined them for drinks. Jo was shocked. She had heard of things like this, but she had never seen them. Despite her shock, she was fascinated. Clay had to touch her arm to distract her attention from the scene.

"I have a table reserved," he told her. "This place has the best food in San Francisco."

She recovered her composure enough to challenge him. "How do you know that?" She forced a smile and tore her eyes away form the red-clad girls.

"I know it," said Clay, as he pulled out a chair for her, "because I own this place. And I have given instructions that the food must be the best in San Francisco." He circled the table and sat down facing her. "Look at this menu," he invited, opening it for her and placing it before her. "Mexican terrapin, Salinas lettuce, tender been filets—not the stringy longhorn beef they serve everywhere else. I've made an arrangement with a rancher in Marin who's imported some eastern cattle. Wines—we have the best French wines. There are also one or two California wines. Now," he leaned foward, smiling, in his wryest manner, "what would you like? It's on the house."

Jo took a long breath. For the first time in days she felt her troubles fall away. She took a deep breath and looked squarely at him. "Clay," she said, "I'm glad you brought me here." His smile broadened.

They had an elaborate dinner, starting with the terrapin and moving on to Pacific flounder for the fish course, and the filets of the beef that Clay had boasted of, together with fresh peas from the beef that Clay had boasted of, together with fresh peas from a ranch down the peninsula, plus a French red wine that dissolved the last of Jo's troubles. They concluded with a French pastry. At the end, they sat back, and Clay smiled again at the pretty woman before him.

"Are you feeling better, Joe?"

"Yes! Yes!"

"I want you to meet Mrs. Corson. I don't think you met her on the boat."

"No, I didn't."

"Then you must meet her. She came out with us from Panama. We're in partnership in this establishment."

He called a waiter and gave instructions. In a few moments, Mrs. Carson, imposing in beads, ostrich feathers, and a towering black coiffure, moved toward them with the regal demeanor of a royal yacht under full sail.

Clay rose and made the introductions.

"Will you join us?" Jo invited.

Mrs. Corson, her chin high, accepted condescendingly. Clay drew up a chair. She folded her large ostrich-feather fan and placed it in her lap. "I didn't see you on the boat," she said to Jo.

"I was—indisposed."

"Humph! I can understand why. That was a rough-ridin' old tub, and it was overloaded and sloggin' along so low in the water you got wet every time you stuck your face out on deck. Well, what are you doin' in Frisco, dearie?"

"She's with her husband," Clay explained. "He's gone to the diggings to see what he can find in the way of business. I've agreed to look out for her during his absence."

Mrs. Corson looked Jo up and down, noting her creamy complexion, slim figure, luminous eyes, and thick dark hair. "Well," she shrugged, "he'd better not stay away too long. That's all I've got to say!"

Jo blushed, and Clay hastily interposed. "Mrs. Morgan's had a tragedy. Her child died on the Isthmus. She's had a rough time of it."

Mrs. Corson was instantly sympathetic. "Well, dearie, you've got to get your mind off your troubles. It don't do no good to bood about 'em. I'm glad to see you're up to comin' out to dinner."

"I agree, Mrs. Corson," Clay said. "She ought to keep busy. I was about to suggest to her that she might want to help us here in the Golden Eagle." He turned to Jo. "How would you like that, Jo? Just until Thad comes back, or as long as you like."

Jo's eyes widened. "Help you here? You mean, work here?" She cast a quick glance at the short-skirted girls around the gambling tables.

After a moment's hesitation, Mrs. Corson followed Clay's lead. "You certainly are better lookin' than any of our regular staff," she encouraged. "You'd be a real attraction for this place, and you'd bring us a lot of business."

Clad hastily interposed. "I wasn't thinking of Jo's being a floor girl. I think she might be the hostess for the restaurant, sort of a female maitre d'." He chuckled. "I think a lot more men in Frisco would want to eat here, in that case."

Mrs. Corson caught Clay's eye and changed her approach. "Why, yes, dearie. It would be perfectly respectable, and this is the West, you want to remember. Women do things here, quite properly, that they wouldn't think of doin' in New York or Boston. Besides, we could pay you a nice little salary. That would help until your husband finds somethin' to do."

"Well, we won't push it, will we, Mrs. Corson?" Clay put in. "We'll let Jo think about it. But," he turned to her, "I hope you do think about it. Both Mrs. Corson and I would like very much to have you help us. Wouldn't we, Mrs. Corson?"

Again the proprietress glanced at Jo's slim figure. "We certainly would. Any time you decide, dearie, come around."

She rose. Her corpulent figure, encased in iron corsets, was as erect as a soldier's. With a saccharine smile that did not extend to her eyes, she departed, sweeping back toward the bar and the gambling tables with the ponderous dignity of a duchess.

"Well, I—" Jo was flustered. "I hardly know what to say."

Clay reached out and took her hand. "Don't say anything now. Think about it. As Mrs. Corson said, we could pay you a nice little salary. You'd feel quite independent."

He stressed the last word and was pleased to see her eye lids flicker as he voiced it. He knew independence would appeal to her, considering how she felt about Thad.

"I'm grateful, Clay, but—"

"Don't talk about it. Tell me tomorrow. Now let's have coffee and think about other things."

They did. His bantering conversation made Jo more light-hearted than she had felt in days. On their way out, they halted to watch one of the short-skirted floor girls with a low neckline bringing drinks to a table full of poker players. Joe looked at the girl, then back at Clay.

He smiled at her and said, "You'd look great in that. And I'd like to see you in it. But that isn't what you'd wear. It would be red, and it would be made of silk, but it would be long and graceful and dignified."

"I just don't know."

"Tell me tomorrow."

He took her back to her hotel and accompanied her to the door of her room. Standing there, hat in hand, he looked tall, amused, and very handsome.

"Good night, Jo. I hope you've enjoyed the evening."

"I have. Oh, I have! Thank you for one of the nicest times I've ever had!"

He turned to go. "Tell me tomorrow about helping us." Clay started down the hall toward the stairs.

Jo stood watching him. Then, in a sudden decision, she called to him. "Clay! Clay, wait!" She ran to him as he stood at the head of the stairway.

"Clay, I've decided! I want to do that. I want to work with you and Mrs. Corson. I've made up my mind!"

He smiled. "Are you sure?" he asked confidently. "Thad'll be back soon."

"I'm not going to wait for Thad! I'm going to do it whether he likes it or not. Yes, Clay, I want to work with you!"

He looked down at her. "I thought you would," he said softly. He waited a moment, then took her shoulders and drew her to him and kissed her soundly.

"Good night, Jo. I'll call for you tomorrow, and we'll start you off at the Golden Eagle."

She stood and waved as he went out the lobby door.

10

It was two o'clock in the morning. Two oil lamps cast a yellow light over the crowded shelves of flour, sugar, bacon, canned goods, and beer in crockery bottles. Thad and Avery Jackson faced the storekeeper across his counter. Thad had his snub-nose Derringer pointed at the man's breastbone. The storekepper was sweating. The beads of perspiration dripping off his nose glistened on his lean cheeks and made him even less attractive.

"What's your name?" Thad demanded. "I've got to call you something, and I've got things to say."

The man shivered with fear. "Johnson," he said rapidly, licking his lips. "My name's Johnson. It's on the storefront. Didn't you see it? Put that thing away, will you?"

"No, Mr. Johnson," Thad said quietly. "I don't trust you. You've called off your men, but only because I threatened to blow you in half if you didn't. They're probably still waiting to bushwhack us outside. If anything goes wrong, I'm going to rouse the town and tell 'em what you've done. I hear they organize necktie parties for thieves and scoundrels. And that's what you are." He gazed contemptuously at the quavering culprit before him. "But now I'm going to give you the chance to be an honest businessman."

Johnson managed to speak. "How—how do you mean that? Put that thing away, willl you? Before it goes off."

"I'll tell you what I mean. I'm going to give you a chance to buy my cows. At two hundred a head. And I've got two-hundred head, give or take a few. That's forty-thousand dollars. I'll take forty thousand dollars for my herd. And I'll take it now."

Johnson gulped in astonishment. "Buy your herd? At forty-thousand dollars? You—you must be crazy! I haven't got forty thousand dollars."

"Oh, yes, you have!" Thad sounded confident. "I think you've got considerable more than forty thousand, and the price will go up the longer we dicker. Right now, it's forty thousand. Fiteen minutes from now it'll be fifty!"

"Oh, come now. Talk about robbery! Who's robbing who? Two hundred a head is ridiculous. I'll buy your herd, but I won't pay any forty thousand."

Avery Jackson pushed up to the counter and stuck out his whiskery chin. "Come on, Thad! Don't let's waste any more time on this varmin! Let's go outside and roust out the town and tell 'em what he done. I got some friends here, and they'll believe me. Come on! He's just wastin' our time!"

"No! Wait!" Johnson sounded desperate. "Look, we can settle this quietly. But let's be reasonable. Let's talk sense."

Thad opened his mouth to speak, but Jackson forestalled him. "Forty thousand is rock bottom!" He glared at Thad, defying him to give in. "He's got it! He's got it in that safe back there! That fifteen minutes is almost up, and the price is going on fifty! Hear that?" He shook a gnarled finger under Johnson's nose. "Hear that? You wait one more minute, and forty thousand won't do it!"

Johnson looked at the angry old man, at the unwavering Derringer in Thad's hand, at the cold determination in Thad's eyes. His voice quivered with rage and frustration as he said, "All right! All right! Forty thousand!"

He turned to the wall safe, put his ear to the dial, and turned it carefully. There were some loud clicks, and finally he swung the door open.

When the deal was completed, Thad and Avery Jackson rode out to where Fernando and his companions were guarding the herd. Thad drew his horse close to the Mexican's.

"he bought. Two hundred a head." He patted his pocket. I have the money right here."

Fernando's face broke into a broad grin. "*Bueno, Señor! Excelente!* Now mi padro has nearly half the money he owes."

"That's right," Thad agreed. "The storekeeper has a ranch about a mile up this canyon, and there's a corral behind it. He wants us to deliver the cows there. After that, you go back and bring two hundred and fifty or three hundred head here. If we can't sell'em here, we'll try another town. But they're salable. We've proved that."

"You are not coming back with us?" Fernando spoke slowly.

"No. I'm going on to Placerville. I hear that's a bigger place. I'll try to have a deal ready for you there, in case Johnson can't buy your second batch. Besides, I have some business of my own."

The Mexican's face was still sober, and he sat his horse silently.

Thad grinned. "I know what you're thinking. That I'm going to take this money and you'll never see me again! Remember our bargain." He reached into his saddlebag and pulled out two heavy rawhide bags, each closed by a drawstring that was triple-knotted.

"Here's the forty thousand. You take it back tot he Señorita. All of it. When your second sale's completed, she can pay me whatever she thinks the trip was worth."

Fernando's dark, mustachioed face broke into a gleaming grin. "Señor, Señor! Accept my pardon for mistrusting you! The Señorita will be happy, and so will Don Petro! You have done much for them!"

Thad smiled also. "You're not the only one who's suspicious. I'm going to see the Señorita on my way back and ask her if you turned that money over to her."

Fernando's grin remained unshadowed. "I am too happy to resent that, Señor. Besides, I have a feeling you did not mean it. The Señorita will get her money, and I will come back with another herd for sale. Who knows? Maybe in Placerville you call get two hundred and fifty!"

Thad and Jackson sat their horses and watched as Fernando galloped dustily off into the darkness, whooping for his companions.

Placerville was even more of a town than the previous place Thad had stopped. Most of its structures were like those of San Francisco and Sacramento—wood-floored and half-walled, with tent tops. There were also a few all-wood buildings going up on the main street, with flase fronts and decent doors. The street itself was wider than most, and some of the chuckholes had been filled and smoothed out.

What attracted Thad was the town's frenetic activity. Men were hurrying about with the same determined concentration exhibited on Montgomery Street. Many were well dressed, with the dust of the street laying heavily upon polished and expensive boots. Gold watches with heavy chains were consulted by hard-hatted men who seemed to have plenty of money for clothes and cigars.

Thad and Avery pulled up their horses in front of a hotel hitchrail. Thad said, "There's business galore here. All we have to do is pick the right place."

Jackson nodded and grinned his snaggle-toothed grin. "I'm glad to see y're thinkin' o' business and not o' diggin'."

"I gave that idea up a long time ago," said Thad. "But I've got to make a lot of money in a hurry. In a hurry."

Jackson looked at him curiously. "Why?" he asked as they entered the hot little hotel lobby.

"It grated on me to owe Clay for the gold he loaned

me to buy your two tickets from Panama to San Francisco, so I paid him back. Now I've got considerable less to work with. I've got to think of a business which will be possible with the funds I have. And I *must* be a success. I must be a success!" He repeated the last sentence almost obsessively. The old man saw Thad's jaw harden as he said it.

Jackson was puzzled. Morgan obviusly had the ability to make money. He had made it, and would make more. But there was something eating him, some unpleasant thing gnawing at his vitals.

They registered at the little hotel, and were surprised at the room charges, which were high for a tiny closet finished in raw wood with two cots and a battered washbasin.

"Well, we can't stay long anyway," Thad said. "We've got to get back to San Francisco. We've got a fandango coming up. Remember?"

Jackson grinned. "I shorely do. With all them b'iled shirts and jewelry."

"So we've got to find out fast what's good and what isn't. Let's spend the next couple of days just going around talking. Let's find out all we can about business here. What's needed and what isn't!"

Jackson nodded sagely. "Good idee. We'll separate, I take it."

"We sure will. You go one way, and I'll go another. That way we can cover more ground."

"I like the way you go at things," Jackson said.

"Business," said Thad, "after all is just doing what people want done, making what they want made, and keeping the price low enough so they can afford it."

"I like the way you go at things more'n never," said Jackson.

They spend the next two days surveying and exploring Placerville. It took longer than they expected, because the level of intelligent activity was high. A shaggy-bearded storekeeper in a red shirt, rough pants, and scarred boots might have considerable wealth in his safe in dust and nuggest. He might also be involved in half a dozen of the town's other businesses.

Thad found a restaurant, consisting of plank tables and benches under a canvas roof, that featured beans and mutton, bread-and-butter, and whose proprietor, an enormous individual in a dirty apron, seemed eager to talk.

"They'll pay three, four dollars for dinner," he told Thad, and think nothin' of it. Some of 'em spend all their dust eatin' and carousin'. A lot of 'em are tryin' to save somethin'. But there's no place for 'em to put their dust. I'm keepin' a lot of it for some of 'em in my back room. But that ain't a very good place. What if we had a fire? Melted gold dust would be runnin' all over the floor, and nobody could tell whose was what."

"What do they want to do with it?" Thad asked.

"They want to send it home or to Frisco or someplace where it'll be safe."

Thad registered that answer in his brain. "What about mail?" he inquired. "Is there a mail delivery here?"

"Durn seldom. We got a pack-mule express, with a few fellers runnin' trains of mules with saddlebags from here to Sacramento and Stockton and down to Sonora. But it ain't reg'lar, and it ain't safe. Mail don't git here on time, and a lot of it's lost. Fer these fellers, who're away from their wives and kids and relations, this is pretty tough. What we need is reg'lar express service to Sacramento and Frisco on stages with a shotgun messenger who can pertect his cargo from the bullyboys and riffraff that hang out in the mountains and who'd rather rob than dig."

"Thanks. How about something to eat?"

"Fine. We got beans."

"Good. Let's have some."

During his meal, Thad continued his probing and unearthed several other pieces of information he filed in his mental cabinet.

After lunch, he met Jackson in the street.

"There's a wagoner down here," said the old man. "Name of Baker. He says they's a firm back in New Hampshire, name of Abbott Downing, that's buildin' some coaches for the trade here, and they're good ones. Concords, they call 'em, and there are some people interested in goin' into the stagin' business, he hears, from Sacramento and Stockton and other places."

"What about the roads? Will they take coaches?"

"The roads are hell," Jackson said. "Why don't we go in this gamblin' joint here in front of us and buy us a beer? I'm so parched, my tongue is stickin' to the roof of my mouth. I got more to tell ye once I've wet my whistle."

Thad laughed. They entered the saloon and ordered beers, which came in cream-colored ceramic bottles that had been shipped around the Horn from New York. The saloonkeeper kept the bottles in a wooden tub filled with the cold water of the spring that ran behind his establishment. The beer was refreshingly cool.

They sat on a wooden bench and talked.

"This stagin' business might be somethin' worthwhile lookin' into," Jackson said. "Trouble is, the coaches—Concords, they call 'em—cost money. Fifteen hundred apiece, delivered here. Then y' got to buy horses, and it takes four to draw one o' these. And you got to have teams stationed along the road every ten, fifteen miles. And you got to have people takin' care of 'm, and you've got to have a place or two on the route where the passengers can git somethin' to eat and drink." He shook his head. "It's a costly business to set up."

Thad did not answer. He was toying with his glass and thinking hard.

"I say," Jackson nudged him, "it looks like it's too expensive to go into."

Thad spoke slowly. "We'd have to borrow money," Thad said. "But I think I know where I could get it. That Benson I met after that thug tried to hold me up owns the Bank of Mission Valley. I think he'd lend me some money. He didn't like my attitude toward dealing with criminals, but I think he'd lend me some money."

Jackson shook his head pessimistically. "It'll take a long time to pay back."

"No, it won't." Thad was definite. "The Bank of Mission Valley is the only bank in California. I don't see why the express business couldn't be a bank, too. It's a natural thing, Avery. Miners want us to carry their dust back to civilization and to their families. We can bank it for 'em too. Once we start taking their dust, we can lend money ourselves."

"Not at twelve percent per month, I hope." Jackson was not enthusiastic.

"No, not at twelve percent a month. Bankers needn't be shylocks. They can be pretty helpful, on occasion. And they're needed in a country like this."

"What do we know about bankin'?"

Thad grined and slapped the old man on the back. "Just as much as we know about the express and stagecoach business! But we'll learn fast. We'll have to!"

Jackson was doubtful. "I thought mebbe you'd start a hardware store, somethin' you know about."

"We can do that on the side." Jackson was glad. Thad was sounding more cheerful than he had for days. Thad's enthusiasm also worried him. You should do what you knew how to do, not risk everything on something you had to learn. But Thad's determination and eagerness could not be brushed aside.

"We'll spend another two or three days here, investigating," Thad said. "But I think we've found it! »I think we know what we're going to do!"

Jackson shrugged. "I've got one more day to find somethin' more sensible for us."

Thad faced him, seriously. "It is *us*, isn't it Avery? That's what I want it to be."

Jackson hesitated, then grinned and held out his gnarled hand. "It's us," he said. "Right down to the day we go into bankruptcy—together!"

They spent another four days exploring the environs of Placerville and asking questions about settlements farther on. The diggings to the north, on the Sacramento River and its tributaries, had attracted more goldseekers than had the diggings to the south, on the tributaries on the San Joaquin. More and more men were moving into the southern regions. Thad filed that piece of information in his now-crowded mental cabinet. He assigned Jackson the task of finding an alternate purchaser for Don Esteban's cattle, and the old man accomplished the job quickly.

"Beef?" he cackled when Thad asked hom how he had done. "They're fightin' each other for it! I had three fellers biddin' against each other! There's more money here than there was in that other place, anyhow. I settled for two-twenty a head. How's that fer good business?"

Thad grinned. "At that rate, they won't have to sell their entire herd. They can keep some for themselves for a fresh start. The girl'll be pleased."

Jackson chuckled. "She won't be the only one. How about her pa?"

"Sure," Thad nodded absently. "He'll like it too." He dismounted from his horse and looped the reins around the hitchrail in front of their hotel. "Now we've got to get crackin'. I hear there's one of those Abbott Downing coaches arrived in Sacramento, and I want to see it before it leaves. Let's pack up and check out."

11

At the Golden Eagle in San Francisco, Clay Moreau introduced Jo to her new duties. He made the transition as painless as possible.

"Here's what you'll wear, that is, if you like it," he said, motioning to the girl who was holding a beautiful bright red dress with fur trim up for Jo to see. "That's been designed by Lucy Cordova. She's the best dressmaker in town. Direct from Mexico City." He stood back, watching as Jo examined the dress. "What do you think of it?"

Jo stepped back. She could not take her eyes from the gown. It was different from anything she had ever seen in Baltimore. It was daring in its flashing color and sweepingly slim design, and low-cut,—but not too low—neckline. It was sleeveless. Jo knew she had pretty arms, but she had never worn anything sleeveless before.

"It's—it's magnificent!" she breathed. "If I try it on, I know I'll never want to give it up. May I try it?"

Clay smiled, partly to himself. "There are some accessories that go with it," he said. "Here." He opened a black-velvet box on the table next to him and held it before her. In it lay a sparkling choker, a diamond bracelet in a platinum mounting, and a tiara, together with rings and a brooch, all glittering like the treasure of Ophir.

"They're not! They can't be *real*! Jo gasped.

"But they are," said Clay easily. "I wouldn't have you wear anything that wasn't real, Jo. You ought to know that."

Jo tore her eyes from the contents of the box and looked into Clay's. "But—but I couldn't accept them."

"Oh, they're not yours," he said. He had been prepared to give another answer, if circumstances warranted. But he rode the current of the conversation, as he had planned to do. "They belong to the house. But you'll wear them. And if there's any of them you decide you want, after awhile, we could make you a pretty good price. After all, they'll be secondhand jewelry." He chuckled. "Try them on, along with the dress."

Excited, and almost speechless, Jo took the dress and box and permitted a short-skirted girl to lead her upstairs. The girl opened the door and ushered Jo into a beautifully furnished bedroom, with a heavy walnut bedstead, a flowered spread, a huge mirror framed in carved walnut, a heavy bureau, and richly upholstered chairs.

"Why—what is this?" Jo turned to the girl. "Is this Mrs. Corson's room?"

The girl smiled with amusement. "No, chickie, it's not," she said. "This is in case a customer gets tired and needs a little rest after dinner. Go ahead, change into your new togs, and come on downstairs. Mr. Moreau doesn't like to be kept waiting." She departed, closing the door after her.

Jo was puzzled by her answer. After a moment, the feel of the red silk in her hands and the glitter of the diamonds in the box drove all doubts from her mind. She excitedly removed her own dress and put on the red-silk confection.

After a few happy moments filled with primping and adjusting the jewelry, Jo stood before the mirror and admired herself. Jo took a deep breath. It could not be she, she was certain. Whoever it was, she was beautiful. Baltimore was never like this.

As she came downstairs, Jo saw that Mrs. Corson had

joined Clay. The two of them watched silently as she descended. She knew she was making an impression, and she exulted in it. When she reached the main floor, she stood before them and waited for their reaction.

It was different from what she had expected, but much more satisfying. Mrs. Corson regarded her with frank admiration, and Clay—Clay the cynical, Clay the amused, Clay with the arrogant half-smile—Clay had lost all those expressions and was staring at her soberly. There was surprise in his gaze.

A long silence passed. "Then: "My God, you're beautiful!" Clay breathed. He reached out a hand and took hers. "You're the prettiest thing in San Francisco!"

Mrs. Corson cleared her throat. "You're an aristocrat, dearie. You'll make these clowns sit up and take notice!"

Clay was still recovering his equanimity. "You'll be a magnificent hostess!" he said. "Absolutely magnificent! Every man in San Francisco will want to come here." He turned to Mrs. Corson. "We've got a winner!"

Mrs. Corson nodded. "Yes," she said. "I think this'll be advantageous for everybody concerned."

The short-skirted girl who had shown Jo upstairs approached. She looked Jo up and down with clear hostility. "Are you going to keep these on or change back into your old duds, chickie? We can't leave your stuff up there in the guest room."

Clay said, "Come back this evening at six. They ate early here. You'll work evenings. We'll see that you get back to your hotel all right. You can take these clothes with you, unless you want to come back here and change."

"I'll take them with me, if you don't mind," said Jo. "I can't bear to part with them!" She looked squarely at Clay. "Clay, thank you for everything!"

Clay smiled back. When Jo had left, he turned to Mrs. Corson. "Well?" he inquired.

She shrugged. "The gold mines ain't all up in the hills," she commented. "We got one right here, with that looker."

"But we'll have to take it easy," Clay warned. "That's the answer. We'll just take it easy."

The hotel clerk in Sacramento City knew where the Abbott Downing coach was on display.

"It's out at Sutter's. You know, the fort. And it's a beauty! Everybody in town's goin' out to see it. Holds nine people inside and twelve of the roof. That's includin' a shotgun messenger. I ain't been in it, but they said she rides like a dream."

"Which way's the fort?" Thad inquired.

The clerk pointed out the doorway. "A couple of miles," he said. "You can't miss it."

"Thanks." Thad rejoined Jackson at the hitchrail and the two mounted, Thad his horse, and the old man his sleek mule. They cantered north side by side.

They were not the only ones out to the Concord. A dozen or so people were gathered around the gleaming vehicle, some of them louts and loafers, conversing loudly and cracking jokes; but some were serious of mien they inspected every coach bolt with sober diligence. Thad noted them with interest, and nudged Jackson.

"We're not the only ones with business on our mind," he murmured.

The coach was a beauty. As graceful as a ship, as it had curving lines, highly polished darkwood panels gleaming hardware, and yellow-ash wheels, and spokes, and wagon frame. It shone with newness and even smelled new. Thad opened a door and ran a hand over the dark-leather seats. "It's mighty goodlooking," he said.

"Looks pretty heavy to me," Jackson said doubtfully. "What's this? Leather?" He pointed to a multiple-layered leather strap arrangement that ran on each side from front to rear supporting the coach's body.

A heavyset man who had been examining the coach carefully heard the question and turned. "Those are the thoroughbraces," he said. "That's what will make this wagon ride easily over our rough roads. Any ordinary wagon with springs would shake itself to pieces in our mountains. But with this thoroughbrace mounting, you don't get your teeth jolted out. Easier on the horses, too, they say."

"I dunno," Avery scowled. "Looks to me mighty expensive and heavy. I sh'd think somethin' lighter would be better."

"Well, we've got mudwagons already running on schedule, but I know what'll happen when these Concords get to running," the heavyset man said. "Everybody'll take a Concord. Hell of a lot more comfortable. I know I would. No question about it!" He moved on.

Thad nodded. "I think he's right," he said to Jackson. "Who wants to ride in a bumpy farm wagon when he can get in one of these?" He took a long breath. "I think we've found our business, Avery! If it's all right with you, I think we've found it!"

The old man shrugged. "If it's all right with me!" he exlaimed. "*I* don't have nothin' to do with it! *You're* the one who decides things that work out. I decided back in Frisco that my chips were on you, right down to the last white one. And they still are! If you think this is the business for us, we're in it—even though I got some doubts."

"What are they?" Thad asked.

Jackson shook his head. "They don't count," he said firmly. "When you got your bed made, you got to know it's goin' to win." He looked up at Thad, squinting. "I know you're goin' to win!"

Thad waited a moment, then extended his hand. "Thanks, Avery," he said. "I'll remember that. And I'll do my damndest to see that we do!"

At the edge of town, as they headed southwest, toward the bay, Thad said, "I've got to see that

114

banker. I figure we'll need quite a loan."

Jackson scowled and shook his head as if to clear it of unpleasant thoughts.

The Golden Eagle was a busy place. During the few days Jo had worked as hostess at the restaurant, it grew even busier than before. Clay told her that, and she was pleased, but she did not believe him. However, true it was. The dignified, erect, dark-haired hostess in the flaming red dress and the diamonds had in the space of a few days, become a subject of conversation in that male-dominated, excitable, free-spending city founded on optimism and tales of treasure that had come true.

At the end of the fourth night, at 11:00 in the morning, Clay came to Jo and said, "You're wonderful! You've paid for yourself already! Business is booming! There's even an article in the *Advertiser* about you. Have you seen it?"

She shook her head, smiling. "No."

"Here. Look." He handed her the four-page paper that did service as San Francisco's journal. She took it and read, in tiny, blurred type:

The Golden Eagle Restaurant on Montgomery Street has a female hostess who is attracting hordes of customers. She reminds every man of his wife or sweetheart, and she behaves in a most proper and dignified manner. She keeps a good distance from the soiled angels who inhabit the bar and the gambling room. The editor recommends that all his readers (that is, those who are free and without encumbrances) go to visit the Golden Eagle Restaurant. It will be a memorable evening.

Jo blushed "I'm sure I don't know what I'm doing to deserve this."

"I know what you're doing," Clay said. "You're being yourself."

115

Elena Sarmiento y Lugo stood on the veranda of the ranchhouse near San Jose and watched the shimmering heat waves rise from the floor of the valley. Two and a half weeks had passed since that eventful day when *los yanquis* had given her an effective argument to ward off Bronson. Bronson had not been back since, but she knew he was counting the hours. So was she.

It had been a move of desperation, she decided, to entrust half their herd to the plan of a stranger. But it had seemed the only thing to do at the time. As the days and hours passed, and the time of reckoning with Bronson came closer, she grew more and more despondent.

What did she know about Morgan? Absolutely nothing. He might be every bit as bad as Bronson himself.

But he had not seemed so—

Don Esteban emerged from the dark, cool *sala* and stood by her side, looking over the flatlands.

"*Que pasa, chiquita*? You do not look happy."

"How can I be? The days are passing, and we have heard nothing!"

"But we will."

"We do not know Morgan and his friends."

"Fernando is with them, and so are Raimundo and Juanito."

"But they are farm boys. They do not know how to deal with someone like Bronson."

"Morgan is not like Bronson." The old man smiled.

"How do you know?"

"I have seen many men. I have learned to discriminate."

She sighed. "I hope you are right." She turned toward the house.

"You are going in too soon," the old man said.

"What do you mean?"

"Look." He pointed toward east. In the shimmering waves of velley heat, were horsemen in a cloud of dust, riding furiously toward them.

116

"If I am not mistaken," Don Pedro said, "that is Fernando and his *muchachos*, coming home without the cattle."

"You cannot see that far. It may be bad instead of good news." Her heart leaped, nevertheless.

Don Pedro was right. It was Fernando and his boys, and they galloped at full speed on their lathered horses right up to the hitchrail before the veranda, coming to a haunch-sliding, dusty stop and whoops of excitement.

Elena was waiting for them when Fernando mounted the steps, his face running with sweat and streaked with dust, his clothing wet with perspiration.

He waved a rawhide sack in the air. "Señor! Señorita! We have it! And there will be more!"

They crowded into the *sala* where Fernando poured out the dust and coins and currency on the big table. "There is half of what you need! I will take more cattle and bring back the rest!"

"How much is there?" the girl asked.

"Forty thousand! Every penny we made from the sale!"

"But Señor Mogan. What did he take?"

"Nothing, Señorita! I could not believe it! He would take nothing! I mistrusted him, and to prove his honesty, he gave me the entire sum!" Fernando laughed, his white teeth gleaming. "He said he mistrusted *me*! He will be back here on his way home to make certain I delivered all to you!"

Elena felt a sudden sense of relief. "He will stop here again?"

"He said so, Señorita."

"I am glad. We must thank him. And pay him—something."

"Well, there is no time to waste. I am to take two hundred and fifty head and go to Placerville, where Señor Morgan is making another deal for us. I must hurry if I am to bring back the money in time."

There was much excitement, loud talking. A feast was spread in an hour, with *carne* and *frijoles* and tomatoes and corn and squash and *tortillas*. Fernando, Raimun-

117

do, Juanito, and Edmundo plunged into it with the air of famished men. There was much talk and much laughter.

Don Pedro leaned toward his daughter. "You look happy for the first time in days, *chiquita*."

Her face glowed. "it is true. I am happy for the first time in days."

He chuckled. "Because of the money or because Señor Morgan has turned out to be an honest man?"

"Because of the money," she said defensively.

He chuckled again. The girl continued to eat, though somewhat absently. He *had* been handsome, and tall and stern and businesslike. Altogether a most interesting and admirable *hombre*.

12

At the Golden Eagle on Montgomery Street, Clay Moreau brought a customer in to introduce him to Jo.

He was a stocky, erect, well-dressed man, with iron-gray hair and mustache, and eyes that twinkled when he saw Jo. She smiled and greeted him hospitably, noting the well tailored clothing, the heavy gold watch chain, and the ruby ring on his thick finger. Here was a prosperous customer Clay would want her to welcome.

"Mr. Benson," said Clay. "Meet Jo, our hostess. Mr. Benson is a banker in town, and this is his first visit to the Golden Eagle. We hope you'll return, sir."

"Well, if everything is as attractive as what I've seen up now, I'll certainly be back," Benson said. He bowed over her hand. "Jo, it's a pleasure!"

Jo led him to a choice table, near a window that overlooked the busy street, handed him an elaborate menu with gold tassels and embossing, and returned to the entrance, where Clay took her arm.

"Be nice to him," he said in a low voice. "He's a very important person in town. Rich as all get out, head of a vigilante outfit that's done more to bring peace to the place than anything the police or marshal did, and he's not married."

Jo looked up. "What do you mean by that?"

Clay shrugged. "Just be nice to him, that's all. If he asks you to do something, do it."

Jo smiled. "Well, that depends."

Clay did not smile. He looked at her with hard eyes. "Do what he asks you to," he repeated. "He's important to us—to me. I'm planning to expand this business, and I'll have to borrow some money. He's got more of it than anybody else in town." He turned away and left her puzzled and somewhat disturbed.

Jo was busy that evening and only occasionally noted what Benson was ordering. He chose lobster, which was expensive, and two kinds of wine. Clay passed her once at the entrance and said shortly, "Be nice to him!" She frowned slightly, but obediently made her way to his table.

"Is everything all right, Mr. Benson?" Jo asked.

"Well, not quite," he said, rising. "The one thing that's missing is you sitting there across from me, sharing a glass of this excellent wine. Please join me. I'm sure your boss wouldn't mind."

The only thing he'd mind, Jo though, *is if I didn't accept your invitation*. She hesitated, then said, "I'll be glad to, for a moment."

Benson seated her in courtly fashion. He chatted amiably, and Jo could sense the force of his personality. Here was a man accustomed to getting his own way and who brooked no interference or interruptions. The range of his conversation was wide. He was interested in many things, and he was careful not to flaunt his wealth or power. Jo found herself enjoying the respite from her duties. Out of the corner of her eye, she saw Clay nodding in approval as he saw them sitting together.

She did not stay with Benson long, excusing herself on the basis of having responsibilities. He rose again, smiling, and thanked her for her company. "If you don't mind, Jo, I'll be back, and I'll expect you to share another glass with me."

"Thank you," she said. "I'll be glad to see you again."

Benson bowed once more over her hand, and again she noted the hard intelligence of his gaze. She would have to be careful with this man. She would have to be absolutely honest and firm. There would be no deceiving him.

Thad and Avery Jackson followed the Sacramento River toward the bay. As they camped at night, Thad spend his time calculating the costs of teams, stage stations, feed, and Concord coaches. As they rode during the day, Thad noted and wrote down the best sites for relay stops, talked to storekeepers who might be willing to augment their income by serving stage passengers (without telling them the purpose of his probing), and charted out routes in his mind. At the upper end of the bay, near Carquinez Straits, Thad told Jackson, "I don't want to take the time to go around by San Jose. Can't we get a boat a little farther along and get over to San Francisco that way?"

Jackson shrugged. "There oughta be plenty of boats, what with all the traffic. We kin try."

"What we might do later," said Thad thoughtfully, "is to buy a boat and make it part of our stage connection. Quicker than traveling all around the south end of the bay."

"Would be at that," Jackson said. He had lost some of his doubt and concern as Thad's enthusiasm mounted. When they passed, dozens of men and much equipment going both directions, moving to and from the mines, Jackson's reservations diminished even more.

At night, by their little fire on the shore of the bay, with the lights of San Francisco twinkling across the white-capped water, Clay was still figuring. At last, he put down his notebook.

"I think I know how much we'll need from our friend the banker," he said. "I've figured a relay stop every twelve or fifteen miles from Placerville. We'll need at least two coaches to start. If we can use the storekeeper we talked to, we'll need only thirty new employees to take care of the horses and help hitch up. We'll also have to have something for rent and feed and food for passengers. We could do it on eighty thousand, but I figure a hundred thousand would be safer."

Jackson removed his hat and mopped his brow. "That," he said, "scares the livin' daylights outa me! We'll be in the same spot as the old don we met on his ranch at San Jose—at twelve percent per month."

"We're not paying any twelve percent per month," said Thad shortly, slapping his notebook shut. "We'll either get a reasonable loan on something approaching eastern rates, or we won't go into business. But I think Benson's smart enough to see that, even on that basis, with a share in the company, he'll make money."

"A share in the company?"

Thad nodded. "That's why I think this thing'll work out. If we combine staging with an express business, it works right into banking. He'll double his banking business. I don't see how it can lose—for either of us."

"He'll be part owner of the stage line—" Jackson said slowly.

"And I'll be part owner of his bank before we get through."

Jackson shook his head admiringly. "I like the way you think, son," he said. "I like the way you think!"

Thad and Avery Jackson arrived in San Francisco the evening of the third day of their journey from the northern diggings. They had not gone by way of San Jose, but had instead found passage on a small sloop two miles west of Carquinez. After a wet and rough trip, lasting several hours across a choppy, gray bay, they landed on North Beach, soaked to the skin, shivering, and in bad humor. They paid the disappointed Argonaut running the ferry service an exorbitant sum and made their way toward the seven hills and their illuminated tents and noise and busyness.

"I'll go to the hotel," Thad told Jackson. "Jo's been

alone long enough. First thing in the morning, let's meet, and we'll see Benson at his bank."

Thad mounted the stairs of the hotel eagerly. He had much to tell Jo. Perhaps, by this time, her bitterness had lessened. Now they could make plans again, as they had in the past. The prospects were good, exciting. This was a great country. If offered opportunities the more staid eastern communities could not equal. Jo had been bored with Baltimore, because there had seemed to be no way to rise above their economic level. In California, one could rise—and fall—overnight.

But Thad did not intend to fall. As he mounted the final steps to the upper hall, he thought of that gigantic bird soaring over the coastal range whose vast wings that would rise above any storm. Those wings could be his. Theirs.

He put the key in the lock of their room and entered without knocking, a smile on his face.

The room was dark. Jo must be in bed, asleep, although it was early.

"Jo," he said. "I'm back. Jo?"

There was no answer. He found a candle and lit it.

The room was empty, the bed unslept in. A sudden sick fear gripped Thad, and he pulled open the drawers of the battered dresser. Sighing deeply, he felt cold perspiration on his body, so relieved was he to find her things still there.

She had not moved out, which was what he had feared. She was still there, in the hotel. But where was she—in the evening? San Francisco was not a town where a lone woman ventured far after dark.

He quickly left the room and ran downstairs to the dining room next to the lobby. She must be having dinner. The dining room was empty. San Franciscans ate early. Unless they were spending the evening in one of the gambling saloons, they went to bed early. They worked hard, and the day started at dawn.

Thad went to the desk. The clerk with whom he had negotiated his arrangements was there, the pompous,

123

chubby little man with the high wing collar and dark, tight suit.

"I'm Morgan," he said. "I'm just back from the diggings, and I'm looking for my wife."

The clerk, whose last mood before his departure had been obsequious, Thad remembered, was now disdainful.

"You won't find her here," he said. "Not at this time of night."

"What do you mean?" Thad demanded.

"She's got a job. Or apparently so. I haven't talked to her about it."

"A job? What kind of a job?"

The clerk shrugged. "Well, I'm not certain, Mr. Morgan. Maybe you'd better ask her. She leaves here every evening, dressed fit to kill, and I hear she's working at that new saloon on Montgomery Street. The Golden Eagle, they call it. I was going to ask her myself what kind of job she's doing. I figured I might have to ask her to leave the hotel. But I hadn't got around to it yet. Now you're here, you can ask her." He looked up at Thad, his pudgy face comically stern. "I'm interested in keeping this hotel respectable!"

Thad felt impelled to hit him but restrained himself. "You say the Golden Eagle's on Montgomery Street?"

The clerk nodded. "Right. Near Market."

Thad wasted no more words or time. He ran from the lobby into the street.

He pushed open the batwing doors of the Golden Eagle with trepidation. The nose, bright lights, thumping piano, and hum of loud voices in drunken conversation gave him a sinking feeling. When he found himself inside that crowded, warm, glittering room, he was even more unsure.

A tall woman with dark hair and in a shining red dress, with sparkling jewelry, approached him.

"May I show you to a table, sir?"

They recognized each other and stared.

"*Jo*! Thad exclaimed.

It took a moment for her to recover herself. "Hello, Thad." She adjusted her hair primly. "I have a job. I'll be home at two."

The only thing he could think of to say was, "I'll meet you."

"Don't bother. Clay walks me home." She lifted her chin and stared squarely at him. There was hostility in her gaze. "*Please* don't bother!"

He was there, nevertheless, at two. After Clay greeted him and welcomed him back and told him what a success Jo was making of herself as a hostess for the restaurant, he walked his wife back to the hotel.

Most of the walk was silent. Finally, he said. "Don't you want to know where I've been? What I've done?"

She shrugged. "Don't you want to know what *I've* done!"

"I can see that," he said shortly. "You shouldn't wear that jewelry on the street at night. It's an invitation to trouble."

"Always the Cautious Katie," she mocked. "Furthermore, it's real. Clay told me."

Thad stopped walking and faced her. "And he gave it to you?"

She smiled maddeningly. "It belongs to the restaurant. But he lets me wear it. Maybe, after I've saved up enough money, I'll buy it."

They arrived at the hotel, and entered. It was a difficult night.

San Francisco in the morning had a choice of two moods. If the fog had not yet rolled back over the Golden Gate and retreated to the Farallones, the mood was gray and cool and overcast. It was a type of grayness that invited activity, and the streets were bustling shortly after daybreak.

If, on the other hand, the fog *had* rolled back, the morning sun shone in a sparkling sky of blue hard to match anywhere else in the world; it, too was an invitation to activity before breakfast.

This was one of the bright mornings. The world—except for Thad—was cheerful. Grimly, he strode through the sunlit streets to the spot where he had promised to meet Jackson. When the older man appeared, Thad said, "Come on. Let's go."

Jackson regarded him with concern. "You all right?"

"Of course, I'm all right. Why wouldn't I be?"

"You saw your wife last night for the first time since you got back. How was she?"

"Fine."

"Is that all? Just fine?"

"That's all. Just fine."

Jackson hesitated. "I was wonderin' if everything was all right."

Thad stopped and faced him. His face was stern. "Look, Avery. We've got a business relationship. And that's all it is, a business relationship. My life is my own, and I'm going to keep it that way."

Jackson retreated. "I was worried, that's all. Sorry."

Thad did not answer but strode on ahead.

They got to the Bank of Mission Valley before its doors were open, but there was movement within. Thad pounded on the door.

A shirtsleeved clerk with arm garters and an eyeshade responded. "We're not open," he said shortly. "We're open at ten."

Thad put his large foot in the foor. "I can't wait till ten," he said briefly. "Tell Mr. Benson it's Mr. Morgan. He'll remember me."

The man locked the door again with a look of deep suspicion and disappeared within only to reappear within a few moments. He opened the door and welcomed them ungraciously. "Come on in. Mr. Benson'll see you."

Thad and Jackson entered, rounded the glass-topped counter where the two tellers worked, and approached a desk. Behind the desk sat Benson, erect, gray-haired, with a neatly trimmed mustache and a large ruby ring on his finger. When he saw Thad, he rose with a smile.

"Morgan!" He pulled out two chairs. "Come on in! Sit down. Glad to see you!"

Thad shook hands, unsmiling. So did Jackson. They took the chairs proferred, and Thad leaned across the desk.

"I'm glad you remembered me, Mr. Benson," he said.

"Why wouldn't I?" the other chuckled. "The moral victim! Damn near got killed, and then tried to keep the thug who did it from a rope! You've got guts, Morgan, and principles that I must admit I don't undersand. But I respect you. What do you want?"

Thad's answer was short. "Money. A loan. I want to go into business, and I've got a project I think you'll be interested in."

Benson's warm smile faded, and his eyes grew cold. "Well," he said, "I like you also, but when I do business, I do business. I don't let personal feelings interfere."

"I don't expect you to," Thad said. "I've got a good deal, and I want you to listen to it."

Benson shrugged. "Go ahead."

Thad told him. He told him about their trip to the diggings what they had discovered about miners who wanted to travel, about miners who wanted mail service, and miners who wanted some place to put their dust and gold. He told him about his calculations, about his trip south from Placerville, about his visits with storekeepers who might be interested in running stage stops, and about his estimates of cost. He told him about his inspection of the Concord coach and its shining panels and its thoroughbraces and yellow-ash wheels. And about the interest of the people who were inspecting it and their eagerness to ride in it.

"I think that ought to be a good business," Thad said. "I think it's a business you ought to be interested in, particularly the banking part."

Benson had listened quietly. At first, his attention

127

had been distracted, and he had played with a pen on his desk and smiled periodically when Thad's words seemed too enthusiastic. But as Thad continued, and as he portrayed the economics of the venture, with its carefully calculated costs, and the precise estimates of the number of necessary horses, the location of stations, and the number of employees required, Benson had grown serious and listened attentively.

"There are a lot of people going into this business," he said reflectively. "I've heard of a few myself."

"But very few have started yet," Thad said. "This is the beginning. By next year, there'll be several competing lines. It's important to be first."

Benson nodded. "You might be right. But it's a hell of a lot of capital to start what is a highly risky proposition."

Thad nodded. "With small capital, you take small risks, and get small profits. You're a businessman. You don't need me to tell you that."

Benson leaned forward. "You sound like a businessman yourself."

"I was. In Baltimore. Hardware." That told him about his previous life, about his bringing mining tools west.

Jackson broke in. "Mister, this feller's the best businessman you ever saw. He not only brought tools with him and made a killing on the docks, he had me selling old newspapers from the boat on the streets before we were unloaded. And now he's got an idee about some boiled shirts and a fandango."

Thad interrupted. "Never mind, Avery. That can wait. We're talking about stage lines now, and that's where I want to put my time and interest."

"What about a fandango?" Benson asked.

"That's another project," Thad said. "It had nothing to do with what we're talking about."

Benson chuckled. "I like fandangos."

Thad noted the relaxation in his manner and felt encouraged. "What about the loan, Mr. Benson? I need a hundred thousand."

The banker sobered, and hesitated. "Well," he said, "let me think it over until tomorrow. I've got a few friends I want to talk to about the staging business.'

Thad rose. "Sorry," he said stiffly. "This is my idea, and I don't intend to have you or anyone else spread it all over town. How do I know you won't work out a deal with somebody else? Either I get an agreement now, or I got elsewhere."

Benson looked up at him with respect. "You'll have a hell of a time finding that amount of money from a single source."

"I've got some funds of my own."

"Then why do you want a hundred thousand from me?"

"Because I think most businesses fail at the outset due to lack of capital. I want this to start right. A hundred thousand will do it. It'll make money for whoever lends me the hundred. If it isn't you, it'll be somebody else. There must be other men of vision in this town."

There was a silence. Thad stood silently, understanding the struggle going on in Benson's mind. The banker looked at him. He was thinking, and thinking hard.

When he finally stood up, Thad held his breath. He knew no other place where he could obtain such a large sum, and by the time he might locate it, someone else could beat him to the punch in this project.

Benson held out his thick, muscular hand and smiled. "You've got your hundred thousand," he said.

Thad smiled for the first time since he had seen Jo. "Thanks!" he said fervently. "You won't regret it!"

"See that I don't," said Benson.

13

Señorita Elena Sarmiento y Lugo found she could not sleep that night. She rose from her heavy carved-walnut bedstead and stood by the window looking on the flatlands of the San Joaquin.

There was bright moonlight. The plain shone pale-blue against a black sky dotted with myraid stars. It was very quiet. The bulk of the herd was en route to the diggings with Fernando and his cowboys. Not even the muttered lowing of cattle, so much as accompaniment to her life, disturbed the nocturnal stillness.

Elena was not thinking of cattle. For some inexplicable reason she had confidence that the cattle deal would work out. For the first time in weeks, she had lost her fear of losing the ranch. What she was thinking of was a tall, stern *yanqui* who had arrived at a critical moment in their lives and had proposed a solution to their problems. She was mature enough to realize that the main reason he dominated her thoughts was because of the fact that he had come as a hero and had left as a hero. Her memory of him had romantic colorations. But when she discounted all of this, there still remained the vision of the stranger who had come, like the white god of the Aztecs, from out of nowhere at the appropriate time to solve their problems.

She stood by the window musing, dwelling pleasantly on the memory of that day.

Suddenly, her attention was distracted by movement in the moonlight plain. It appeared to be horsemen, two of them, galloping through the night toward the ranch.

She wondered who it could be. Her pulse quickened. Surely, it must be the tall *yanqui* returning from the mines! According to Fernando, he said he would stop in on his return.

It must be!

Hurriedly, Elena threw a robe around her shoulders and hastened to the front door. She flung it open and peered into the shadows.

There was no question but that the two horsemen were heading for the ranch. She could hear the hoofbeats of their horses, and they were coming fast.

Their haste puzzled her. Surely, they had a long journey from the diggings, and their mounts would be tired. Also, why would they be traveling at night? Unless, of course, they had felt they were close enough to the ranch to avoid another night out in the open.

A small twinge of disquiet rose in Elena's consciousness, but she quelled it quickly. Who else could it be? Who else but the tall, solemn man who had had the idea which was saving their estate, and who had refused to seize his reward?

She stood on the veranda, the night breeze fluttering the robe her slim ankles.

The two horsemen were nearer now, pounding up the lane leading to the veranda. Suddenly, she felt a catch in her throat. The figure on the lead horse was not tall and erect, but rather squat and chunky. The rider of the second horse was lean and stooped and menacing.

It was Bronson and his hired gun.

Elena was terrified. Fernando and the cowboys were gone. She and her father and Marie were the only ones at the ranch. Why had she not thought of this possibility and kept at least one of the cowboys for protection? Hastily, she turned and ran into the house, slamming the big door behind her and dropping the crossbar into place. She hurried to the wall and lifted off the rusty old

131

muzzle-loader that rested there on pegs. She had no idea of whether it was loaded, but it was a gun, and it looked dangerous.

The hoofbeats had stopped just outside the veranda. She could hear the horses shuffling and the muttering of human voices. She was rigid with terror as she stood by the big dining table, the gun in her hands.

There was a pounding on the door.

She did not respond.

The pounding repeated, and Bronson's voice called. "Open up! Open up in there!"

She remained silent.

The pounding resumed. Someone kicked the door with a heavy boot. The voices sounded drunk. Elena was sure Bronson and his man were both carrying a heavy load, judging from their slurred words and growls.

She debated what to do. If she answered, they would know she was awake. She was certain, in their minds, she presented no danger to them. If, on the other hand, she kept silent . . . .

She decided to remain silent. Perhaps they would tire of knocking and pounding on the door and go away.

They did not. The pounding grew louder, and so did the angry voices and mutterings. They were both intoxicated enough to fly into an easy rage. She had seen it happen to *vaqueros* who had had too much mezcal or tequila. When it did happen, they became completely unreasonable and did stupid things.

Elena wondered if the gun she held was loaded. She held it up and tried to peer into the breech. There was rust on the mechanism. She had heard of old guns exploding. Even if this one were loaded, it might be dangerous to shoot.

The pounding grew thunderous. Bronson shouted, "Open up or we'll break the door down!"

She hurried to the door, which was shaking under blows and kicks. It was of massive timber construction, with wrought-iron lock, opened by a massive key that now hung upon the wall next to the door; there was also a heavy wooden bar across it that fitted into two wrought-iron cradles. Both the bar and the lock were secure.

The door, she was convinced, would hold, and Elena felt a slight sense of relief.

Someone touched Elena's shoulder, and she jumped nervously. It was Maria, the household servant, whose corpulent figure in a voluminous Indian blanket. Her black hair in nighttime braids framing her round, brown face was trembling with fear.

"¿*Que es esto*? What is this, Señorita? Who is trying to get in?"

"Señor Bronson," Elena said curtly. "And his friend. They are *borrachos*—drunk."

Maria's fear gave way to anger. "Those *perros*! They must not enter! They will harm you! I saw the way the little fat one held your arm. They must not get in!"

She scurried from the room into the huge kitchen, returning a moment later with a huge meat cleaver that she held threateningly, shaking it at the door.

The door shook with the blows. Then the pounding stopped. The two men muttered between themselves, and Elena could hear footsteps.

Suddenly, there was a crash of glass. One of the wooden chairs that rested on the veranda came flying through the broken window. Bronson shouted. "That'll do it!"

The tall gunman carefully chipped away the sharp edges of the remaining glass and vaulted into the room. He helped Bronson, who puffed and struggled and swore as a glass fragment pierced his hand.

They were inside. The tunman lit a candle on the table, and the two men faced the two cowering women, Elena holding the big muzzle loader and Maria with the cleaver in her hand.

They laughed.

"We came," said Bronson in slurred tones, "to take a look at my property. It ain't mine yet, but it will be

133

soon. I want to get a close look at it. I ain't never really had a close look at the inside." He advanced a step.

"Get out!" Elena shouted. "Get out of here! It is not yours yet, and it will never be! Now get out before I shoot!"

Drunk as he was, Bronson was sober enough to notice the gun. He laughed. "You'll never shoot that thing. If you do, it'll blow up in your face. And it would ruin that pretty little face of yours. Now, come on, Señorita. We had a long hard ride to get here, and it's late. I want to go through the house and see what you got, so you don't cart away any of this stuff before I take over. Mack," he turned to his aide, "you got your pen and paper so's you can take inventory?"

The tall gunman searched through two pockets before he found what he sought, a stubby pen and a small sheaf of paper. "Ink," he muttered. "Got no ink."

"There must be ink around here someplace. Señorita, where's the ink?" Bronson demanded. He stepped forward again, tripping on the rug, and caught himself from falling.

Elena's father came out of the bedroom in a white nightshirt and carrying a candle. His white hair was mussed. He was only half awake.

"¿Que va?" he demanded. "What is this? Who are these men?" Then he recognized Bronson and in a moment was fully awake. "Señor! You! What are you doing here at this hour?"

Bronson waved a thick hand as he stood weavingly before them. "No reason for anybody to get excited. I'm just checkin' up. Thought it would be a good idea to take inventory before you had a chance to get away with any of this stuff that's goin' to be mine in a few weeks."

The old man, ordinarily mild and amiable, scowled. "No, Señor! You have no business coming here, especially at this hour! I will not have you in this house! Do me the favor to leave *pronto*! *¡En Seguida!*"

A brief silence ensued, as Bronson digested the old man's hostility. There was movement from the

134

shadows. The tall gunman growled an imprecation and moved swiftly forward. He took a full-armed swing and slapped the old man on the side of the head with resoundingly.

Don Pedro sprawled on the floor, where he lay dazed and moaning. Elena screamed, dropped the muzzle-loader, and ran to her father's side.

Maria lifted the cleaver and sprang forward toward Bronson, who retreated precipitately. The felling of the old man, coupled with the girl's scream and the maid's attempted assault seemed to clear his brain. He shook his head irritably and held up his hands.

"No, no!" he said. "We'll leave. Come on, Mack."

The tall gunman blearily regarded him. "But what about inventory?"

"We'll take it later," said Bronson, suddenly sober. "Come on. We'd better go."

The two men made their way to the door and exited. There was conversation and some swearing on the veranda as they sought to mount their horses. One of them apparently slipped from the stirrup and fell heavily to the ground. After more thumps and curses, the horses trotted off. There was silence once more in the household, save for Don Pedro's heavy breathing.

Elena was still kneeling by his side. Maria dropped the cleaver and hurried toward her. "How is he, Señorita? Is he all right?"

"I don't know! I don't know!" the girl said. "Come. Can you help me get him to his bed?"

With effort, the two lifted the limp body and carried Don Pedro to a huge wooden bedstead with a fringed canopy above it. The old man was breathing heavily. As they laid him on the bed, his eyes opened.

"Where is he?" he muttered. "Where is *el perro sucio*?" He struggled to rise. "I must get my gun."

"No. No!" Elena said. "They have gone. Lie back, Father. Everything is all right now."

The old man sank back with a moan.

She laid a hand on his brow. "Are you feeling better?

135

How are you feeling?"

"I—I could not get my breath," he muttered. "The blow surprised me, and I could not get my breath. But I am better now."

"Then lie still until you are recovered."

"Are you sure they have gone?"

"I am sure."

He closed his eyes, and she rose and reentered the *sala*, where Maria was already sweeping up the broken glass from the window. She had already picked up the cleaver and laid it on the table. Maria pointed a fat finger toward it. "We will leave that there!" she promised. "Just in case they return! *¡Quel animales! ¡Borrachos!*"

"Yes," said the girl. "They are. And Fernando must get back with the rest of the money, and he must get back in time. I would like again—" she hesitated.

"Yes, Señorita?" Maria encouraged.

"I would like again to see the *yanqui* on his return from the mines."

14

Thad and Avery Jackson departed from Benson's office treading on air.

"We're ready to go!" Thad exulted. "We've got it!"

"You haven't got it in your pocket," Jackson objected.

"Benson will keep his word. That's no problem. The problem now is to plan how to get this thing in operation as fast as possible. We'll need men, at least twenty to start." He halted on the street and faced Jackson, jabbing a forefinger into the older man's chest. "You'll be better at hiring men than I will, Avery. I don't know how I know that, but I do. This afternoon I'll get some of the money from Benson and head up the trail to Sacramento. We've got to pin down some of those state stops that we saw. You get the men, and we'll get 'em staffed in jig time."

"What are you going to do until this afternoon?" Jackson asked suspiciously.

Thad permitted himself a grin. "I'm going to put in an order for four Concord coaches. We'll have two trips up and two trips back a week. With that kind of service, we'll freeze out all competition."

Jackson was unaccountably grumpy. "What about the b'iled shirts and the fandango?"

"They'll have to wait until we get the stage line started." Thad turned away and started at a fast pace toward town.

"Where are you going?" Jackson asked.

"I'm going to tell Jo!" Thad said, exultingly. "I'm going to tell Jo!"

But when Thad arrived at the hotel, Jo was not there. He waited for a time, then, disappointed and worried, he left for the post office, where he knew there were advertisements for Concord coaches and the address of the manufacturing company in far eastern New Hampshire.

That morning, Clay had knocked on Jo's door. She came, surprised at his early arrival and serious expression.

"What is it?" she inquired.

"Benson wants you to go for a ride with him," he said shortly. "I'd like to have you do it."

Jo hesitated. "I'm afraid Mr. Benson has a mistaken idea of my ability to go riding with other gentlemen. After all, I'm married."

Clay looked at her, unsmiling. "Jo," he said, "have I been your friend?"

She nodded eagerly. "You certainly have! You've been *our* friend. You saved us in Panama."

"Then will you be *my* friend and go riding with Benson?"

There was a long silence. Jo raised her eyes and asked, "Does he know about Thad?"

Clay said flatly, "No, he doesn't. And I don't want him to." He moved closer to her in the doorway. "Jo, I must borrow money from Benson, and I want him to be pleased, very pleased with the Golden Eagle. You can help me to get a loan from him—if you do what I say."

Another silence.

"That's all he wants? Just a ride?"

"He's got a team of beautiful horses he wants to show off. You'll have a picnic lunch. How can you possibly object?"

"Well," she said, "it isn't customary for a married

138

woman to go picknicking with a single man who isn't her husband. What must he think of me when he finds out?"

"He needn't find out. I'll have my money before that. And that's all I want—my money!"

Jo regarded Clay with surprise. This behavior did not fit her image of him. She frowned slightly. "That's all you want? Money?"

He tried to recover. "Well, that isn't exactly the way I meant it. What I meant was, if you're nice to him now, and he's pleased with the Golden Eagle and with me, it'll be much easier to get a loan."

He took her arms in his hands. "Jo, I've got big ideas for this city. The Golden Eagle is just a beginning! There's a fortune to be made here, many fortunes!° And you'll be in for a share, if you do what I ask now!"

Benson did have a beautiful team: two massive grays, in sharp contrast to the roans, and sorrels, and palominos of California. They were hitched to a two-wheeled cart, and he had had them trained to keep in step. High-stepping prancers they were. Attached to the bridle, each wore on its brow a large red plume that jogged and swayed with each hoofbeat. Everyone looked at them with admiration and astonishment. The team performed like circus animals. Benson sat erect and proud in a gray derby and an English tweed riding coat. He handled the reins like an expert. Jo had donned the traveling suit she had worn from the East Coast, which had been cleaned and refurbished. Her pert hat sat forward on her piles of dark curls, and she could not help but share the exhilaration of the fast, high-stepping ride.

Furthermore, Benson was a good conversationalist. He had talked about things that kept Jo from thinking too much about her possibly embarrassing position. They left the city on a narrow road heading toward the southwest, quickly mounting the range of hills that formed the spine of the peninsula. The hills were covered with a thick growth of chaparral and trees, kept green by the constant, shifting fogs from the sea.

They found a shady glade near a trickling stream, and Benson pulled up the team, gave the lathered horses two nosebags, and opened a large, well-stocked hamper. He spread a canvas on the ground, opened up two camp stools, and invited Jo to sit.

"Oh, I'd like to help!" she said. For a moment, the beauty of the wooded scene, the brisk air filtering through the green foliage, and the sight of the picnic basket revived memories of her childhood. She busied herself with the plates, food and flatware.

Benson had not been niggardly with his provisions. There was a roast chicken, cold pork chops, tomatoes, pickles, Spanish olives, a watermelon, grapes, potato salad, long loaves of French bread, a red wine with a French label on it, and champagne.

"How in the world do you expect us to eat all this?" Jo wondered.

Benson grinned. "I don't," he said. "I just didn't know what you liked, so I brought several things. Select what you want, and leave the rest. There are birds and animals around here who will enjoy what we don't."

"I hardly think they're used to champagne."

"That we'll finish," Benson winked. "Also the wine. I guarantee you'll like them."

They had a pleasant time. Jo felt relaxed for an hour. Then her conscience began to gnaw again. She wondered what Thad would think if he saw her in this setting.

It was strange, she thought. For some time she had not worried about Thad or what he would think. Her misery had prevented that. She had blamed him in her mind for everything bad that had happened. Clay had dominated her days and evenings, and she had been charmed by him. Now her idyllic image of him was marred by the coldness of his eyes as he told her to be nice to Benson. When he spoke of money, she began to wonder if she had been reading Clay correctly. That thought made her wonder if she had treated Thad fairly.

In any case, despite the luxurious viands, Benson's easy conversation, and the beauty of the sylvan setting, Jo felt more and more uncomfortable. She wanted the picnic to end.

As they were sipping champagne, Benson moved his stool closer to hers. "Jo," he said, "I don't know you by any other name, so you'll excuse the familiarity. I find myself enjoying your company very much."

She hesitated before answering. "Thank you," she said primly.

He raised his brows. "Isn't there anything more you have to say, like you enjoy mine, too?"

Again she hesitated and felt even more uncomfortable. This had been a bad idea, and it had been Clay's. Clay had no business forcing her to do this.

"Of course, I enjoy your company, Mr. Benson. And this has been a very pleasant excursion. But I really think we ought to be getting back to the city. I must change my clothes and be ready for my position at the Golden Eagle."

He smiled and shifted the stool even closer. "No, you don't, Jo," he said confidently. "I talked the matter over with Mr. Moreau, and he told me not to worry about getting you back on time. In fact," his hard, piercing gaze fixed upon her and she drew back, "he said, if you didn't come to work at all tonight, it would be all right with him."

There was a frozen silence.

Jo rose from the stool and tried to keep her voice steady. "Well, it may be all right with him, but it's not all right with me!" she managed to be firm. "This has been very pleasant, Mr. Benson, and I thank you, but I really would like to go home!"

He stood up and faced her. His eyes searched hers, and he could see the determination in her gaze.

He made one more attempt. "I'd like very much to get better acquainted with you, Jo," he said gently. "I

141

could do quite a lot for you, and I'd be glad to."

Her chin rose. "I don't know what kind of person you think I am, sir!" she flared. "Please! Will you take me home?"

Benson gazed at her for another long moment, then sighed and turned away. He picked up the hamper and tossed the plates and silverware into it carelessly. He put it and the canvas in the back of the cart, untied the horses from the bush to which he had tethered their bridles, stood aside, and bowed grimly as he gestured toward the cart. Jo climbed in stiffly and wordlessly. Benson snapped the reins angrily, and the cart descended the road they had come up, both of them sitting bolt upright and in hostile silence.

As they turned the corner from Montgomery Street into the street where Jo's hotel was located, the cart came within inches of a man hurrying around the corner toward the hotel.

Jo glanced at him, then looked again and drew in her breath sharply and tried to turn her face away. But it was too late. Thad had seen her. She saw him halt in his stride as if thunderstruck and stand with his mouth open in astonishment, his hands clenched into fists.

At the hotel, Jo jumped from the cart without a word of goodbye to Benson. She looked over her shoulder at the corner to see Thad, who had been hurrying toward the hotel. He hesitated, then reversed his steps and disappeared around the corner.

Alone in her room, Jo hurried to the window. Thad was nowhere in sight, and Benson was lashing the horses angrily as he drove the cart around the same corner. She had begun to feel unsure of herself before; now she had a strange mixture of feelings. Guilt was making her angry, angry both at Clay's insistence that had caused all this dismay and at Benson and his expectations.

The thing that bothered her the most, she realized, was Thad's misunderstanding, the expression on his face as he saw her and Benson together, and his turning away from the hotel and disappearance into the crowded city.

Suddenly Jo's misery returned, but it was not the same. Now it was blame for herself, for the way she had dealth with her husband and the way she had allowed Clay to use her. And the way she had trusted him.

Thad found Avery Jackson on the waterfront, talking to two men who were obviously on their uppers and trying to get work on one of the numerous ships tied up at the rickety wharves.

"We can offer y' good wages and a growin' business," Thad heard him say. "If you know how to handle horses and can count money, you'll have a good job."

"Where is it?" one of the men asked.

"It's up inland, on the way to the diggin's."

Thad interrupted. "Sorry boys, we don't have any jobs."

The three men turned to him with astonishment. Jackson's was the deepest.

"What do you mean?" Avery demanded. "I just about got these two lined up, and I got two others all signed."

"Well, unsign 'em."

"Tarnation! Why?"

"We have no money."

"What about Benson?"

"I'll tell you about him." He turned to the other two. "I mean it boys. There's been a change of plan. We did have some jobs an hour ago, but no longer. You might as well look for something else."

The two shrugged, looked at each other, and departed.

"Now, what do you mean?" Jackson was scowling. "What in hell's happened to change the scene this quick?"

Thad's voice trembled. "I wouldn't borrow a nickel from Benson!" His fists were tightly clenched, and his face was white with rage.

"But why? Fer Pete's sake, why?"

Thad swallowed. His anger was so great, he could hardly speak. "I saw him out riding. Out riding with Jo!"

Crestfallen, the old man gazed piercingly at Thad. Then, seeing his misery, he shook his head.

There was a long pause.

"Sorry, boy," he said finally. "We'll think o' somethin' else."

15

It was another blistering day near San Jose. The sun shone brassily from a hot sky. The live oaks were dusty and motionless. Puffs of choking dust rose from the hoofs of Thad's horse and Jackson's mule, and the riders were silent and grim.

Jackson had tried to occasionally draw Thad out in conversation by suggesting plans for refinancing the project, but Thad was morose and uncommunicative.

"There are bankers in Sacramento who might do the same thing for y' as Benson," the old man said.

"We looked into that when we where there," Thad said wearily. "Don't you remember? Interest ten per cent per month on anything at all. It's a boom town. You can't make any money with a loan hanging over you like that. Maybe we'll have to go to mining ourselves."

"No, sir!" Jackson was vehement. "I learned my lesson! When they's a boom goin', you *don't* do what everybody else is doin'! The odds are agin y'! No, we'll think o' somethin'."

Thad sighed. "Well, I don't seem to have a thought in my head."

"What about those salt flats we just passed? Last time ye seen 'em you was interested."

"That would take money, too. You can't mine salt with your fingernails."

They lapsed into silence, making a silent and gloomy camp south of the pueblo. The next morning they plunged into the baking, dry, forbidding hills guarding the San Joaquin Valley.

A shadow cast an outline before them. "There's that bird again," Jackson observed, halting his mule and pointing to a dark object soaring over the coastal range. "The condor."

Thad drew up his horse and shaded his eyes with his hand. The huge bird fascinated him. It moved without a tremor of its vast wings, effortlessly seeking the air currents that kept it in the blue. It seemed to be descending gradually toward the hazy crags in the distance.

Then, even as Thad watched, without warning the gigantic bird moved convulsively. One wing lifted sharply and a flutter of feathers floated away from the dark body. The wings turned downward, and the condor arced into a steep dive toward the earth. As it did the *crack*! of a gun came to Thad's ears.

"Consarn!" Jackson exploded. "Some eternal idjit's shot him! Look! He's fallin'!"

There was another *crack*! as the delayed sound of a second shot reached them. Within seconds, the condor disappeared into the mist blanketing the surface of the mountains.

"Some bastard's'll shoot anything!" Jackson grumbled. But it's a doggone shame! There ain't enough of them birds left to harm anybody. And they're too purty to shoot!"

Thad still sat his horse silently. The shot that had sent the majestic bird plummeting to earth seemed an omen to him. That bird, and its image had possessed his mind ever since the day he had seen it from the deck of the *Darien*. It represented to him the untouchable security, the sureness those massive wings guaranteed. Gold would be his wings! Once he had spread those wings, he would be able to fly above all storms! He had convinced himself of it!

But now, the image was destroyed. The gigantic bird,

146

which had seemed so invulnerable, so calm, so secure, so invincible in its size and strength, had been blasted to earth. Not even its huge wings or its altitude above the earth had been able to save it. The cold realization came to him that the same thing could happen to him. No living thing was invulnerable. Even wings of gold could be destroyed!

Thad had been away from Jo for too long. There was no reason why a beautiful woman should waste herself waiting for a fortune-seeking, or loitering, husband to return. His search for gold might be forever elusive. He must get back to Jo. He must resolve their differences before it was too late. Already, someone may have taken his place. The very thought made Jo more desirable.

Late that afternoon, descending the eastern slopes into the ovenlike flats, from which heat rose in waves that shimmered the purple-hazed Sierra in the distance, Thad and Avery halted under an oak to rest their lathered mounts.

"There's that ranch we was at," Jackson said, pointing to the patch of green in the distance ahead of them. "Mebbe we ought to see how the gal and the old man is doin'. And they have pretty good chow."

Thad nodded absently, and they walked their horses through the gathering dusk toward the Sarmiento ranchhouse. They dismounted at the hitchrail without seeing anyone, although there were horses in the nearby corral, and a wisp of smoke was coming from the brick chimney over the *cocina* oven.

"Looks like somebody's home," Jackson commented as they mounted the veranda and knocked on the huge, hand-hewn door.

Maria, the rotund cook, answered. Her face brightened as she recognized them. "*¡Bienvenido bienvenido! ¡Venga!* Welcome! Come in! I shall tell the señorita and the señor!"

Maria urged them into the large, cool *sala* and bustled toward the rear of the house. In a moment she was

147

back. With her was Elena, who hurried to Thad and held out her hands. "*¡Nuestro amigo!* We have wondered how to reach you to thank you for all you did for us, but we did not know where you were."

Thad could not help but smile, so evident was her joy. Her face was flushed, and her dark eyes gleamed with pleasure.

"We're on our way back to the diggings," Thad said awkwardly.

"Do not speak of where you are going!" she exclaimed. The important thing is that you are here. You must stay as long as you can. We will celebrate by serving you something special to eat. I must tell my father."

She hurried from the room. In a few moments, she brought back Don Pedro, whose face reflected the same sincere pleasure that had shone in the girl's eyes.

"Welcome, welcome! *¡Mi casa es su casa!* It pleases me much to see you. Elena and I are most grateful for all that you have done for us!"

They seated themselves, while Maria bustled back and forth, preparing the table for dinner.

"The second sale went well?" Thad inquired.

"Better than the first! We paid off our entire loan and still have some cattle left with which to build a new herd. We owe you so much. And you have not even collected your commission! Besides giving you that, we want to think of some additional way to repay you."

Thad was embarrassed. "To know that it went well is all the thanks I want," he said. "There is no need to do anything further. I am glad you are free of debt. If you ever have to borrow again, don't go to the Yankee moneylenders. Go to a regular bank. Most of them are honest, and at least you will have more reasonable interest. High interest rates are very bad for any business. These private moneylenders can ruin you in short order."

"We know, we know!" Don Pedro nodded vigorously. "We are not accustomed to *yanqui* ways."

"Being dishonest is not a *yanqui* way," Thad protested. "You just ran into a bad apple. There are dishonest people in every land, but they are not in the majority."

The girl became impatient. "I do not want to talk about *yanqui* ways!" she said. "I want to talk about *you*! Where are you going? What are your plans? How long can you stay with us?"

Thad smiled. "Not long. We'd appreciate bedding down for the night, like we did before. But tomorrow we ought to be on our way."

Jackson interrupted. "We got a business proposition we're interested in, and we're lookin' for some financin'."

Thad frowned. "This won't interest them, Avery. We've got our problems, they've got theirs." He turned back toward the girl. "One thing we do know, we're not going to spend our time mining. My friend here," he jerked a thumb at Jackson, "has firm ideas on the subject. We'll go into some kind of business."

"And you need money?" Elena asked.

"Every businessman needs money. We'll find it. That's why we're going back to Stockton and Sacramento."

"But if we could—" Don Pedro leaned forward, but Thad raised his hand and interrupted.

"I'm glad your problems are solved," he said. "Now I've got a few, and I intend to solve them in the same way. The only favor I'll ask of you is supper and a place to sleep. We'll be mighty grateful for that."

Later, in the room off the big, flowered patio that had been assigned to them, Thad told Avery, "They just paid off their loan. They haven't got any money. This is the first time they can take a deep breath. I don't want 'em to feel obligated, and I certainly don't want 'em to think we've come here for money. How would they get it, even if we wanted it?"

"They got land and cows," Avery grumbled. "A lot o' land, and probably a hell of a lot more cows than

149

they think they've got. They could sell a few or borrow again."

"Borrow! They almost got ruined borrowing!"

"But you said not all bankers was dishonest. I'll bet interest rates on ranch land wouldn't be nearly so damn high as interest rates on a business related to minin'."

"You might be right at that," Thad said. "But if you think I'm going to borrow from these people after the experience they just had, you've got another think coming. Now let's get to bed. I want to get to Stockton tomorrow."

Jackson muttered something under his breath, and the two went to bed in their underwear.

In another room in the big house, Elena lay awake, thinking other thoughts that did not have to do with money. They concerned a tall *yanqui* who had done them a large favor and who wanted nothing in return, and whose blue eyes looked upon her as a piece of furniture.

She did not look upon him that way, she realized. She knew he had filled her thoughts since their last meeting to an extent that doubtless merited confession to Padre Serafino, the friar at the Mission San Jose.

After a large *desayuno* consisting of tortillas and eggs with chiles and tomatoes, Thad and Avery started out again toward the valley flats. The morning was still cool, but the cloudless sky gave promise of the day being another scorcher. They paced their mounts quickly to cover as much ground as possible before the torrid heat of the day enveloped them.

Elena and her father and Maria stood on the veranda as they departed. Elena remained standing there even after her father and Maria had reentered the house. Even though she stood there until they were tiny moving figures in the distance, she did not see the horsemen on the hills behind the ranch, standing their horses in the shade of the live oak clump that had sheltered Thad and Avery on their first trip to the San Joaquin. Bronson and his hired gun sat their horses and watched as the two travelers disappeared in the distance.

Bronson, his pudgy features flushed with anger and his tiny eyes cold with hatred, turned to his companion. "That's the damn Yank that robbed me of this ranch! I'd know him anywhere—even a mile away!"

The tall man with the drooping mustache lifted a heavy brow. "Want me to go after him?"

Bronson hesitated. "It'd be too easy to connect me with it. But," his little eyes narrowed, "tell you what you can do. You can follow him and see what he's up to. Go on with him to the diggings, if you have to. I won't need you for a few days. Maybe we can figure out something where he'll have to pay us back."

The tall man waited for a moment. "You mean it?"

Bronson scowled. "Sure I do! Go on, beat it! Find out what he's up to!"

In Stockton, Thad and Avery went to the largest bank in town. It was in a false-fronted frame building consisting of a counter, a safe, and two men in eyeshades. A large horse pistol lay on the counter in ready reach of the teller.

The latter eyed them suspiciously and put both hands, palms down, on the counter. "Goin' to deposit?"

"Nope," said Thad. "I want to talk about a loan."

"Twelve percent a month; ninety days limit."

"No, no," said Thad. "I'm talking about a big loan. Hundred thousand, or more."

"See the cashier." The man jerked a thumb toward the other eyeshaded individual who, in a dark frock coat and flowing tie, waxed mustache and pomaded hair, was working on a ledger.

Thad was followed by Avery. The man did not invite them to be seated, although there were two hard chairs by his desk. Thad told him what he wanted.

"What security?" he demanded.

"Some boiled shirts and jewelry in San Francisco, and I've got some cash of my own to put into the venture."

The man leaned back in his chair and regarded Thad with a frown. "You must think I'm crazy."

"No, I don't think you're crazy. And I'm not either. I'm trying to sell you an idea, a good one that'll make us both money."

"Well, it isn't good enough." The man turned back to his work.

Thad paused a moment, deciding whether it was worthwhile making another argument, decided it was not, and departed with Avery at his heels. Out in the street they faced each other.

"If'n ye're so bound not to do business with Benson, then ye should have talked to the old rancher. I bet he'd have thought of somethin'."

Thad's jaw tightened. "We'll go to the other bank." He strode off.

They met with the same reception, although the banker was slightly more friendly. He told them he had thought about staging as a good investment, but it took experience. All the experienced stage drivers were already in the business, as it was expanding fast. He smiled slightly when Thad described his security but turned him down with a degree of courtesy Thad appreciated.

Out in the street again, Thad said grimly, "We'll try Sacramento!"

Avery clutched his sleeve. "You know you're wastin' time for both of us! Nobody's goin' to lend us money on the terms you're proposin'. Only reason Benson did it was 'cuz he knew you, or thought he did, and thought he owed you somethin'. We got to think o' somethin' else."

"You tired of following me around?"

"Hell, no! It's just that I think we're wastin' time."

"Well, don't waste any more of yours. I'm going on to Sacramento. I'll see you back in the city sometime.

That is, if I come back." Angrily and stubbornly, Thad turned on his heel and moved off up the street.

Jackson reached out a hand. "Now, wait, durn it!" Then he withdrew it and watched Thad stride away.

"Feisty critter," he muttered. "Feisty. And kind of stupid when he's mad." He shrugged. "But ain't we all?"

He watched Thad disappear up the street.

16

Two days later, Avery Jackson was back in San Francisco at the door of the Bank of Mission Valley. He hesitated at the portal, took off his hat, put it on again, squared his thin shoulders, and entered. He was not used to bankers.

He went directly to Benson's desk, where the banker was talking to one of his employees. Benson finished his conversation and looked up. He frowned. "Don't I know you?"

Jackson nodded. "I come here with Thad Morgan a few days ago. You know, the feller who wanted to enter the stagin' business."

Benson's expression cleared. "Oh, yes. And by the way, what happened to him? I thought we had a deal. He hasn't shown up. Are you representing him?"

"Well, in a manner of speakin'."

"I'm glad you are, because you can tell him that I waited a day for him to show up and then didn't wait any longer. I made another sizable loan, and right now I'm not in position to produce a hundred thousand for him. Why the hell didn't he show up?"

The old man's face fell. He took off his hat and twisted the brim in his hands. "Well, I was agoin' to tell ye about that, but now I guess it don't make no difference."

"Tell him I'm sorry, but a banker makes money by keeping his money at work. When a good deal came along, I had to take it. Maybe sometime later we can do business. I'll be liquid again in a couple of weeks. I think he's honest and has the makings of a good businessman, but right now I'm up to my loan limit and can't do anything for him. Sorry." He turned back to his desk, and Jackson waited a moment. He failed to think of anything to say and turned to depart.

Jackson took two steps, then turned back. "I got a question to ask."

Benson, his gray brows pulled together in a second frown, looked up. "Yes, what is it?"

Jackson took a long breath. "Are you still squirin' that hostess from the Golden Eagle?"

Benson was taken aback and gazed silently at the old man. "Did I hear you correctly?"

"You sure did. Are you still squirin' that hostess from the Golden Eagle? The one in the red dress and the jewelry?"

Benson stood up slowly and came to the side of his desk, where, despite his middling stature, he looked down upon Avery's seamed face. Jackson was uncomfortable but game. He swallowed and stood his ground.

"Before I throw you out," Benson said angrily, "I'll ask *you* a question. What the hell business is it of yours, and why are you interested?"

"A simple reason," Jackson retorted. "A simple reason that might make you add two and two together."

"All right. What is it?"

"That purty gal is Thad Morgan's wife!"

Again, Benson was shocked, this time to the extent of gazing upon Jackson with open mouth. Then he recovered himself and slowly returned to his desk and sat down behind it. After a moment, he remembered Jackson and waved a careless hand at the chair beside the desk. "Sit down, old timer."

"Why?" said Jackson. "They ain't nothin' more to talk about if you loaned out all your cash. I just thought you oughta know."

"Well, sit down anyway. I won't be at my loan limit

for very long." Benson leaned forward. "I assure you I didn't know that girl was Morgan's wife. In fact, I didn't know she was anybody's wife."

"That'll help," Jackson nodded, but he refused the chair. "I'll see that he gets that information."

The two men stared at each other for a long moment. Then the old man turned to go. At the door, he faced Benson again. "You ain't answered the big question," he said. "Now that you know she's somebody's wife, are you goin' to keep right on squirin' her?"

Benson reddened. "That's none of your damned business!" he flared. "I don't like your implication!"

"Morgan didn't like the idea either," Jackson said. "That's why he didn't show up." He turned on his heel and left the bank.

At the corner of Montgomery, Jackson hurried out of the way as a fringed carriage, driven by a Mexican in *vaquero* garb and carrying two passengers, and old man and a girl, trotted swiftly by.

Jackson paid little attention, but when the carriage had passed, he halted and swung around. "By gollies," he muttered, "that looked all fired like Fermando and the old Don and his daughter!" He stood musing. He was certain Don Pedro would strive to be of help if approached. But he recalled Thad's firmness when he had broached the subject. Avery Jackson debated with himself whether to try to follow the carriage, then shrugged and walked off in the opposite direction. He hoped, although he was not at all certain, because of Thad's stubbornness, that Thad had calmed down and was on his way back to the city. But when he thought of Thad's expression when he had told about Jo being with Benson, he was not so sure.

In Sacramento, Thad made the rounds of the banks and received the same answer he had got in Stockton. Stubbornly, grimly, he went on to Placerville and after that to Coloma, to ask the same question and get the same answer.

156

In a tent-roofed hotel in Sacramento, Thad re-inventoried his assets. He had about $8,000 in cash remaining from his San Francisco ventures, and there was a smaller amount due him from the Sarmientos as a result of the sale of their cattle. That, however, had yet to be collected.

He sat on the edge of the sagging cot, thinking. Beside him, a candle stuck in a saucer burned on a small table that held a pitcher, a bowl, and a small tarnished mirror. He looked in the mirror and was surprised at what he saw. It was his face all right, but with a three-day stubble of dark beard, unkempt hair, worry and fatigue lines around the eyes and mouth. He looked down at his boots. They were scuffed and dusty. He didn't wonder bankers were turning him down right and left. He didn't look as if he were solvent, to say nothing of being a good risk for a large, long-term loan.

He sat back and gazed absently into the dark shadows in the corners of the tent-roofed, board-floored cubicle. Outside, voices rose in drunken dispute, and in the distance a shot was fired. Horses galloped by on the busy street. From half a block away, the tinkling of a barroom piano filtered through the other sounds.

Why was he here, and what had happened to him in the last few weeks? He shook his head. It was hard to realize that the little shop on Charles Street in Baltimore was less than two months behind him. He remembered how pleasant summer mornings could be in Baltimore, with the fresh cool air redolent of the fields outside of town; the morning greeting from Mort Gimbel, the apothecary next door, as he swept his brick walk; the first customer, usually a housewife, hurrying to buy a dish or a hook or a washtub, and usually interested in an exchange of words.

It had not been a bad life, and the arrival of their daughter had been a tremendous event. But Jo had never been satisfied, never happy. The little apartment over the store that held happy memories for him apparently held none for her. She had constantly complained about its small size and compared it with her family's big house on a large farm near Silver Spring.

But now, in a tent hotel without Jo, with brawling, drunken miners outside, with the stifling heat of the Sacramento Valley imprisoned in the tent and flies buzzing maddeningly about his perspiring face, what had brought him to this? It was Jo, after all, Jo who had caused this change. He had willingly accepted it, if it would make her happy. But all it had brought was tragedy and separation.

All of the thoughts and regrets and sadness and bitterness that had assailed Thad during the last few weeks tumbled in his brain. He rose from the cot and stood staring out the dirty little windows, his fists clenched. He should have done things differently, he knew. He should have insisted on being with Jo, on her being with him. He should not have left her alone. He knew why he had behaved as he had. He could not bear the thought of losing her. He had posponed the showdown again and again, fearful it would turn out wrong.

A feeling of hopelessness and helplessness overcame him. His stubborn anger vanished, and he felt almost afraid. There seemed to be a conspiracy of hostile forces against him. The fates were frowning. Whatever he did turned out wrong. Whenever hope brightened his prospects momentarily, they were dashed. For a time, the staging business and his contact with Benson had seemed to indicate that the cards were falling his way. Then. . . .

He shook his head angrily and rose to pace the board floor of the little shelter. The sight of Jo with Benson, with another man had been too much. He could not bear to think of it or to recall the choking misery that had followed.

He sat for a long time thinking. There were several courses open to him. He *could* start mining, but Jackson had pretty well convinced him of the disadvantages of such an endeavor. He could go to work for somebody else. They always needed clerks and barkeeps, but his spirit rebelled. He had been his own man for too long; he was not in the mood to become an employee, even to keep from starving, and he was nowhere near that extremity. He could, of course, go back east and leave Jo to her new banker friend.

The bitterness returned. Thad rose and paced the creaking board floor. He sat down again, his head in his hands. He thought of the voyage and the high hopes that had accompanied it, the long hours at sea.

Suddenly the vision of the huge bird that soared effortlessly above the dry coastal mountains came to him. What was it Avery had called it? A condor? Its wings were so vast they enabled it to rise above the storms. Those wings were what he needed. He immediately related them to the moneybelt about his waist. That was what he needed, the broad wings the gold would bring. That was what would enable him to rise above the storm.

His mind cleared, and calm returned. If he could not start his business on a large scale, he'd start it on a small one. He'd buy some mules tomorrow and get started. He'd begin a pack-mule express. Even without wheels and the shiny newness of a Concord coach, he would be able to start the business that had brought him to the diggings. Furthermore, there was a chance that, once he had those broad wings, he could persuade Jo to return. Perhaps she had not even left. After all, he was the one who had angrily departed. He turned over on the cot and slept soundly for the first time in days.

Three weeks later, Thad drove his string of eight mules up to the hitch rail of the Rancho Santa Elena. He looped the lead leather of the team over the rail and dismounted from his horse. The place looked the same, solid and stable and beautiful. Its tiles gleamed rose-red under the hot, bright sun; roses climbed up the whitewashed walls; the well with its long sweep in the yard shone dusty green with its vines.

The big door to the *sala* swung open, and the girl

came running out. "Señor!" she exclaimed, hurrying to his side. "I did not see you coming or hear you! Please come in! Fernando will take care of your horse and your mules." She gazed at the string of eight, with their heavy pack-saddles. "You are carrying mail?"

"And dust." Thad smiled at her excitement. "But I don't talk about that. At least not very loud! It's good to see you."

Elena looked up at him worshipfully, then reddened under his friendly gaze. "*Mi padre* has been wanting to see you."

Thad followed her into the cool *sala*. Don Pedro was equally pleased and excited at his arrival. "I have some news for you, some good news," the old man said. "After our dinner, we will discuss it!" He seemed to be bubbling with a pleasant secret. Thad felt a mild curiosity, then dismissed it from his mind.

At the dinner table, which as usual was loaded with food from the lush gardens and orchards of the rancho, Don Pedro said, "I have recently seen your friend, Señor Jackson, and he wished me to tell you where he was staying, in case you decided to look him up." He hurried over to his desk, drew out a piece of paper, and handed it to Thad. On it was a San Francisco address.

Thad felt uncomfortable. He regretted his angry departure and his virtual dismissal of Avery. He had awakened in the night more than once, filled with remorse. The note did not make him feel any better. Indeed, it deepened his regret, but he was relieved to know that Jackson bore no hard feelings and might even look forward to a renewal of the partnership.

He could use a partner. Traveling alone down lonely mountains trails with gold dust worth thousands belonging to others was not Thad's idea of a relaxing occupation.

With the meal finished, after the *postres*, Don Pedro eagerly leaned forward. "You are driving mules, but you wish to run stagecoaches to the mines." His old eyes twinkled.

"You've been talking to Jackson."

"That is right. I saw him in San Francisco. He was very worried about you, and he wanted me to be sure to tell you where he was."

Thad looked away. "I'm glad to hear that. We shouldn't have parted. I was feeling a little low, and we had an argument."

"One should not have arguments with friends."

Thad nodded.

"But you need money for stagecoaches. Since you helped us pay our debt to Señor Bronson, I am now in a position to borrow money at better rates from a good bank."

Thad raised a stubborn hand. "You got into trouble borrowing before. You're clear now. You shouldn't borrow anything. You should just run your ranch and enjoy it."

Don Pedro shook his head. "That is not the way to progress. If I have learned anything from you *yanquis*, it is never to sit back and do nothing. I am looking for a good investment in a good business. One might always have a bad year for crops or cattle on a rancho, and it would be wise for me to protect my daughter's future by having another business interest. But one must find a good businessman in whom to put one's confidence."

"That certainly is important," Thad said.

"I think I have found one."

Thad's jaw tightened. "I don't want to be responsible for your going again into debt."

"It is too late."

"What do you mean it's too late?"

"I have already borrowed the money. It is in my account at my bank in San Jose. It is doing nothing but earning small interest. I must produce more income from it, or I will be in trouble again."

Thad was aghast. "You've already borrowed it? For what?"

"For you. I was sure you would come this way again, and both Señor Jackson and I have been watching for you." Don Pedro pushed back his chair and stood, his seamed face stern and dark against his white mustache and beard. "Señor, I am a man of honor. You have done me and my family a large and important favor. For centuries, my family has acquitted itself honorably in such situations. You must permit me to do the same. This is a matter of honor, and I will not take no for an answer!"

Thad glanced at Elena. She was leaning tensely over the table. "Please!" she said. You must let us help you!"

There was a long silence.

Finally Thad said, "How much did you borrow?"

"One-hundred-thousand dollars."

"And how much interest are you getting?"

"Six percent."

"And how much are you paying?"

"Eight percent."

Thad shook his head. "You must pay the money back right away, so you will lose no more. Don't misunderstand me. I appreciate what you've done, but I can't let you do this."

Don Pedro reseated himself and peaked his fingers triumphantly. "Señor, if I pay the money back within one year, there is a—what did the banker call it?—a ten-point penalty. Señor, I cannot afford that. You must make some money for me!"

There was another long silence. Then there was talk far into the evening. At midnight, Thad rose and said, "I must get these mules into San Francisco as fast as possible and look up Avery. Then we'll get those stages and go to work. I'm glad we can do it, but I'm sorry we're doing it this way. What if I lose your money for you? All of my effort up at the mines with your cattle will have gone for nothing."

"You will not lose." Don Pedro was confident. He turned to his daughter. "Will he, Elena *mia*?"

She looked up at Thad, her eyes glowing. "You will not lose, Señor. And, we will see you often!"

Thad checked his mules and his horse, then went to bed in the comfortable room off the patio where he had slept before. He spent some time lying awake, worrying thoughts rumbling through his mind. His most troubling thought was of going to San Francisco where he would look up Jo. Was she there? Would she be glad to see him? Or was she with Benson? Or Clay?

The last thought bothered Thad more than any other. It was long before he slept, and then it was a restless, tossing slumber, interrupted by many awakenings.

Once he thought he heard horses. He sat up in bed. The grandfather clock in the hall, brought around the Horn by a *yanqui trader*, struck three.

Earlier that afternoon, even before Thad had arrived at the Santa Elena with his mule train, Bronson's droop-mustached hired gun galloped up, dusty, his shirt dark with perspiration, to Bronson's office in a false-fronted building in San Jose.

The room was hot and buzzing with flies. The man threw himself down in the one rickety straight chair that stood before Bronson's desk. Bronson was there in his shirtsleeves, sweat circles under his arms, his cuffs held up by purple sleeve garters. He was smoking a twisted black Mexican cigar.

"Well, it's about time, Mack. I about gave you up. What'd you find out?"

The tall man took off his hat and mopped his dripping brow with a blue bandana. "He's runnin' a pack-mule express. And he's doin' well. Better than some who've been at it longer. He's got business from several towns—Placerville, Whiskey Flat, Slumgullion."

"Well, where do we fit in?"

"He's carryin' a lot of dust. And he's alone. That dust is now in the barn at Santa Elena."

Bronson sat up and took the cigar from his fat lips. His eyes narrowed.

"He's not expectin' anything tonight, is he?"

"Not a thing. There are two Mexes there, but they'll all be asleep."

Bronson grinned slowly and winked at his colleague. "I think a moonlight horseback ride would be good for us, Mack. How about it?"

The tall man nodded. "I'll go get a little shuteye. I covered quite a few miles this afternoon.

As the clock finished striking, Thad swung his long legs out of the bed and went to the window. The barn was a dark shadow, but there were other dark shadows, smaller and moving, by its side.

Thad rushed to the chair where he had placed his clothes, threw them on, grabbed the five-shooter he had purchased in Placerville when he knew he would be guarding his cargo by himself, checked it to make sure it was loaded, and swung out of the window. He bent low, so his dark form would not be silhouetted against the whitewashed wall of the house, and moved rapidly and circuitously toward the movement he had seen.

There were two horsemen, he saw. One was still mounted, watching the other, who was at the closed barn door. The bunkhouse, where the ranchhands slept, was 50 yards away, and there was no light or movement from that quarter.

There was only one answer to what he saw. Someone had heard of the dust in the packsaddles and was planning to help himself.

Thad moved silently toward the two shadows. As he approached, the man at the barn door swung it partly open and slipped inside. Time was pressing, and Thad had a difficult time swallowing the surge of anger that rose in his throat. He uttered a war whoop for Fernando, then fired his five-shooter above the head of the horseman still mounted outside the barn. The man turned. His blocky figure told Thad his identity. It was Bronson, the moneylender from San Jose who had

164

attempted to swindle Don Pedro out of his property.

Bronson pulled a gun a fired twice. Thad felt a blow like a mule kick in his left shoulder. The impact whirled him around and slammed him to the ground. He was hit, he knew, with a heavy-caliber bullet. He lifted himself with difficulty on his right elbow and, head swimming, tried to fire again. The last thing he remembered was another figure emerging from the barn, lugging two sets of saddlebags. Then he lost consciousness.

When he awoke, it was bright morning. The girl was tending his wound, and Fernando, sweaty, dusty and angry, was standing at her side with one of the other ranch hands.

"Ah, Señor! You are awake! God be praised!" The girl's voice trembled.

"And we have the bullet!" Don Pedro was leaning over her shoulder. "It is a clean wound, but you must lie still for awhile, Señor."

Thad groaned. He still felt weak and sick. "Did they get away with anything?"

Fernando stepped forward. "I am sorry, Señor. We chased them, but they got away. By the time we got our horses, they were too far ahead."

Thad groaned again. "What did they get?"

"Two sets of saddlebags. They left three bags behind."

"The ones that had dust or mail?"

Fernando hesitated and looked away. "They must have had dust, Señor. The ones that are left have the mail."

Thad gazed up at the whitewashed ceiling with its rough beams and felt as if the bottom had fallen out of his world.

17

At the Golden Eagle, Jo went to work that evening
feeling, as she had for some days past, worried and
remorseful. The experience with Benson had wrenched
her back to a semblance of emotional normality after
the shock of her baby's death. Once again, she was
thinking of Thad, and she was thinking, too, of things
she had not thought of before, such as the lack of consideration she had shown for her husband, the
complaints, her discontent with their Baltimore exis-
tence. Watching the men come to the Golden Eagle in
large numbers, watching them with the red-skirted floor
girls, watching them climb the stairs to the plush rooms
above, had given her a new perspective. She was forced
to conclude that she had been fortunate to have a
husband who was loyal and generous and hard-working
and principled. There were obviously many men who
were none of those things.

Now that she was beginning to have these thoughts,
now that she was appreicating Thad in a way she never
had before, it seemed to be too late. She remembered
the expression on Thad's face when he had seen her in
the carriage with Benson. It was so full of pain and
anger that she could not erase the vision from her mind.
She had not seen or heard from him since. He had even
deserted his old partner, Avery Jackson, who had come
to see her more than once. They had inquired of each

other if either had news of Thad. Neither had.

That evening, as she arrived at the Golden Eagle, the beautiful red dress no longer thrilled her, and the diamonds about her throat seemed like shackles rather than ornaments. Nor was Clay the same as he had been. Since she had rejected Benson's advances—and she had told Clay about it—he had been unfriendly. He treated her with a cool, businesslike mien and never mentioned the incident. He was no longer warm and admiring, and she was rapidly arriving at the conclusion that she had misjudged him also.

Tonight, as she entered the swinging doors, Clay was there to meet her. He obviously had been waiting for her. He took her by the arm and led her swiftly aside.

"I'm glad you're here," he said. "Benson's here, too. The first time he's come since you threw him over."

"Clay, I didn't throw him over."

"Whatever you did, it didn't help. Now you have a chance to make up for it. He's sitting at the same table he had before, and he's ordered the most expensive things on the menu. He's looking around, obviously looking for you." Clay stood back. "What are you going to do about it?"

Jo was at a loss for words. "What do you expect me to do about it?" she asked, falteringly.

Clay's eyes narrowed, and his faced turned hard. "I expect you to go over there and be nice to him. If necessary, apologize for the way you acted. I want to do business with him, and I want him to keep coming here. It's up to you to see that he does!"

Jo was silent for a long moment. "And if I don't?"

"Then you needn't come back to work tomorrow. Think about it. Thad's gone, I understand. You're on your own. There aren't any more jobs like yours in this man's town. All you can get is something like that." He gestured toward one of the floor girls, who was urging a new acquaintance to buy her a drink.

They stood looking at each other for a long moment as Jo's misery deepened.

"Well?" Clay demanded. "What's it to be?"

Wordlessly, helplessly, Jo turned away and moved slowly toward Benson's table. When he saw her coming, his face brightened. He smiled, rose, and gallantly held a chair for her.

"Well, Jo," he said. "I was afraid for a minute you weren't here. I came back to see you."

Her heart sank, and she glanced at Clay. He was standing by the door with a mirthless smile on his face, watching both of them.

For a moment Jo debated whether to rise again and leave the Golden Eagle. Then the clutch of fear gripped her. What was she to do? Her money was almost gone. Living in a high-cost town like San Francisco had used up most of her salary. She closed her eyes for a moment, then turned to Benson.

"Good evening, sir," she said.

"Oh, come on!" he said, smiling. "Let's not be formal! Will you share a glass of wine with me this evening?"

She hesitated again, then nodded. She was sure the hole thing was beginning over again. Benson was about to make another attempt, and this time there would have to be a decision. The decision would be made under the cold gaze of Clay, who was still standing by the door, watching.

Benson was fully at ease and was mking light conversation about the weather, about the menu, about things that Jo did not hear, so troubled was she about the situation. Finally, Benson stopped talking and leaned across the table. He was smiling. "You're not listening to me, Jo."

"I'm—I'm sorry," she said.

"Is it because that boss of yours is watching us?"

"Well, no. I—"

"Or is it because he's told you to play up to me, and you're afraid I'll invite you on another picnic?"

She stared at him. He was laughing at her, but his eyes were kindly.

He reached across the table and took her hand. "I'm not going to invite you another picnic, Jo," he said. "I found out you're a married woman, and I don't monkey around with married women. I have a feeling you're not the kind who goes out with men other than your husband, either—except that your boss made you." He glanced toward Clay, still standing at the door. "Am I right?"

She could not find her voice.

"Don't bother to answer that," he said. "I came here this evening because your husband tried to borrow some money from me and never showed up to claim it. I guess he misinterpreted our buggy ride. I've got the money for him now, and I'd like to do business with him—and you, too. Will you tell him that?"

"I—I don't know where he is. I haven't seen him since—since—"

"Since he saw us together, eh? That's too bad. But I'm sure he'll show up. Nobody in his right mind would walk away from a woman like you." He rose from the table. "When you see him, tell him." He patted her hand. "By the way, your boss wants to borrow some money from me, too. I didn't give it to him. Does he know you're married?"

She nodded, unable to speak.

"Well, that clinches it. I don't like people who force other people to do things they don't think they should do. Goodbye, Jo. Don't forget to give your husband that message when you see him. And you'll see him."

Jo watched Benson as he walked away. She saw him halt briefly by Clay's side and speak to him. He nodded in her direction as he did so. A sense of disaster came over her. He was probably telling Clay what he thought of him, and now she would be discharged.

"I'm still considering that loan proposal, Moreau," Benson was saying to Clay. "Hiring people like Jo, over there, shows you have sound business judgment. I'll let you know shortly."

Clay seized his arm. "But when, Mr. Benson? When?

This proposition I told you about won't keep."

Benson winked at him and extricated his arm. "As long as you've got Jo on your payroll, I'll be back, and we'll talk further. See you soon, Moreau." He clapped his hat on his head and exited.

He left Clay standing by the door, looking at Jo. Jo returned his gaze with trepidation. He walked over to her, and she steeled herself for the bad news.

"Well," said Clay grudgingly, "you seem to have warmed him up. See that you keep on doing it. Watch for him when he comes back. If I don't see him, let me know immediately when he arrives."

He turned on his heel, and Jo, her head swimming with puzzlement and relief, gathered herself together to greet the half-dozen new customers who were standing at the door.

Thad Morgan returned to San Francisco in a hurry. Equally hurriedly, he looked up his former partner Jackson at the address given him by the Sarmientos. Jackson was glad to see him, but edged carefully into the conversation.

"Well, I thought you'd never git back here," he began.

"Let's not waste time, Avery," Thad said. "I'm sorry I got mad, and I'm sorry we split up. I understand you'd like to join up again. Is that right?"

The old man's gnarled face broke into a snaggle-toothed grin. "That's right, pard!"

Thad permitted himself a brief smile. He stretched out a hand. "We'll shake on it. And if we're partners again, we've got to get busy. Here's what's happened."

Quickly he told Jackson about the loan from Don Pedro, and the situation that had forced him to accept it.

"You got the money for the stages! Whoopee!" Jackson slapped his leg with glee.

"It isn't the way I wanted to get it, but we've got it.

We've got to use it and make it pay off. Or, rather, *you've* got to do it. You know as much about it as I do. You go hire the men and reactivate those orders for stages."

Jackson looked puzzled. "Why? What are you goin' to do?"

"I'm going hunting," Thad said drily. Again, quickly, he explained about Bronson and the robbery of the dust he had been carrying in his express packs.

"I'm sure it was Bronson and that hired gun of his," he concluded. "I've got to go after 'em. I've got customers in the diggings depending on me to keep their dust safe for 'em. I haven't done it, and I've either got to get it back or pay 'em off. I can't afford to pay 'em right now."

"You goin' back to San Jose?"

"That's where Bronson is."

Jackson scratched his head. "I ain't so sure he'd try to change that dust into cash in his home town. 'Specially, if news of the robbery got out. More'n likely, he'd come to San Francisco."

Thad scowled. "I've got to start somewhere. All you've done is broaden the field. Anyway, you get busy organizing our stage line, and I'll see if I can get that dust back. I've got some mail to deliver first. And sometimes later today I want to see Jo."

"Ain't you goin' to see her first?"

Thad shook his head. "I'll—I'll look her up later," he said. He did not say what was on his mind, that he was almost afraid of what he would find at the hotel. She might be gone. She might have moved out. She might again be with . . . Benson. They made arrangements to meet later that day, and Thad hurried off. He delivered his mail to the place he had arranged for, a general store in the middle of town with a safe. Then he bought some more ammunition for his new five-shooter and set off grimly for the hotel.

Jo was not there, although she was still registered as a guest. The latter piece of information gave Thad such a

171

sense of relief that he closed his eyes for a moment and did not trust himself to speak.

"You all right?" the hotel clerk asked worriedly.

"I'm all right," said Thad. "Thanks for the information."

"You want I should give a message to Miz Morgan when she comes in? Won't be till late."

"No," said Thad. "I'll be back in a day or so. I'll give her the message myself."

Jo was still there. Somehow, that news meant a great deal more to Thad, he realized, than he thought it would. It meant she was still around, and it also meant she might still be waiting for him.

He set out for the south with a heart lighter than it had been for days. The fog was rolling in as he departed from the city. He did not emerge from the fog until he reached the spot on the bay shore where Coyote Point stretched eastward with its brushlands and scrub trees. He had not, he knew, adequately prepared for this trip. He was short of food and water, and his horse was already tired from the long trek from the diggings. Yet, he pushed himself. It was only out of consideration for his horse that he halted in the shelter of a live oak and forced himself to rest.

The tree was a short distance off the main trail. As he sat there holding his horse's reins, he heard hoofbeats approaching from the south. There were two horsemen. For some reason he could not explain, even to himself, Thad dismounted and held his horse's muzzle to prevent it from whinning. He pulled the animal farther into the shadows of the live oak and strained his eyes to see the riders.

He could not believe what he saw. Yet he knew he had almost been expecting it, after Jackson's warning. The two riders were Bronson and the tall thin associate who carried his gun low on his hip. Avery Jackson had been right. Bronson was not prepared to risk disposing of the dust in his home town.

Thad let the pass and move a mile to the north before

he started to follow. Then he followed them carefully. In San Francisco, they left their horses at a livery, and so did Thad. Then they started what seemed to Thad to be a pub crawl. They went to three saloons, staying only a short time in each. Thad concluded they were less interested in liquid refreshment than they were in information. After all, saloonkeepers were well-informed men, usually, especially about the darker aspects of the town's activities.

After the third saloon, a disreputable establishment near the waterfront, Bronson and his aide stood for a time outside discussing something very seriously. Then they moved back toward the center of town.

Thad debated whether to enter the saloon to see if he could find out what they had been talking about or to follow them. He decided on the latter course. After all, if he lost them now, he might never find them again, and this particular saloonkeeper might be close-mouthed.

Cautiously, he followed. He was pleased they were still unaware of his presence.

The fog was low now, and a chill was in the air. The mist drifted in wisps and fingers above his head. Lights were going on in the tent-topped buildings of the city, giving it its characteristic Japanese-lantern appearance. As the dusk deepened, Thad found it harder to keep his quarry in sight. Once, he almost lost them in a knot of passersby, and frantically, he darted down two streets before locating them again.

They turned on Montgomery and headed toward—again, Thad found it hard to believe—Clay Moreau's Golden Eagle Saloon and Restaurant.

Thad swore under his breath. Of all places in town, that was one he could not enter. Jo was there, and she would recognize him immediately. So would Clay. Bronson would see him, and there would either be an immediate confrontation, with probably small results, or the thieves would change their plans.

He did the only thing he could think of. He circled the

173

building and crept up along its side in the deepening gloom, hoping he would find not only the side of the building where his quarry was located, but also that a window would be open.

Clay Moreau welcomed Bronson and his aide coolly. "Who told you about me?" he asked sharply.

"Otto Milner down on Broadway," Bronson said, smiling artificially. "He recommended you as a feller who likes a private deal once in awhile that might be profitable for all concerned."

Clay shrugged and studied Bronson's thick face with its mean little eyes. "What kind of private deal?"

"A private private deal," Bronson chuckled. "He said you bought dust once in awhile."

Clay looked at the two for a long moment, then nodded toward an office. Once inside, he closed the door. Still standing, he asked, "Is this one of those deals where everybody remains anonymous?"

Bronson chuckled. "Now you got the idee! Cain't we set and talk it over?"

Clay nodded and slid behind the desk, while the two thieves sat down in straight chairs.

"My commission's pretty high for anonymous deals," Clay said.

"How high?" Bronson wanted to know.

"Forty percent."

"Oh, come on now!" Bronson scowled. "Let's be reasonable! Forty percent! It don't pay to do nothin' on that basis!"

"You know what they do around here to people who steal dust?" Clay bit the end off a gnarled Mexican cigar and lit it. "The risk's high. It's got to be paid for."

"Well, you're not stealin' it."

"No, but I'm dealing with crooks like you who have. It's forty percent. Take it or leave it. And if it isn't a sizable amount, it's not worth the trouble, anyway."

Bronson leaped to his feet, kicking the chair over backward in his anger. "What do you mean, callin' me a crook? You got a loose mouth, mister."

Clay smiled mockingly at him. "Well, aren't you?" He puffed out a cloud of acrid smoke and rose to his feet. "Look, I don't want to argue about your character. If we've got a deal, let's talk business. If we haven't, I've got things to do out on the floor."

For a long moment, he and Bronson gazed into each other's eyes. Then Bronson's gaze wavered, and he stepped back. "We got a deal," he grumbled. "But, my God, forty percent! A real shylock!"

They bock sat down again and bent over the desk. Thad, looking in through the edge of the window, could no longer hear them as they lowered their voices, but he recognized the rawhide bags Mack pulled out of a canvas sack and laid on the table for Clay's inspection.

That night, two dark figures returned to the alley next to the Golden Eagle. The shorter of the two pulled a lump of what seemed to be putty from his pocket, pressed it carefully onto the lower pane, drew a sharp instrument in a circle around it with a rasping sound, and pulled out a circle of glass that he laid carefully on the ground.

"You must have been a second-story man," Thad murmured.

"I do a lot of readin'," said Jackson, grinning in the darkness. He reached inside the window frame, opened the latch, and raised the sash. It made some noise, but after they had waited for several minutes, they were convinced that they had not been overheard.

"I see the safe," said the old man. "It's agin the right wall. Now you stay out here and warn me if anybody's comin'." With an agility unusual for his years, he clambered through the window. He studied the safe for a moment, then returned to the window and murmured to Thad, "Damn thing's only got a key lock! Your

175

friend ain't as smart as I thought he was. This won't take me more'n a minute."

It was more than a minute. In fact, it was closer to ten. Once during that time, Thad heard people approaching down Montgomery Street. They paused at the mouth of the alley to converse loudly in drunken tones and then moved on. Thad heaved a sigh and resumed his vigil.

The night was chill with a low overcast. The air was fresh with a breeze from the sea. Thad shivered.

Finally, after a time span that seemed far longer than it was, Jackson grunted his way back through the open window. He reached in and hauled out a large canvas sack that weighed him down considerably. Thad helped him carry it, and the two hurried quietly out of the alley.

In the street, Jackson paused. "I wanta go back and close that window."

"Why? It's got a hole in it. He'll know somebody was there."

"Sure enough: Let's go."

"Where are we heading? I want to go to the hotel and see Jo."

Jackson halted again. "You won't want me along on that trip," he said. "Help me git this sack over to my place. It's only three blocks from yours, and I'll guarantee to have it for y' for an early-morning delivery. I'll sleep on it, and I've got a gun."

Thad nodded, and the two of them moved rapidly down the street. He was concerned that they might be stopped by a member of a vigilante group or someone else who claimed official responsibility. Although he was certain of his own position, carrying a sack full of gold dust with other men's names on it at 3:30 in the morning on a foggy night was bound to raise suspicions. But the streets were unusually quiet. Only once did they encounter people—two men, clearly under the weather, who greeted them warmly and teetered on in another direction.

Thad saw Jackson safely located in his room, insisted

that he check his gun to see that it was loaded, and then headed back toward his own hotel, where he had not been for some time.

It was four o'clock. He mounted the stairs with trepidation, his recently recovered assurance evaporating rapidly. At the door he halted, debating whether to use his key or to knock. He remembered Jo's hostility over all these days since Panama, her bitterness, her turning to Clay for comfort. Most of all—and most unpleasant of all—he remembered seeing her with her perky hat sitting erect and beautiful at the side of Ezra Benson in the two-wheeled cart being drawn by the plumed horses.

His hand was raised to knock, but he withdrew it. She had not left town, and he had been mightily relieved to know it, but there could be several reasons for her remaining, some of them as unpleasant as the thoughts that had been running through his mind. There was no reason for him to believe she had softened toward him. Indeed, his angry absence was cause for additional rancor on her part.

The dark corridor reflected his gloom. There was a musty smell and no sound at all throughout the hotel. At four in the morning, even San Franciscans were asleep. Should he use his key and burst into the room, demanding that Jo listen to him, demanding an explanation of her being with Benson, demanding to know what was happening between her and Clay?

However he entered, what would happen after that was critical. It would mean the continuation of his marriage—or the end of it. He took a deep, shuddering breath. He was, he decided, not willing to face that decision yet. It might go wrong.

Thad stood for a long moment, gazing at the door. Then, silently, cursing the creaking floorboards, he retreated and descended the stairs and exited to the street. He headed back toward Jackson's lodgings. He'd bunk with Avery tonight. He needed to do some more thinking before he confronted Jo. He had to figure out better arguments than he had. He was not good at talking to a woman, and he could not lose her.

"What the hell you doin' back here?" the old man demanded, rubbing sleep from his eyes. "Didn't you see your wife?"

"No," said Thad. "And shut up about it. Tomorrow, after I deliver that dust, we'll get busy on that stage line. That's next on my list."

Jackson gazed at Thad in the darkness, as the latter removed his boots. He shook his head. The next thing on Thad's list, he knew, was neither the dust, nor the stage line. It was a dark-haired girl in a hotel room three blocks away, to which Thad had the key.

18

The next few days convinced Jackson that Thad was able to concentrate on the task at hand. They were terribly busy days, with interviewing men and hiring them, trying to keep from being swindled by horse traders, and waiting impatiently for information about the delivery of the three Concords Thad had ordered from Abbott Downing in New Hampshire.

The two of them made a quick trip to the diggings in the company of some of their new employees in order to locate and make arrangements for stage stations. This was accomplished rapidly because of the groundwork Thad had laid on his previous trips.

Back in San Francisco, they were overjoyed to receive an answer from Abbott Downing. "We won't have to wait six months for delivery!" Thad exulted. "There are two coaches in San Diego. The stager who ordered 'em went broke, so we can have them! We'll go down and drive 'em north! You take one, and I'll take the other!"

"Hell of a trip!" Jackson grumbled. "How do we know they's a usable road all the way through?"

"There must be!" Thad said. "The old mission road, El Camino Real, has been used for a long time."

"By horses and armies. Not by coaches."

"Anyway, we're going to try it. We can root out the bad places on our way down and find alternate routes."

"It'll still be a hell of a trip."

179

"But profitable!"

"What do you mean profitable?"

"We're going to bring a full load of passengers in each coach! We'll make the trip more than pay for itself and get a down payment for the coaches out of it! They'll each carry twenty-two! Think of it, Avery! The first stage trip from San Diego to San Francisco! We'll have all kinds of people wanting to come!"

The old man clapped a hand to his brow. "Oh, my God! You don't believe in askin' for trouble. You go out an' dig it up! What you're talkin' about ain't never been done!"

Thad clapped him on the back. "I know. That's just why it'll pay off!" He suddenly sobered and gripped the old man's shoulders. "You're still with me, aren't you, Avery?"

Jackson forced a grin. "Sure, sure. You just scare the liver outa me with some of your idees. But let's go! Might as well die doin' somethin' crazy as somethin' sensible."

Thad again clapped him on the back. "You're the one who told me not to do what everybody else was doing! I'm just following your advice!"

"I never woulda given it if I'd'a known."

Bronson and his partner returned to the Golden Eagle three days after their first interview, and their mien was troubled. Clay, considerably more courteous than he had been during their first interview, invited them into his office.

"You got my money yet?" Bronson demanded.

Clay cleared his throat. "It takes awhile, a deal like this."

"Well, somethin' happened that bothers the hell out of me." Bronson squinted his tiny eyes, and his fat jowls shook with emotion.

Clay shifted uneasily in his chair. "What's happened?"

180

Bronson hesitated. He had noted the names of some of Thad's customers on the sacks of dust, and he had made it a point to talk with two of them. They were extremely pleased with the express service. Those who had sent the sacks had, in some cases, made hidden marks indicating the weight, so it could be checked on arrival, and not a grain had been missing.

How had they got the dust, if Moreau had it in his safe?

Bronson looked out the window. "You sure that dust is still in your safe?"

Clay reddened. How had this character come to suspect the robbery of his office? He had, of course, discovered it immediately the following morning, and had quickly had the glass pane repaired, while at the same time alerting all of his many contacts on the edges of the town's respectable population. So far, not a word of information had come to him. None of the known criminals in the city seemed to be involved. He had not bothered to weigh the dust when Bronson left it with him. All he had done was count the sacks. He had no idea how much was involved. He had been planning to get an accurate estimate the following morning, and that morning he had arrived in his office to find a neat hole cut in one of his windows, the sash raised, and his safe open. The dust was gone.

Clay looked away. "Certainly the sacks are still in my safe," he lied. "I'm trying to get you a good deal. The one I tried yesterday didn't seem to me to be a high enough offer. I looked in the sacks. This is pretty high-grade metal. You want the best deal you can get, don't you?"

"Sure, sure." Bronson was still frowning suspiciously. "I got reason to believe that gold ain't in your safe anymore."

Clay became even more uncomfortable. The tall man with the low-slung gun seated expressionlessly next to Bronson did not reassure him. "What makes you think that?"

181

"Well," Bronson hesitated, "I got that gold from a feller who was supposed to be makin' some deliveries here in San Francisco. I found out a couple of those deliveries was made. How could that be, if the stuff is still in your safe?"

Clay took a long breath. He had hoped to have a couple of days' respite with the idea of probing San Francisco's underworld to see who was responsible. Bronson was now making that difficult.

Clay leaned forward, his intelligent eyes serious. "Listen, Bronson, I know you stole that gold. You wouldn't have come to me to dispose of it otherwise. So let's stop fooling around. Somebody broke into my office last night and stole it. Was it you, hoping to get a double payment?"

Bronson's fat face empurpled. He sprang to his feet. Mack rose with him, more slowly, his long fingers hovering around the butt of his gun.

"*Stole*! You mean to say the stuff's been stolen?" Bronson was apoplectic with rage.

Clay was on his feet. "That's what I mean. And I think you did it. You were the only one who knew it was here, you and your friend. Knowing the likes of you, it's the kind of thing you'd do!"

Loud and angry argument ensued. Clay's accusation threw Bronson off balance, and he found himself quickly on the defensive. After much more loud talk and considerable swearing, Clay permitted himself to be convinced that Bronson had not stolen his own gold.

"Then who did?" Clay demanded. "Tell me who you got this from. Maybe he followed you."

Bronson hesitated again. It took a deal of talk to persuade him to divulge any more information. But he did, seeing no alternative to losing all of the profit he had hoped to make from the robbery.

"Feller named Morgan. Thad Morgan," he grunted. "Runnin' a pack-mule express. I had reason to want to do him some damage, and this seemed a good way to do it. I'm not in the habit of stealin' dust. I'm a businessman. But this feller Morgan swindled me out of a big piece of property down San Jose way, and I swore I'd git even! Now you have it! What can you do about it?"

Clay was not prepared to answer. The news struck him like a thunderbolt. Morgan! Running a pack-mule express! Back from the mines! And he had not yet returned to Jo. He was silent for so long that Bronson finally had to jerk him back to attention.

"What's eatin' you, Moreau? You know Morgan?"

Clay nodded. "I do, and he's such a stubborn, hard-driving son-of-a-gun that I think he's the one who got into my office. He must have followed you without your knowing it. The more I think about it, that must have been what happened, particularly if the deliveries were made. If some crook had broken in here, he wouldn't have delivered the dust to the customers. He'd have kept it."

They were all silent for a log moment.

Clay snapped his fingers. "That's what happened! That's the only thing that could have happened!"

"What about my dust?" Bronson's fat chin jutted belligerently.

"*Your* dust?" Clay laughed easily. He had taken Bronson's measure. Now that the picture was clear, he could see other possibilities. "Your dust has gone, and it's not my fault. It's yours, for letting yourself be followed. Anyway, if what you're really after is to get even with Morgan, I've got a bone or two to pick with him as well." He gazed directly into Bronson's evil little eyes. "Maybe we can do business together. And who knows. Maybe there'll be a little profit in it also."

Growling and muttering, Bronson permitted himself to be led back to his chair, and the conversation continued.

The trip to San Diego to pick up the two Concords did not turn out the way Thad had planned. There was only one coach, not two, as had been reported, and by

183

the time Jackson had finished his arguments, Thad was persuaded that a five-hundred mile trip over uncertain, and perhaps missing, roads, would probably rack it to pieces and render it unserviceable for the kind of luxurious travel he contemplated for the northern diggings.

They located a vessel that was large enough to carry it as deck cargo, and Thad paid what he thought was a horrendous freight charge. But they saw it safely and firmly stowed and wrapped in tarpaulins and took passage themselves on the same vessel, which got them back to North Beach within two weeks, after a stop at Monterey.

Back in San Francisco, Thad got posters printed:

NEW STAGE LINE TO THE GOLD FIELDS!!!

MORGAN & CO.

Ride our new luxurious Concord Coach, manufactured by the famous Abbott Downing Co. of Concord, New Hampshire. Drawn by a six-horse team! Soft leather seats! Twenty-two passengers, with luggage!

Overnight to Stockton! Day and a half to Sacramento!! Placerville! Whiskey Flat!

Ride speedily in comfort in this magnificent new Concord coach!!

Stockton $8. Sacramento $12. Placerville $20. Leaves every Monday! Make your reservations NOW!!

"We'll run one trip up and one trip back, and then—"

"Then what?" Jackson demanded.

"Then we go up and get our boiled shirts and studs and arrange for an inaugural ball to start off our new stage line! But I want to make sure everything's working well first, and I need a few days to round up the commandant at the *presidio* and some leading politicians.

That constitutional convention's been going on down in Monterey, and a lot of those fellers are going to want to be seen so they can get elected to the new legislature. We picked the right time! The state's getting started, and so are we!"

Jackson shook his head wonderingly. "Where you git all your idees, I don't know!" he marveled. "All I got to say is, let's not bite off more'n we both can chew!"

"We won't," Thad promised. "But I can handle a pretty big mouthful, and so can you!"

As Jo was winding up her chores at the Golden Eagle, Clay approached her.

"Jo, let me walk you back to the hotel."

She raised her brows. "It's been some time since you've done that."

"I know." He smiled apologetically. "I've been treating you pretty rough. Benson bothered me, and I thought you'd killed a deal that was pretty important to me. But he's friendly again, and although we haven't done any business yet, he keeps mentioning it every time he comes it. And he comes in to see you."

"Is that the only reason you're walking me home? If it weren't for Benson, I could walk by myself."

Clay smiled his most compelling smile and took her arm. "Come on, Jo. You know what it is to be worried. I've seen you worried, and you weren't as nice to people as you might have been."

Jo swallowed and looked away. Clay knew exactly how to probe until it hurt.

"All right," she said. "I'll get my cloak."

A bewhiskered waiter came up. "I'm ready to walk Miz Morgan home, sir."

Clay smiled at Jo. "You won't be needed tonight, Frank. Or from now on." He walked her to her hotel. At the door, he faced her. "I'm sorry, Jo. I apologize again." His eyes narrowed. "Where's Thad?"

"I don't know," she said. "He hasn't come back,

185

since—"

"Since what?"

"Since he saw me with Mr. Benson."

Clay nodded thoughtfully. "So that's it." He turned to her. "Well, if he hasn't thought enough of you to come back—"

"Don't say that, Clay!"

He shrugged. "You're getting mighty careful of his feelings in absentia. You didn't worry much about him when he was here."

"I know. And I was wrong. Wrong!"

"I'm not so sure. After all, he brought you west, you and that baby girl who couldn't survive the trip."

"Don't talk about that!"

"But that's what he did. And you blamed him for it. Why have you stopped blaming him now?"

"Because I was unfair. He only came West because I didn't like what we were doing or the way we were living back East."

Clay was silent for a long moment. "But he's not here now. And I am."

He drew her toward him. For a moment she yielded, then pushed him away. "No, Clay! I've been wrong! And I shouldn't have come to work for you."

"How would you have lived otherwise? Has he supported you? Has he come back to ask how you were getting along?"

She was close to tears. "I don't know! I don't know!"

"Well, I do. He's treated you miserably. You don't like it, and I don't like it." He took her hands and looked at her piercingly. "Jo, come home with me tonight. I've got a nice place, and I'll never treat you as he's treated you."

Jo looked at Clay Moreau for a long moment. Her thoughts were tumbling in her brain. Then she withdrew her hands and moved toward the door. "No, Clay. Good night."

"Will I see you tomorrow? At the Golden Eagle?"

186

She regarded him soberly, then nodded. "I'll see you tomorrow at the Golden Eagle."

When he turned away and walked swiftly down the street, Jo watched him for a moment, then entered the hotel.

In her room she wondered if she had done the right thing. Clay offered her security—for a while at least. And Thad? Where *was* Thad? Why didn't he return? She had always considered that Thad was hers, that he would always return, that he would always be at her beck and call, no matter how shabbily she treated him. In fact, he had responded in that manner for a long time. But now, she was surprised at his absence and was suddenly fearful. For the first time, she began to imagine what life without Thad would be like. The vision was not pleasant.

There was always Clay, of course. But Clay had lost some of his luster. His insistence upon her playing up to Benson, for instance, had provided her with a new view of his character. And his sullen unfriendliness during the last weeks and days after her refusal to follow his instructions was another enlightening experience.

Jo could not help but compare Clay with Thad—Thad the magnanimous, Thad the unselfish, Thad the dependable, Thad the moral and upright and unquestionably loyal. Clay suffered in the comparison. She sighed and mounted the dark stairway, lit by only a single oil lamp fixed to the wall in the upper corridor. She unlocked the door of her room and swung the door open with the same anticipation she had had during the last many days.

Would Thad be there? Would he be sitting waiting for her, as he always had been?

The room was dark. She lit the candle on the dressing table with the same dull disappointment she had experienced in recent nights. Thad's merely being around had meant more to her than she had realized. She took off the red dress, giving it hardly a second glance, and she removed the jewelry and tossed it carelessly on the table's surface.

Without Thad, things were different. Neither Clay nor anyone else she had met seemed able to fill the gap he had left.

19

"I got Mr. Colton and Mr. Gwin to promise to attend, if we hold it on a night they can be here," Thad told Jackson. "They gave me a list of dates when they could come. Let's book up that saloon for one of these dates and get things moving."

"That hotel's the same place Jo's stayin'," Jackson reminded him.

"I know," said Thad. "And I'm not ready to have a talk with her yet. So I think you'd better conduct the negotiations."

Jackson winked, screwing his face up into an elfin grimace. "Are ye thinkin' now about that purty señorita in San Jose?"

Thad scowled. "No, I'm not! And, Avery, you keep your nose out of my private life! We're business partners. And that's all!"

"All right, all right!" The old man hunched his shoulders and moved toward the door. "No offense! I can see it ain't the señorita you're thinkin' of."

"And keep your conclusions to yourself!" Thad ordered. "Now go see if you can get us a good deal with that hotel man who's part owner of the saloon next door. Remember, I mentioned five hundred. Don't pay him a cent more! And while you're there, check on the boiled shirts and the jewelry. See if they're all right."

The old man hustled out of the hotel room, leaving Thad alone with his thoughts.

They were simple. They were all of Jo and what he was to say when they met, wondering when they should and hoping against hope that she would be glad to see him when they did. He was angry with himself frustrated, that his words never came easily in situations such as the one he envisioned. He wished fervently that he had Clay Moreau's smoothness of manner, his ease with the ladies. But Thad knew his words were bumbling, his pauses too long, his inability to think of the right thing to say self-evident.

When he saw Jo, he would *have* to say the right thing, he would *have* to convince her of his love, and he would *have* to leave that interview a winner.

If he did not . . . Thad shook his head to rid it of the awful thought. He had to do it right, and he had to plan it right. But he still needed some time.

Clay Moreau was on his way to the Golden Eagle next morning when he paused before a poster on the wall of the new, raw-wood post office at Portsmouth Square. "New Stage Line to the Gold Fields! Morgan and Co.!" it read. And Clay knew beyond a doubt that the Morgan was Thad.

He read the poster twice, then went to the City Hotel where he inquired at the desk for Mr. Bronson. He hoped Bronson was still in town.

"Sure," said the clerk. "Mr. Bronson's still here. But he ain't in his room at the moment."

"Tell him I called," Clay said, scribbling a note with the scratchy hotel pen. "And tell him I'd like to see him as quick as he can get over to the Golden Eagle."

"The Golden Eagle!" the clerk gaped in awe. "You the owner? By gollies, everybody's talkin' about that place! Well, it's a pleasure to meet you, Mr.—"

"Moreau," said Clay. "Moreau. With a 'u.' "

"It's a real pleasure!" The clerk stuck out his hand and Clay took it unenthusiastically.

"Tell him, and give him this." Clay thrust the note

into the outstretched hand.

"I sure will! Depend on it! Pleasure to meet you, Mr. Moreau!"

Clay forced a grin. "Come on by, and there'll be a drink—on the house." He knew the message would get to Bronson.

As he walked back to the Golden Eagle, Clay reviewed several things. He remembered, and realized that wishful thinking probably exaggerated it, Jo's hesitation before she refused his invitation. He thought again about Thad's absence and his not having gone to Jo, even though he was in town. He also mulled over Thad's new venture: staging. There were opportunities galore for trouble for anyone who wanted a stage line.

Thad had new posters printed, large, colorful ones with big red-and-black curlicued letters:

INAUGURAL BALL!!

To Celebrate the New Morgan
Stage Line to Placerville

MONIHAN'S UNION HOTEL ANNEX

Formal. $25.00 per Head

MUSIC!! DANCING!!
REFRESHMENTS!!

All Moneys Collected Above Expenses To Go
To Miners' Benefit Fund

Come and Inaugurate San Francisco's Newest
Connection to the Diggings!!

8 P.M. September 24

"What's the Miner's Benefit Fund?" Jackson asked.

"I just thought it up," Thad explained. "We'll start a bank account with a hundred-dollar deposit, and whatever profits we get from the ball will go into it. It isn't the ball we'll make money from; it's the boiled shirts and the jewelry." He rubbed his chin thoughtfully. "We've got to have some engraved card invitations for important people, like the politicians and leading business men, and we'd better send those out right away, so we can get some word-of-mouth advertising."

"Where are we goin' to sell the boiled shirts?"

Thad grinned. "Right next door to our new stage ticket office on Union Square. You're going to handle that, Avery. I'm going to make a haberdasher out of you."

Jackson dramatically clapped a hand to his brow.

The days passed, an preparations for the ball went apace. Thad spent money on decorations for Monihan's Saloon, which he was careful to approach from the direction away from the hotel lobby, so he would not inadvertently run into Jo. More than once he headed for the hotel door, determined to confront her, and then grew afraid, concluding he was not yet ready. He was a coward, he knew, about the prospect of losing her. As long as he delayed their meeting, he could cling to the hope that things would work out.

Meanwhile, the ball promised to be a great success. Many tickets were sold right off the street as a result of the posters. The prominent citizens who received the engraved invitations also responded with more acceptances than refusals. Mr. Gwin, who had given signs of running for the United States Senate once California joined the Union, was pleased to accept. Sam Brannan, who had brought the first news of the gold strike in Sutter's mill race, said he would be there with bells on, and with a belle of his choosing. Ezra Benson, who had received an invitation only after Thad had given it much thought, responded promptly and affirmatively. Thad held his response in his hand for a long time and wondered bitterly whom he would bring. He also sent Clay Moreau an engraved card, and he accepted.

Jackson set up a canvas-covered stall next to the Morgan Stage Company's ticket office and fronted it with a large sign:

FORMAL WEAR FOR THE BALL!!!

Formal Shirts!!!
Formal Collars!!!
Formal Cuffs!!!
Formal Studs!!!
Formal Cuff Links!!!

When they sold like the proverbial hotcakes, Jackson persuaded Thad that they might as well stay in the haberdashery business. He rustled up additional shirts from a more recent shipment, and even some black broadcloth suits and cutaway and swallowtail coats that could in a pinch, double, for formal clothing. A week before the ball, Jackson was sold out and was unable to locate any more supplies. He closed the shop with satisfaction, counted the profits, and told Thad, "The Miners' Benefit Fund is safe. There ain't no need for us to collect a nickel from the ball."

Thad hired a group of musicians, including a barroom pianist who, although he made his living by playing honkytonk, preferred the classics, plus two violinists, and a bass fiddler. He tested them out before he firmed up the arrangements. After a little practice, they sounded exceedingly good, and he urged them to emphasize waltzes and more sedate dance numbers rather than mazurkas and frontier squares.

As long as he could keep his mind on the preparations for the event, and while he was busy making arrangements, Thad was able to keep Jo off his mind. But as the days passed, he knew he would have to see her.

Either she would come to the ball with him, or he would take no one.

He spent many hours in the evenings, lying awake and thinking what he would say, planning his approach.

It *had* to turn out right! It had to.

20

Clay approached Jo in the smoky, noisy atmosphere of the Golden Eagle. A piano banged away in the barroom, diners were waiting in line for a table, the red-skirted floor girls were hustling for drinks, chips and cards were spread over round tables amid the loud obligato of half-drunken conversation.

"Your former husband's giving a ball," he said, by way of introduction.

Jo bridled. "He's not former. He's my husband."

"Has he asked you yet?"

She shook her head and turned away.

"You know about the ball, don't you? It's to inaugurate his new stage line. He's moving fast."

"Everybody knows about it. It's the first big social event this town has ever had," she said. "It's about time, and I'm surprised that Thad thought of it."

Clay laughed easily.

"It probably wasn't his idea."

"Don't be too sure," Jo said. "Even after living with him for several years, he surprises me."

There was a pause. Jo ushered a couple to a table, the man bearded and with the horny hands of a miner, the woman flashily dressed and obviously not his wife. When Jo returned, Clay said,

"Would you like to go to the ball?"

Jo looked at him silently for a long moment. Clay knew what she was thinking. If Thad hadn't asked her, whom was he taking? He knew she did not wish to go with Clay, but the desire to be there and to see Thad and know who he was with caused her to hesitate.

Clay turned away. "You don't have to answer that question yet, Jo. Think about it. Tell me tomorrow." He smiled at her. His peaked brows and watchful eyes gave him the expression of studied insolence that at one time had appealed to her. He walked away, but halted and said over his shoulder, "You'd like to know who's there, wouldn't you?"

She reddened. Yes, she would like to know who went to the ball. She would like to know, very much, if Thad had a new interest. Perhaps that was the explanation of why he had not come to since his return to the city would be there at the ball.

She said, "Thank you, Clay. I'll think about it."

"Tell me tomorrow."

"Tomorrow." Two new customers arrived and saved her frm the necessity of talking further about the matter.

That night, Jo lay awake for many hours debating with herself. She did not wish to go with Clay. The last thing she wanted was for Thad to see her with another man. It was seeing her with Benson that had sent him away.

The next evening she went to work at the Golden Eagle with trepidation. She had worried all night and all the following day, and she had not yet made up her mind. Clay approached her, as she knew he would. Clay, with his half-smile, his quizzical brows, his knowing eyes. He intercepted her as she came from the cloak room where she had left her coat. She was dazzling, as usual, in the red silk dress with the fur trim. The gleaming diamonds were on her neck and in her dark hair.

He regarded her admiringly. "Jo, you are the most beautiful thing west of the Rockies," he mused. "Have you decided?"

She looked away. "No," she said. "I haven't."

The smile left his face. "Whether you have or not, are you going with me to Thad's ball?"

195

She was silent.

"It's two nights from now. If he's going to ask you, he'd have done it by now. You know that, don't you?"

She nodded miserably.

"Are you going with me? I want to know now, so I can ask somebody else if you won't."

She took a long breath and looked up at him. He was still the handsome, appealing man who had saved them at Panama, who had sympathized with her on the death of their baby, who had given her a job when she badly needed something to do. He had been there when Thad wasn't. He was selfish and crass and cruel, she knew. But he had been all of those other things, too.

She looked up at him again. "All right, Clay. I'll go with you."

He smiled and took her hands in his. "We'll have a wonderful evening, Jo. Maybe you'll find out where your best interests lie." Then he turned away and thoughtfully did not approach her for the rest of the evening.

Clay walked Jo home, but he did not enter the Union Hotel lobby with her. He bade her goodbye on the stret and reminded her of the ball to come.

She nodded and thanked him absently. Then she climbed the stairs alone, wondering if she had done the right thing.

She had to know about Thad! She had to know if he was turning to someone else. This was her only way.

Jo turned the key in the lock of her room and swung the door open. The lights were on, and Thad sat there, hat in hand, looking uncomfortable, the candlelight harsh on his craggy features. A thin film of perspiration shone on his forehead. His brow was creased in a frown. When she entered, he stood slowly and held out his hands.

"Jo," he said quietly.

Suddenly she was angry. Why hadn't he come one day sooner? Why hadn't he come three weeks ago? What right had he to make her worry and wonder and finally yield to a man she had no wish to yield to? Where had he been?

He *always* did the wrong thing. *Always*!

They stood facing each other for a long moment. "Jo," he said, and his voice shook. "I'm having a ball to inaugurate our new stage line. You'll go with me, won't you?"

She took a deep breath. The ready anger that was always seething close beneath the surface erupted.

Jo regarded her husband coldly, even though she wanted more than anything else to go to him. "No," she said. "I'm going with Clay."

Thad stood there for a moment longer, running through in his mind the exhaustively rehearsed words he had intended to use. None of them fit this present situation. That was always the case, he reflected miserably. He was never ready. He never had the right words to talk to a woman, and he never had the right words to talk to Jo.

He looked at her sadly, noted the familiar angry glint in her eyes, the stubborn set to her attractive chin.

He reached out his hands, helplessly. "Jo," he pleaded.

She drew back. "I'm going with Clay," she said again. "You're too late. You're always too late, Thad. I'm going with Clay."

His jaw became set, and the same cold anger rose in him that had risen when he saw her with Ezra Benson. Wordlessly, he picked up his hat and moved quickly toward the door. Without looking in her direction again, he left the room. She heard his heavy steps descending the shaky wooden stairs.

On Thad's departure, Jo's anger evaporated. She stood looking at the closed door helplessly. She had had her chance, and she had spoiled it. Spoiled it forever, she was certain.

Slowly, she blew out the candle and sat down in the darkness in her shining red-silk dress. A faint light came in through the window from a saloon sign across the street and glinted on the diamonds around her neck and in her hair.

Thad and Avery drove the Concord up to Placerville and back, checking the stage stops, the horses, the station crews, the food for the passengers, and the usability of the road. They returned to San Francisco, knowing it would work.

On their return, they found an excited city. It was easy for San Francisco to get excited, and a fandango was excuse enough. Thad believed in publicity, and he had provided a great sufficiency. There were posters and handbills, in addition to engraved invitations to the important people. The San Francisco press, what there was of it, pounced on the ball as a tremendous answer to the problem of filling columns. Thad found his biography—several versions of it—in more than one edition of the local press. Avery excitedly reported to him hourly on the talk in the streets and saloons and city squares.

"You got somethin' goin', mister," he exclaimed. "I ain't never seen people so talkative and friendly. Ain't nothin' like this so upsot 'em since Sam Brannan said they was gold on the American River!"

"We had to have more tickets printed," Thad said. "That room's going to be so crowded, I don't know how people will dance."

"Don't you worry none about the crowd," Jackson advised. "From what I heerd about California fandangos, everybody's goin' to have a good time, even though they're out in the street and ain't able to git in!"

Thad was silent for a moment. Then he asked, "Are we ready for trouble?"

"What you mean, trouble? This is a party, ain't it?"

Thad nodded. "Just the same, you go hire a couple of the shotgun messengers from our new stage line, and have 'em here with their guns. And have 'em show themselves—*and* the guns."

Jackson frowned in puzzlement. "I dunno what you're expectin', but I don't see no trouble."

"Have the shotgun messengers there anyway," Thad ordered. "Two at least. Maybe three."

Jackson shrugged, and grumbled off.

Buck Bronson entered the Golden Eagle shortly after noon of the day before the fandango.

"Where the hell have you been?" Clay demanded irritably. "I left a message for you three days ago!"

Bronson drew his brows over his tiny eyes. "I ain't a houn' dog to come when I'm whistled at. What's eatin' you? You shorely ain't got my gold back?"

"*Your* gold!" Clay sneered. "You told me yourself it had already been delivered to Morgan's customers. Certainly I haven't got it. But I've got a proposition for you, if you want to do him a dirty turn."

Bronson's face lit up. "Now you're talkin' my language! Where can we set?"

Clay nodded toward his office, the same office with the safe that had failed to secure the dust he and Bronson had deposited in it. Except for a few sidewise glances at the big green metal box, Bronson said nothing. He jerked off his hat and sat, prepared to listen.

Clay leaned forward.

"Morgan's starting his stage line. This fandango that he's having is to celebrate it and give him some advertising. But," he said, "and this is the important part, Morgan isn't just running a stage line for passengers. He's also got an express business. He's carrying dust from the mines. I had one of my people talk with his partner. It's pretty clear Morgan is figuring on making more money out of the express business than out of passengers."

Bronson looked interested. "Where do we come in?"

"Like this. One of you ought to go to Placerville and nose around and find out when he's carrying a particularly big shipment. When he's got a good-sized one—"

"Yes, what then?" Bronson sneered. "We do the dirty work and split with you? Is that your idee?"

"No, of course not!" Clay shook his head impatiently. "I'll help. You two need somebody to help you think. We'll plan this out right and walk off with his gold. Then we'll wait for another big shipment and do it again! This time, in a different place and under different circumstances, so he'll never know what to expect."

"Well," said Bronson, scratching his head, "if you're goin' to involve yourself, all right. But I want more than just promises. It's a hell of a long time to wait. Might be weeks before the right conditions came along."

Clay smiled. "I'm not through talking. This fandango. He's sold most of the tickets beforehand, and I suppose he's got the money in a bank. This is a rich crowd coming to that party, and they'll have money and jewelry. Most of 'em will be half drunk." He sat back and waited.

Bronson slapped his leg. "Mebbe we won't have to wait after all!" Suddenly, he frowned. "But I don't wanta be recognized in any deal like that. I got a business to keep up. I can't afford to git a bad reputation."

"We can hire this one done. Your friend here," Clay nodded toward the tall, saturnine Mack, "can keep an eye on those we hire."

There was a long silence. Then Bronson leaned forward and said, "We oughta talk about details."

Clay grinned. "Fine," he said. "That's why we're here."

21

The fandango in Monihan's Saloon to inaugurate the Morgan Stage Line drew hundreds of people to Union Square, and they arrived early.

It was a motley crowd. There were red-shirted miners who had not bothered to equip themselves with party clothes, but who had washed their shirts and put new and clean patches on their pants. There were wealthy citizens in formal attire who paid no attention to those who did not match them in sleekness, but freely mingled among them. Some citizens wore cutaways, and there were even a few swallowtail coats among the attempts at dressing up. Mustaches and beards had been trimmed, tallow had been rubbed on boots until most of the scuffing was less evident, shaggy locks had been shorn. Also, as one of the events that made this occasion so unusual, baths had been taken.

As to the women, this was the first event in San Francisco that had attracted the "respectable" ladies of the town, who remained largely in seclusion most of the time. There were more arriving every day, with husbands and families. The boisterous high spirits of the tent-city with its saloons and dance halls and gambling hells and ladies of the evening did not encourage the more-dignified members of the female community to venture out often onto the streets. Here, however, was an event that promised to be generally respectable, with form dress urged and an orchestra with real violins in it, plus a promise of an attractive punch bowl rather than bottles of corn whisky or tequila. Moreover, it was associated with a solid business enterprise, a stage and express line, and not only with some sleazy saloon.

No sooner had darkness fallen than the crowd began to arrive. They came on horseback, in carriages with servants bowing out ladies in voluminous skirts and cloaks and gentlemen gleaming in black broadcloth and white linen, in wagons singing lustily and waving bottles already half empty, in carts with blankets carefully spread on the seats so the women would not soil their dresses, and walking from other parts of town. There were Americans, Englishmen, Mexicans, Californios in bell-bottomed *pantalones* lined with silver along the legs, white silk shirts, and broad-brimmed black hats. There were some, although not in the majority, short-skirted belles of the dance halls.

Thad noted the early and enthusiastic arrivals and ordered the orchestra to start an hour before he had previously arranged. Avery came to his side and said, "Mebbe if they come early, they'll go early."

Thad shook his head. "These people are so hungry for something like this that they'll come early and stay late. I hope we don't run out of food."

"It ain't the food I'm sorried about, it's the punch," Jackson responded. "As long as they git some liquor under their belts, they won't worry about eats."

As the throngs arrived, Thad moved to the front door of the building to greet his guests. He had chosen a long black coat, a dark flowered vest, shiny half-boots, and a gleaming white shirt with soft collar and a black flowing tie. He had had his hair shortened, although it still flowed to his collar, and his face had been clean shaven by the sharpest razor in town. He stood by the door, erect, dignified, handsome, welcoming his guests.

"Mr. Gwin," Thad gripped the tall, bearded man's hand. "I'm glad you could come. Next time you're here, we'll greet you as Senator."

Gwin smiled. "Oh, come now! No politicking tonight! I'm here to have a good time, and so is everybody else!" He moved inside, accompanied by his wife.

There were several people whom Thad knew, bankers he had talked to, businessmen he had sought advice from as he organized his staging company. He greeted them warmly, and they reciprocated the respect he showed them. After all, none of them had thought up such a tremendous event to launch their own businesses. Thad deserved their respect and consideration.

Suddenly, over the heads of the crowd, Thad saw a familiar face. It was square with a gray mustache. The black hat, black formal coat, and gleaming linen indicated prosperity, while the calm eyes exuded confidence. It was Benson.

Thad tried not to look as if he were peering at the woman on Benson's arm, but he could not help himself. They were too far away for him to identify her, but she was of Jo's height and slimness. She was bundled in a long coat, so identification was difficult.

Jo had said she was going with Clay, but she had been angry when she said it. It may have been only the first cruel thing that came into her mind. Thad tried not to show his turbulent feelings. His stomach was revolving, and he felt almost sick. What would he do if it *were* Jo? How could he stay in this convivial gathering, pretending to be calm and cheerful, when inside he was a maelstrom of bitterness?

He swallowed. With an effort, he turned his eyes away. When they came up to him would be time enough to decide what to say. The people Thad greeted as he awaited Benson and his companion made no impression on Thad's consciousness. He mumbled some words he hoped were the right ones, but he did not see them, could not remember them, was unaware of their identity.

He wondered, for a moment, if this would be a good time for him to leave the doorway and check on the punch or the orchestra or the tickets, or something. Then he drew himself up and made up his mind he would not be driven from hosting his own party. There were some things a man had to do, some things that he had to face. This, Thad knew, was one of them.

Benson approached rapidly, with the girl on his arm. He came before Thad, removed his hat, looked up into Thad's face—Thad was a good half-head taller—and smiled in friendly fashion.

"Good evening, Morgan. I'm happy to come to your party, and I'm pleased that you invited me."

Thad shook the proffered hand. "I'm glad that you came." As yet, he had not dared to look at the woman at Benson's side.

"Allow me to introduce," Benson said, turning to the girl, "Miss Alice Enslow. She recently arrived with her parents, who are going to set up in business in this city. Miss Enslow, will you meet Mr. Morgan, who, if I'm not mistaken, will shortly be one of our leading businessmen?"

Thad reaction was seismic. He felt a cold sweat break out on his body; the feeling of relief he experienced left him almost numb. With an effort, he turned to face the girl. She was an attractive blonde, much too young for Benson, he thought, but he felt too good to hold any negative reaction in his brain.

"I'm—I'm pleased to meet you, ma'am," he said awkwardly.

"You know," Benson said, clapping him on the shoulder, "I have some money for you. Any time you want it. You didn't come by to pick it up before. But it's there for you, any time."

Thad thanked him, and the next several people who went by were again anonymous. He could not have remembered any of them to save his life. He was feeling too relieved, too euphoric, too grateful, to see anything around him. Jackson had to shake him by the arm to draw his attention.

"Yes, what is it?" Thad finally pulled himself together.

"I got those guards. Four of 'em. Where you want 'em?"

"Around the building. One on each side. And tell them to watch out."

"For what?"

"I don't know, but I have a funny feeling. I think something's going to happen."

"It's happenin'. It's happenin', but it's all good!" said Jackson gleefully. He waved a gnarled hand at the lively crowd, already packed too tightly on the floor to do more than sway in time to the music.

"This is a good evening," said Thad, "and I don't want anything—anything—to spoil it! Tell 'em to watch out sharp!"

Jackson squinted up at him. "You're feelin' better!"

Thad laughed. It was the first time Jackson had heard him laugh like that in weeks. He clapped the old man on the shoulder. "This *is* a good evening!" he said again. "Let's keep it that way!"

Jackson elbowed his way through the noisy throng and did as Thad ordered. The four hired guns, out-of-work Irishmen who had just arrived without funds, vanished into the darkness. Jackson made his way back to the ball, bumping against a couple arriving from the other direction.

"I'm sorry, ma'am," he said, then looked again. "Miz Morgan!" he exclaimed.

Jo nodded toward him. "Hello, Mr. Jackson," she said. Clay, at her side, nodded impatiently and moved toward the door.

Jackson shook his head. Thad's pleasure was to be shortlived, he reckoned.

Thad saw them coming and steeled himself. They halted before him. "Hello, Thad," said Clay easily. "I thought Jo ought to see this shindig, so I asked her."

"You beat me to it," said Thad. "I asked her, too, but I was too late." He did not look at Clay but kept his eyes on Jo. She faced him defiantly, saying nothing.

The two of them moved onto the dance floor as Thad followed them with his eyes. He was so preoccupied that someone caught him by the elbow.

"Will you greet your friends, Señor?" Smiling and gleaming in a black *charro* suit with silver trim, Don Pedro held out a friendly hand. Thad pulled himself back to the task at hand and greeted the old man warmly.

Don Pedro shrugged. "Who would miss a fandango such as this one?" He nodded sidewise. "My daughter wouldn't either!"

Thad turned toward the girl. She stood there, in pale-blue flowing silk and black shawl and mantilla, her dark eyes and hair in sharp contrast to the creamy whiteness of her face. Thad glanced again at the dance floor. Clay and Jo were dancing and looking into each other's eyes.

"Señorita," said Thad, "will you dance with me?"

The girl's face brightened. "Oh, Señor! I would like nothing better!"

Don Pedro watched them, beaming, as they moved onto the crowded floor.

Now it was Jo's turn to turn away from Clay and watch Thad and Elena looking into each other's eyes as they danced. Thad did not see it. He was suddenly enjoying himself. Elena smiled at him. She had a very attractive smile, Thad reflected, and she looked more appealing than she had in her riding clothes on the ranch. Funny what a party dress could do to a girl.

There was a shot from the rear of the room and the sound of breaking glass. A woman screamed. There was shouting and stamping, and the music stopped.

Thad ran to the clot of turbulance. Jackson was at his side. Two men were struggling on the floor. One was an armed Irishman. He was on top and busily engaged in pounding his opponent's head on the floor. The vanquished one was a ragged Sonoran, who gave up groping for his knife just as Thad arrived, and subsided into unconsciousness.

The Irishman looked up at Thad. "He was comin' in the window," he reported, rising and brushing off his trousers.

"Then there'll be others! Get outside quick!" Thad ordered. He excused himself to Elena, who had followed him to the scene of action, and motioned Jackson to go out the other door. As he passed the orchestra, Thad signaled to them to start again. As he reached the door, the strains of a Spanish melody filled the air over the babble of voices.

Clay was standing at the door, looking out into the darkness. He seemingly had forgotten Jo, who stood a short distance away by herself. Thad brushed by him, then suddenly halted and looked him squarely in the face. Clay frowned and looked away. Thad's suspicion was evident.

Thad ran into the narrow alley beside the building. No one was there. Lights from the windows of the saloon cast warped yellow rectangles on the ground.

He moved forward. A dark shadow detached itself from a darker shadow and slithered up behind him. Thad swung around, and the gun butt, raised high in the shadow's hand, pounded his skull. Thad sank to the ground as Jackson ran forward. The shadow melted into the darkness and disappeared. Jackson's cries brought help, and Thad was carried into the back room of the saloon. He opened his eyes and painfully tried to relate himself to his surroundings.

"Don't let the music stop!" he begged. "Keep the party going!" He struggled to rise, then, nauseated, sank back on the couch they had laid him out on.

The music continued, and the noise of the ball went on, the murmur of conversation, the loud babble of voices of people having a good time filled the room. Thad's head pounded, and stabs of pain went through it. He could still see Clay's interested eyes peering out into the blackness when the disturbance started. Clay was his problem. Clay was with Jo. Clay had done him much damage.

Elena burst into the little room and ran to his side. Jo was close behind her.

"Oh, Señor!" the girl exclaimed. "Are you hurt?

207

Where are you hurt? Oh, *Dios Mio!* That such a thing should happen to you!'' She knelt by the couch.

Jo was at her side. She pushed her roughly. "Get away from him!" she commanded. "He's my husband!" She bent over Thad and demanded, "What happened?"

Thad opened his eyes with an effort. "My head!" he groaned. "My head!"

Elena's face flushed with anger as she came close to Jo's side. "He may be your husband, but you have not treated him like a husband!" she flared. "You were not with him when he needed you! Get away from him now!"

Jo turned to her. "What right have you to give orders? Or to have anything to do with him?" She advanced menacingly upon the girl. "I am his wife."

"In name only!" Elena exclaimed. "You have not been a wife to him! You haven't helped him when he needed it!"

"What has he told you?"

"He has told me nothing! But a woman can see."

Jo raised her hand and, in a full-armed sweep, slapped Elena's face resoundingly. The girl, her face red from the blow, turned white with anger and plunged both hands, clawlike, into Jo's hair. The two fell to the ground, struggling, while the men, awed and helpless, stood back and muttered in confusion.

Thad was only half aware of events around him, but he saw the struggling women and forced himself to open his eyes and rise upon an elbow.

The two women rolled apart. Elena's mantilla was gone, and her dark hair was awry. An angry scratch was on her cheek. Jo's red-silk dress was torn; her face was bruised. They scrambled to their feet and stood, crouching, facing each other like angry cats.

Elena turned to Thad. "We are here!" she cried. "Which do you choose? This woman who has turned from you or me?"

Thad struggled to a sitting position. Blearily he

surveyed the room. Jackson was there. He shook his head to clear it, and a spasm of pain shot through it. He winced.

"Did they stop the holdup?" he demanded of the old man.

Jackson nodded. "The party's goin' on fine," he reported. "Nothin's happened."

Thad turned back to the two women, who had not moved from their positions. He looked at Elena, the scratch on her cheek, the mussed dark hair, the pain in her dark eyes. Then he turned to Jo, who was facing him with troubled mien.

He thought for a long moment, hoped his head was clear. Then he said to Jo, "This time *you're* too late." He turned to Elena, who rushed to his side and embraced him recklessly.

He was sitting on the couch, his head in his hands, Elena by his side, when Jo turned silently and left the room. He could guess where she was going.

The ball was a great success. So was the beginning of the Morgan Stage Line.

Thad sat in the little office in Union Square, totted up the receipts, and sat back with satisfction. The way things were going, Don Pedro's loan was secure. Thad would be able to cancel out that obligation within a matter of months. This realization relieved him considerably. He tapped his pencil on the desk and pursed his lips thoughtfully. Elena was the problem. He did not want to be obligated to the Sarmientos. Elena was already behaving possessively toward him. Although he was deeply grateful to her and her father, he frankly did not know what the future held for them. He wanted to owe no man—or woman.

Avery Jackson clumped in from the street, his gnarled face split by a broad, snaggle-toothed grin. "Got some news from the diggin's," he said conspiratorially, pulling up a chair by Thad's desk. "Real big news."

209

"What is it?"

"Whisky Flat. Big strike at Whisky Flat. Nuggets at big as baseballs. Dust so thick it makes you sneeze. They're prizin' out pure gold from the rocks with jack-knives."

Thad shrugged. "I don't believe everything I hear."

"But this is legitimate!" Jackson pounded the desk. "I got it from two, three fellers. They're all tellin' the same story! Talk's all over town!"

"Well, if that's the case, we'll probably have some valuable express business before long."

"Yer damn tootin'!" Jackson agreed. "But," he leaned forward and lowered his voice, "seein' as this news is all over town, it's bound to interest some people who know we're goin' to be carryin' some o' that gold!"

"So?"

"Don't ye see?" Jackson was irritated. "Every ragged-pants would-be stage robber in California will be thinkin' o' this! I think we ought to take steps to see that run don't git into trouble!"

Thad nodded. "You may be right. What do you think? Carry two shotgun messengers?"

"Well, that's an idee. But ain't there some other way we culd make it real hard for that stage to be robbed?"

"Well, we can bolt the box to the floor."

"Sure, but that's been done, and every highwayman's comin' with a full kit o' tools now. I wisht we could think o' somethin' that would really throw 'em back on their heels!"

Thad rubbed his chin. He mused, "If that strike's happening now, next week we'll begin getting gold on the express run to bank here in the city."

"Right. We ain't got very long to get ready."

Thad straightened. "Is there a smelter in that town?"

Jackson shook his head. "I dunno. There might be. There's a little one in Placerville."

Thad rose and paced the floor. "If we could get to a smelter—"

"Yes?" Jackson looked up eagerly. When Thad looked like that, he usually had a pretty good idea.

"If we could get to a smelter, we'll give whoever tries to rob us a big surprise!"

Jackson stood up. "How?" he demanded.

Thad told him.

It was as well that Thad and Jackson were discussing the problem, because, at the same time, just a few blocks away on Montgomery Street, others were also talking of the strike at Whisky Flat.

"I think this is our chance," Clay told Bronson. "That strike will load up Morgan's express boxes with dust and nuggets, and they'll be running heavy the first week or so, even if the strike turns out to be shallow. There's a Morgan Stage run from the northern mines to Sacramento and Stockton next Tuesday. If I'm any judge, that'll be the time to move in."

Bronson scowled and shifted uncomfortably in his chair. "I don't know that country," he said. "If it was only somewheres around San Jose."

"I have a map." Clay pulled a large sheet of paper from his desk drawer and unfolded it. "Here are the mines. Here's Whisky Flat. Here's Placerville. Here's the road to Sacramento. It comes out of the foothills right here." He pointed with a pencil. "You and I will take a ride up there tomorrow and come back Saturday. We'll pick the best place. We can figure what time the stage will get there, too. Dusk would be about right. Hard to see then. Are you game?"

"Well, if you're goin' to help and not leave all the dirty work to me and Mack—"

"I'll help," Clay assured him, rising. "Tomorrow, six o'clock, we'll get going. We'll fix Morgan's wagon."

He let Bronson out of the office. Jo was standing there, closed by the door. Clay looked at her in surprise. "What do you want?" he asked.

She lifted her chin defiantly. "I was just coming to

211

get some more menus."

"I'll be with you in a minute." He gazed at her thoughtfully. "How long have you been standing there?"

"I just got here." She flounced away.

Clay's gaze followed after her. His eyes were deeply suspicious. After a moment, he turned again to Bronson and followed him to the door.

"Was she listenin'?" Bronson asked.

"I don't know," said Clay. "But it doesn't make any difference. She doesn't like Morgan either."

"I don't like women messin' around in things like this."

"Neither do I," said Clay. "But she won't cause any trouble. I'll see that she doesn't."

That night, Thad gave Don Pedro a financial report and handed him a sack of coins and currency. "That's from the ball," Thad said. "Not from the tickets. We gave that money to the Miners' Benevolent Fund. This is from the sale of clothes and suits and boiled shirts." He laughed. "I want you to begin paying off that loan, even with the points. I don't want you to be in debt on my account."

The old rancher beamed and patted the sack with his veined hanf. "That will not be necessary, Señor. This is far more than the eight percent on my money for the time that has passed. I can make the payments easily, and you will have the capital to work with. Please, Señor, I insist! I must clear my conscience. I owe you so much."

Thad shook his head. "You owe me nothing. I have your friendship, and that is enough." Elena, standing by her father's shoulder, caught his eye.

"It is not only my father's friendship that you have," she said.

"I know," Thad said uncomfortably. "I greatly appreciate the friendship of both of you. But I wish,

Señor, you would tell me the name of the banker from whom you obtained the loan. Perhaps I could at least talk him into a lower interest rate. Once he knew how profitable my business is becoming, I suspect he would be willing to lower the rate with the hope that I might add to that loan in the future."

The old man shrugged. "I would prefer, Señor, that you just let me give you the money and do not worry about the financial details. Things are working out well, and there is no need to make adjustments."

"But it is silly to pay eight percent when we might get it for seven, or six. It would help me, too. I would not owe you so much."

Don Pedro raised his white brows. "Yes," he nodded. "that is so. Well, if it will help you, Señor, I will give you the banker's name. But do not worry, I beg you, if he will not agree with your proposal."

"All right," said Thad. "Where did you get the money?"

"I got it," said Don Pedro, "from a place called the Bank of Mission Valley, which is owned by a man called Benson. Señor Benson is one of the busiest bankers in San Francisco, and he is well known here."

Thad's jaw tightened. Two white spots appeared on his cheekbones. Elena saw the change in his expression and frowned.

"I know," said Thad. "I know Mr. Benson."

Jackson found Thad alone in the little office on Union Square. He had not lit the oil lamp, and the fog, drifting in as was its custom in late afternoon, made the little room gloomy.

"You can't see to work in here!" Jackson exclaimed, throwing himself into a chair beside the littered desk. "Too damn dark!" Then he saw that Thad was not working. He was sitting staring into the gloom. "What's eatin' you?" Jackson demanded."

Thad turned to him. His voice sounded choked as he

spoke. "I've been building my business on money from Benson! *Benson!*"

Jackson saw that Thad was taut with emotion. "Well," he waved a deprecatory hand, "what of it? Benson said he'd never have gone out with Jo if he'd knowed she was your wife. Never woulda gone out with her if he'd knowed she was *anybody's* wife." He glanced sidewise at Thad, wondering what effect that statement would have, hoping it would ease the tension.

"When did he say that? He told *you* that? When did you talk to him?"

"Right after you didn't pick up that first loan he offered you. I went to see him, hopin' I might salvage somethin'."

"And he said he wouldn't have gone out with Jo if he'd known she was married?"

"Right!"

Thad was on his feet, pacing. His fists were clenched. "That makes it worse! That means Jo didn't tell him."

"Why should she? Moreau made her do it."

Thad stopped his pacing and confronted the old man. "How do you know that?"

"I don't. But it's a damn good guess. Moreau's tryin' to borrow money all over town. He's got some big ideas. Stands to reason he'd try to butter up Benson."

There was a long silence. Thad slowly sat down again at the desk and stared thoughtfully into space. Then he turned to Jackson. "All right. I'll keep going on Don Pedro's loan, which he got from Benson. I guess I've got to, or I'll ruin him as well as myself. But we're going to pay that off *fast!* And as far as Clay is concerned—"

"Now you're talkin'!" Jackson nodded vigorously. "I think that smilin' sonofabitch has been doin' you dirt right along!" He stood up. "They got a smelter in Whisky Flat. A little one."

"Does it work?"

"It works."

Thad nodded. "Then you and I will start for there in an hour."

"In an hour! What about dinner?"

"Get a sausage and some bread and cheese. We'll eat as we go."

Jackson cackled with laughter. "I have a feelin' Mr. Moreau will git a surprise."

"Moreau!" Thad turned, frowning. "What's Clay got to do with it? We're getting ready for stage robbers. You don't think he's one, do you?"

"I got deep suspicions o' Mr. Moreau," Jackson insisted. "He's capable of anything. And he's been doin' you a lot more damage than you realize!"

"I think you're wrong about that," Thad scoffed. "Let's get started for Whisky Flat."

"Before we start," Jackson said, fumbling in his pocket, "I got a message for ye."

"A message?" Thad frowned. "Who's it from?"

"Well," said Jackson, crinkling his eyes as he handed a folded slip of paper to Thad, "it says it's from a Friend."

Thad opened the note. " 'I have reason to believe the Morgan Stage from Whisky Flat will be robbed,' " he read, "It's signed 'A Friend.' " He looked up.

"That's what I told y'." Avery squinted quizzically at Thad and said no more. He knew Thad was wondering about the handwriting. Someone had tried to disguise it, but it still resembled writing that looked very, very familiar.

In the *sala* of the Rancho Santa Elena, Don Pedro explained to his daughter that he had made the first payment and sizably reduced the loan he had taken from Benson to help Thad.

She frowned. The frown did not destroy her beauty, but it made her look older than her years.

"Do not pay it off too soon, padre mio," she begged.

The father smiled and nodded. "I think I know why you say that, *cara mia*. But that is not the way to win a man. He must be tied by other bonds."

"I think I will need all the help I can get," Elena said. "His wife—who is no wife—he still looks at her as if under a spell."

"If that's the case, no loan or anything else will draw him away. Please," Don Pedro took his daughter's hand. "Do not fix your mind on something you cannot have."

She gazed at him stubbornly. "Do not pay off the loan too soon, *por favor!*"

Don Pedro sighed. Women were so unreasonable, even Elena who had inherited his common sense.

22

The Morgan Stage left Whisky Flat for Placerville on the afternoon of August 24th at four o'clock. It had been due to leave at two, but there was a puzzling delay, considering that the stage office had announced it would accept no express shipments of gold later than the previous afternoon. Miners had thronged the office and deposited their hard-won dust and nuggets in the brass-bound express box, each in a rawhide bag with knotted drawstring and tag. But that had been the previous day, and apparently everything was ready when the stage arrived.

The stage was a shiny new Concord. Its door panels shone under their many coats of varnish; its yellow-ash wheels and undercarriage glistened brightly in the late afternoon sun; the six fresh horses snuffled and shorted and pranced restlessly in their gleaming new harness and brightwork. Only six passengers had been accepted for the trip. This was unusual and occasioned much irritation among those who were turned away. The six accepted were all male and were all armed.

On the box was Thad, holding the reins of the six restless horses. By his side was Jackson, a five-shooter in his belt, and a loaded short-barrelled shotgun between his knees. The station-agent at Whisky Flat, a bearded giant named Foster, with shaggy hair and corduroy pants, stood in front of the office and grinned and shouted through his beard, waving his slouch hat as Thad picked up the reins and slapped the horses' rumps. There was the usual crowd around to watch the stage depart.

A man at the edge of the crowd saw the stage loaded, then ran to his own horse that was tethered in the trees behind the town and galloped off to the southeast.

Thad nodded to Foster, slapped the horses' rumps again with the reins, called "Gee-up!" and snapped his whip thunderously over their heads. They sprang into eager action. The beautiful coach lurched and clattered into rapid motion. The onlookers cheered and waved their hats as the stage rattled off in a thick puff of dust.

Once out of town, Thad paced the horses into a steady trot. The country was open for a few miles, then the road climbed one of the Sierra foothills, where scrub trees and chaparral obscured the turns. Thad kept watching, his gaze darting from one side of the road to the other. Jackson did the same.

"Three miles ahead, the road curves around that brush-covered hill!" Thad shouted to Jackson over the clatter of the hooves and the rattle of the wheels. "Remember, that's where we thought something might happen."

Jackson did not try to be heard over the noise of the coach but merely nodded and gripped the shotgun tighter.

As the road wound upward, the horses' pace slowed. The odor of pine needles and an occasional waft of sage fragrance filled the air. The horses nodded and strained at their harness, and the coach, on its leather thorough-braces, rocked and rolled like a ship at sea. The air was hot and dry. Thad could feel the perspiration creeping down his back beneath his shirt. Part of that, he knew, was not due to the weather, but to the tension building up inside him. He was almost certain something was going to happen. If it did not, of course, all their preparations would have been in vain, and they would feel somewhat foolish. But Thad had a hunch of a sort that had seldom led him astray in the past.

This was the logical trip for a stage robbery to take place on. They were carrying the largest load of metal that would come out of Whisky Flat; it represented the first richness of the strike. News of the strike had shipped lashlike over all of California. That knew Jackson wsa right. Every down-at-heel hoodlum in the area would be thinking of the express boxes loaded with gold that were bound to come down from the diggings to the San Francisco and Stockton banks.

Thad peered into the trees and thought he saw movement. No, it was only a shadow from the lowering sun. Something would happen. He could feel it in his gut.

The beautiful, shiny Concord clattered on. One of the passengers stuck his head out of the window and called up to Thad, "Ain't we comin' to that spot you told us to watch out for?"

"Right," said Thad. "Another half mile." He pointed. "That hill ahead to the right, covered with brush. Road curves around it to the left. Sharp turn at the tip of the promontory. If I were doing it, that's where I'd do it."

The head disappeared inside the stage, and Thad could hear the clicking of gunbolts.

The stage rattled on, faster as it descended a declivity, and then slower as the road rose toward the brush-covered hill. The sun was lowering, but it was still above the hill, a bad plce for it to be for the stage driver, since it shone directly in his eyes as the hill neared. Thad squinted and felt his muscles tense as the stage veered around the blind curve.

A gun roared from ahead. The lead horses reared. Two figures, wearing floursacks over their heads with holes cut out for eyes appeared in the middle of the road. One was clutching a pistol, the other had a sawed-off shotgun.

"Halt!" one shouted. "Stand and deliver!"

Thad pulled up the team. His only other choice was to run over the highwayman, who then would have tried to use his shotgun. There was a half-smile on Thad's face as he did so, however. His hunch was borne out. He had guessed right. He made sure not to seem overly reluctant to surrender. Nor did Jackson, on the box beside him, even with his shotgun; nor did the passengers, inside the coach, seem unduly disturbed. They docilely alighted under orders from the flour sack-covered robbers and stood with their hands in the air. Immediately, they were relived of their arms by one of the bandits, while the other kept them covered.

The latter, a squat desperado with a sweaty shirt and brown pants stuffed into half-boots, gestured with his gun muzzle at Thad and Avery. "Git over there and jine 'em!" he ordered. Thad and the old man obeyed.

The other bandit, taller and clad in dark clothing below the flour sack mask, laid his revolver carefully on a rock and disappeared inside the coach. He busied himself for a moment, then called out.

"Here's the box, and it ain't even bolted down."

"Good!" the man holding the gun on Thad and his companions sounded jubilant. "Empty it out and we'll be on our way!"

There was a silence, a surprisingly long one, considering what had been said. There were thumps and scrapes from within the coach, and it rocked on its wheels. The sun bore down hotly from low in the sky, just tipping the trees on the western foothills, but it stil carried considerable summer authority. Insects buzzed in the heat, and Thad felt the perspiration trickle down his body. Not a leaf rustled. There was no breeze, no sound, except from the insects and the thumps, scrapes, and muttering from within the jiggling coach.

Thad and Avery looked at each other and smiled.

It gradually grew upon the highwayman holding the gun on them that something was wrong.

"What are you smirkin' about?" he demanded of Thad. Then he shouted at his colleague. "What's goin' on in there? What the hell's the matter?"

The tall, dark-clad man scrambled out of the coach

220

and came to his side.

"Thought you said the box wasn't even bolted down. What's wrong? Cain't you git it open?" the armed one demanded.

"I got it open all right." The tall man was panting with effort.

"Ain't the gold in it?"

"Yup."

"Then what the hell's the matter?"

"It's mercury amalgam, and it's in one piece. It must weight a ton. Can't budge it!"

The gunholder forgot himself sufficiently to turn a surprised face toward his associate. Then he snapped his gaze back toward his prisoners. "One piece!" he shouted. "How could that be? One piece?"

"They smelted it down. It's a two-foot brick. Take an army to lift it."

The short highwayman swore a series of oaths that further heated the hot summer twilight. He gave the shotgun to his accomplice. "Here! You hold this on 'em while I go take a look."

He angrily stumped off on his short legs, clambered into the stage, and busied himself within. In a moment he was out again. Thad wished he could see the expression on his face under the floursack and the color of it. He guessed it was red with rage. The man snatched his shotgun back from his colleague and addressed his prisoners.

"Goddamn smart alecks! Oughta kill you all, and maybe I'll damn well do it."

He was becoming so angry, he would be unpredictable. Thad gave his own right arm a sharp twist and jerk, receiving into his hand the snub-nosed derringer that slid down his sleeve. He glanced at his passengers and toward the pile of sidearms that had been taken from them. They were in a heap on a flat rock 20 feet away. He nodded slightly, as a signal to his companions, then fired the Derringer from waist level. The bullet hit the robber's right arm, surprised him, and swung him around. The robber swore in a thick voice and dropped the shotgun, stooped to grab for it. He was halted by Thad, who was now at his side and straightening him up forcibly with a strong grip on his collar.

Thad could hear his colleagues scrambling for their guns. In order to see what was happening, he jerked the squat robber around. All was in order. The tall, dark-clad man had already been relieved of both his shotgun and his pistol and was standing with both hands in the air. To wind up the action, Thad poked his own shorter prisoner in the back with his gun muzzle and pushed him closer to the others. The man swore again, gripping his bleeding right arm with his left hand.

Standing side by side, now captives themselves, the two highwaymen presented an undignified, almost a comic, picture. The flour sack masks made them look like Hallowe'en figures; and the height of one and squatness of the other made for a ludicrous contrast.

Thad stepped forard and jerked the mask from the short man. He had guessed right. It was Bronson. Bronson's face was red, his blond hair mussed, his little piggish blue eyes under their blonde brows darting venom at his captors. Jackson, meanwhile, had pulled of the mask of the taller man. While Bronson fumed, Mack maintained a stoic silence.

Thad moved close to Bronson. He looked down into the purple, sweating, angry face. Then, on an impulse, he drew him aside, out of earshot of the others, and asked in a low voice, "Who sent you? Who told you to set me up?"

Bronson glared. There was a short silence while he thought over the problem of whether he should divulge this information or whether he could use it for bargaining. He squinted up at Thad. "If I tell you, how about lettin' us go?"

Thad shook his head. "No," he said flatly. "I'll find out anyway. But you might as well save me the trouble. Your friend, however he is, let you down. He didn't give you enough information. He let you make fools of yourselves."

Bronson choked out, "That he did! It was your friend Moreau. He promised to buy whatever dust we got from your express box, for cash. He got us your stage time table and paid some feller in Whisky Flat to let us know when the stage started out."

That was enough for Thad. He pulled the short prisoner back toward the others and confirmed to Jackson, "You've been right all along."

Thad's jaw was set and his eyes determined as he herded the two captives toward the stage. The two blundering highwaymen were hustled inside the coach, under guard, and Thad climbed onto the box with Jackson. He snapped the reins briskly, and the horses lunged forward, jerking the stage into motion. Again, the beautiful shiny vehicle, rocking on its leather thoroughbraces, rolled down the rough and rocky dirt road toward Placerville.

Jackson cast a sly glance at Thad. "Are things clearin' up in your mind?" he asked.

"They sure are," said Thad. "They sure are. There's just one thing, one thing that still bothers me." He shook his head as if to cast an unpleasant thought out of his mind.

Jackson didn't bother to as. He knew what it was.

Back in San Francisco, with Bronson and his aide in jail, the newspapers were running sreaming headlines and lengthy columns about the coup and the capture.

The cleverness of Mr. Thaddeus Morgan, president of the Morgan Stage Lines, foiled two would-be highwaymen out of a rich haul on the stage run from Whisky Flat to Sacramento. Mr. Morgan smelted down the gold with mercury into amalgam, and carried it in one solid piece, after weighing the gold from each of his depositors so full value could be returned to them after the mercury was steamed off. The single piece proved too heavy for the robbers to lift or carry, and in the ensuing developments, Mr. Morgan personally attacked and disarmed one of the outlaws, thus giving an opportunity for his passengers to seize and make prisoner the other. . . .

In their little office, now glinting with golden morning sunlight, Jackson confronted Thad. "Next?" he demanded. "I kin hardly wait to round up that sneaky-eyed sonofabitch who's done you so much dirt and made up to Jo."

Thad did not respond but stared moodily into space.

"How you plannin' to do it? I hope I can help," Jackson persisted.

Thad stood up and shook his head wearily. "I'm not going after Clay," he said dully.

Jackson's mouth gaped. "Not goin' after him? Why, with what you know, and all the witnesses, you canput thim in the calaboose for twenty years! What do you mean you're not goin' aftger him?"

Thad seated himself again, slowly. His face was drawn and tired. Jackson knew a struggle was going on inside him.

Thad finally spoke. "If Jo wants him, I'm not going to hurt him."

Jackson was aghast and showed it. "But if she thinks she wants him, you can show her what kind of a snake he is, and git her back! What's eatin' you, Thad? Your thinkin's all twisted."

"If she wants him, I won't hurt him. That would hurt her too."

Jackson could see Thad's mind was firming on the decision, and he talked fast. "But if he's a no-good, you shore don't want *her* to be hurt by him! And that's what he'll do. He'll hurt her. That's the kind of feller he is!" He went on fuming, but Thad finally quieted him with a lifted hand.

"Avery, I know you're trying to be helpful, but I've made up my mind." Thad shook his head stubbornly.

"I could never get her back by damaging Clay. Maybe, if I let him alone, he'll behave himself."

The old man threw up his hands. "You're beyond me, pard! You're beyond me! I cain't see how your mind's workin'." He talked on, fruitlessly, and finally stamped out of the office, red-faced and angry.

At the Rancho Santa Elena, the late summer night was warm, and Don Pedro and his daughter were sitting with Thad on the veranda, looking up at the icy-white twinkling stars above the San Joaquin Valley.

"You did not need to make a special trip for another payment on the loan," the old rancher said for the second time. "You are taking it too seriously. You are making much money, and I am more than able to pay the interest."

"I want you to do more than that," Thad said. "I want you to get most of that loan paid off quickly, so the penalty payment when you wind it up won't be large."

Don Pedro leaned forward in his rocking chair. "Wind it up? But I do not need to wind it up! I am making the payments easily and have already reduced it by a fourth."

Thad shook his head and smiled sympathetically. "Unless you and your other Californio friends begin to realize that you can't solve problems by owing a lot of money at high interest, you're going to lose your land."

Elena, sitting close to Thad in the darkness, said, "We almost did. And you saved us."

"Well, however that may be," said Thad, "you must realize that a little borrowing is all right, but a lot of borrowing is dangerous. You're not in a bad position now, but you shouldn't owe money any longer than necessary. Eight percent piles up very fast."

They talked on. The old don finally excused himself, leaving Thad and the girl alone on the veranda. Thad found himself with his old trouble—not knowing what to say in the presence of a woman. She sat there in the darkness, her perfect profile silhouetted by the reflected light from the *sala* window. Thad knew she was waiting for him to make the first move, and he knew it was his place to make it. He had come to the ranch knowing that this opportunity would present itself, and he had deliberately come to test himself. If Jo were lost to him, he would have to stop thinking about her. The best way to do that would be to look at someone else.

Thad knew he should have been grateful for Elena's availability. He was not. His mind was in turmoil. On the long saddle ride down from San Francisco to San Jose and beyond, he had thought more than once of the gigantic condor winging its silent and graceful way among the crags of the coast range. Above the storms. Above the storms. With wings big enough to stay above the storms. He had always felt that his wings were in his moneybelt, that golden wings would carry him as easily above the weather as the condor's dark feathered ones.

Yet he had found it was not true. He now had his golden wings, and they were growing and strengthening rapidly. His moneybelt was satisfactorily heavy. His stage line was prospering. He had established an express business that he had saved, through foresight, from ruin by criminals, and he was operating a banking business himself, which also was growing apace. His future in California seemed secure. He had his golden sings, but they were not carrying him above the weather.

"Elena," he said finally, "I wish I could say the right thing in the right way. You know my situation, and I—"

"Oh, Señor!" she swung toward him gratefully. "I know, and you need not talk of it. I only pray that it does not keep us apart!" He reached awkwardly for her hand. She laughed softly. "There is no *duenna* here tonight. Otherwise this would not be permitted."

They sat silently for a time. Finally, the girl said, "I do not wish to be the one you turn to because you cannot go to the one you really want. I hope that is not the case."

226

Thad did not answer. His lack of response made her look quickly toward him. "I don't want that either, Elena," he said finally. He withdrew his hand from hers. "I suppose it is better that we do not talk of these things."

Her mood changed. She was now sober-faced in the darkness, as she peered searchingly at his face. Suddenly, she felt a coldness between them, a barrier that was due to more than Thad's difficulty with words. She opened her mouth to speak, then closed it.

Thad was not behaving as a suitor should. Nor was he behaving even as a man on the rebound would act. He was too silent, too sad, too gloomy. She was there, but she might as well not have been, for all the effect it had on his emotions.

She had thought of him, dreamed of him, welcomed his visits, hoped for just such a time as this. But now there was a barrier she could not surmount.

Elena sat for a long moment longer. Then she rose. "Good night, Señor," she said softly and sadly. "Good night, Thad." She knew it was the last time she would call him that.

Thad did not answer as she went quietly into the *sala*. He was still sitting there as Elena extinguished the lamps, leaving only one for him to see his way down the hall to his own room off the fragrant, flowering courtyard.

Jo sat alone in her room in the Union Hotel, looking out the window at the first wisps of low fog swirling in over the Golden Gate and destined soon to cast a thick, rapidly-moving, mysterious pall over the city. She had more than an hour before she had to leave for the Golden Eagle. She did not want to go. She was depressed and miserable. The thickening fog with its building gloom matched her spirits.

Where was Thad? Why did he not return to her? Thad the dependable, Thad the loyal, Thad who had been her slave?

As the weeks passed, she had told herself, he was gone for good. That was the reasonable, sensible, logical conclusion. There could be no other answer. Yet her heart refused to accept that final, terminal fact as true.

Jo gazed around the little hotel room. She had attempted to make it attractive. There were vases and some flowers from the street vendors who were beginning to set up shop year-round on the corners of the streets of San Francisco. There was a new and colorful quilt on the bed. She had added a lamp and a table to the hotel's spartan furnishings. She realized now that, ever time she had bought something for the room, she wondered how Thad would like it.

She was miserable, and felt sorry for herself. In recent days, another feeling had been added to her consciousness. She realized she herself was at least partly to blame. This was a new sensation to her. It was uncomfortable. She had never felt that way before. If things went wrong, it was always someone else's fault, never her own. She knew that this wrongness, the larges and most massive problem she had ever experienced next to the death of her daughter, was there because she had not only let it happen, but had encouraged it in a spirit of perversity and bitterness.

Much to Jo's regret, it was time to to go work. She donned the red-silk dress, placed the jewelry in her purse, put on a long cloak over the finery, and descended the stairs to the street. As she passed the desk, the clerk looked up appreciatively. She was the most beautiful thing he had ever seen, and he looked forward to her nightly descent of the stairs. She seldom spoke to him, seldom even nodded. Tonight was different. She smiled at him somewhat sadly. She seemed to have something on her mind.

She hung up her coat at the Golden Eagle. It was already noisy with the early-evening crowd, its tinny piano pounding out raucous tunes of the day. Jo took up a sheaf of the expensively printed menus in her hand

and stationed herself at the entrance to the restaurant. She hoped Clay was not there. She did not wish to talk to him. He was becoming more open in his approaches to her. Almost every time he saw her, he made a slurring reference to the husband who had deserted her, expressed a snide hope that she would be able to get along on her own without a man's help. She was growing to dislike Clay. He was handsome and he could be charming, but in her mind was the fear that she would lose her job before she had money enough to return to Baltimore. Ship's passage was high and getting higher. Even if she had the money, she was almost afraid to go alone in the motley throng of down-at-heels adventurers returning bitter and penniless from the diggings, as well as the professional con men who traveled the route regularly, making victims of the passengers, not to mention the drunken rowdies who looked on an unescorted woman as fair game.

Occasionally, Jo had awakened in the middle of the night, gripped with a fear bordering on panic. She was at the ends of the earth, among dangerous people, and Thad was not with her.

Customers were arriving, and she gave them the set smile, the courtesy, the attention that Clay swore had doubled the restaurant business since she had arrived. A stocky, thickset man with gray mustache, expensive clothing, and shiny boots arrived and doffed his hat to her.

'Mrs. Morgan, how are you?"

She was instantly uncomfortable. "Good evening, Mr. Benson. May I show you to a table?"

"Indeed!" He smiled in friendly fashion. "Your husband is to be congratulated. He has a sharp eye for business. Going to be a tycoon before long!" He chuckled as he seated himself and accepted a menu.

"Do you see him often?" Jo's voice trembled, and Benson noticed it.

"Yes, of course. You know we're doing business together." He hesitated. "You sound as if you don't."

She bit her lip. "He is not with me."

Benson's brow shot up. "Not with you? The man must be out of his mind. What's the reason?" he asked directly, then drew back from the question. "That was presumptuous of me to ask." He gazed at her thoughtfully. "Will you join me in a glass of win? It would give us a chance to talk. And I assure you it's under different circumstances than the last time. Then, I didn't know how things were. I do now. The invitation is for conversation, nothing else."

Jo was silent for a moment. Benson's square, strong, intelligent face, and his eyes with their powerful, direct gaze, his confidence-inspiring manner gave her a sudden, desperate desire to talk to him. She could trust him, she felt. It was different from before. Then he was courting. Tonight he was playing the role of a friend.

She nodded. "Thank you."

He rose with alacrity and pulled out a chair for her, then seated himself as he motioned for the waiter. "Last week I found a wine that I would like to pour for you." When the wine came, he toasted her with a courtly gesture, and then leaned forward to ask a personal question. "What's come between you and your husband? He's smart, tough, and honest, and I have a lot of respect for him. And you, you're the prettiest thing west of the Rockies. It's not right to have trouble between two such remarkable people. What's the problem?"

Jo looked down at the tablecloth. It was some time before she answered. "I've been waiting for him," she said brokenly. "And he hasn't come."

There was a lengthy silence between them, and he took up the conversation as if the subject had never been brought up. He tried to cheer her with anecdotes of the city, succeeding in making her smile at least twice. He issued no more invitations, thanked her for joining him, and, after he finished his dinner, bade her adieu.

That night, as Clay walked Jo home in the darkness, he said, "Jo, I've come to a conclusion."

She did not answer.

"Aren't you interested?"

"Does it have to do with me?"

His voice hardened. "It certainly does. You're playing me for a fool. This arms-length treatment has got to stop."

"Arm's-length treatment? I'm at the Golden Eagle practically every waking moment. I've given it everything I have. You can't have forgotten the columns about me in the *Advertiser*!" Her heart sank and she felt a shiver of fear.

Clay's voice, always smooth and compelling, now had a note of anger in it that she had not heard before. "That, Jo, is not the point," Clay retorted. "Your husband's deserted you. He's not coming back. When are you going to realize it?"

"Don't talk that way about Thad!"

"You've certainly changed your tune. Not long ago you wouldn't even speak to him."

"I was a fool."

He paused in the fan of light before the open door of the Union Hotel. "You're still a fool, Jo. But you're not going to make a fool of me. I saved you and Thad from being marooned at Panama. I gave you a job when you needed one. Now I want something back."

She felt cold. She had known this was coming but had determinedly not thought about it. Now it was here.

"I've built a house on Russian Hill, as you know. It's a fine house. There's room in it for more than one man and a couple to help." He turned to her and faced her squarely. "there's room in it for you, Jo, and I want you to come."

In his mind was the memory of his last talk with Benson. "I've decided against loaning you any more money, Moreau," Benson had said. "You're moving in circles that are a little too fast for me."

"Fast circles?" Clay had challenged, attempting a

231

nonchalance about what appeared to be a fast-fading proposition. "I've been running full steam trying to keep up with you!"

"Our worlds are different," Benson had responded. "The people you run around with may be all right for you, but they're wrong for me. There's talk. This isn't a big town, and there's talk."

The loan had fallen through. Clay no longer had to consider what Benson might think of his relationship with Jo. There was no longer anything to keep him from her.

Jo took a long breath, studying Clay's face in the streak of light. His satanic brows were uptilted; the dark, intelligent eyes, hard and unyielding; the handsome face cold. He had clearly served her an ultimatum. Still, she detected a degree of blankness in his demeanor, as though his thoughts were partly on something else. Her thoughts, too, were racing.

"Russian Hill is a splendid address, Clay. But what if I don't make the move?"

"Then, Jo, I think we will need a new hostess at the Golden Eagle."

They stood in the yellow fanlight from the lobby, the fog fingers swirling above their heads, the mutter of the late-night city around them. The illuminated tents glowed up and down the street; an occasional pedestrian, drunk and unsteady on his feet, shuffled by.

"Can I tell you tomorrow?" she asked.

"It'll have to be tomorrow." He tipped his dark, broad-brimmed sombrero to her, smiled sardonically, and utterly without humor turned on his heel and departed. His long black coat and shiny black boots were visible for half a block in the half light.

Jo stood there motionless, watching him. He did not look back. Grimly, she entered the hotel and climbed the stairs to her room.

23

The morning sun shone brightly through the window-panes of the Bank of Mission Valley. The panes were made of rolled glass that had been shipped around the Horn. The view through them was rather wavery. A corner had been broken off one of the largest panes in transit, and it had been covered by a diagonal wooden corner.

Ezra Benson sat in his flowered vest in his office. His back was straight, and papers were spread in front o fhim, but he was not looking at his desk work. There was a small frown on his brow. He went to the door and spoke to his secretary in the outer office. "Has Thad Morgan been in?"

The secretary, a severe-looking woman with square spectacles and hair pulled sharply back into a tight bun, shook her head. "No, sir. Not today."

"Well, when he comes, make sure that he doesn't get away without my seeing him."

She assented, but he stood ther ein the doorway for a moment longer. "We know where he lives, don't we?"

"Yes, sir. He's in a hotel down by Portsmouth Square."

"Well, send a message to him. Tell him I want to see him. Today."

Benson returned to his office and resumed his work. He could not rid himself of the memory of Jo's face when she said, "I've been waiting for him. But he hasn't come."

He shook his head and bent to his desk. Shortly before noon, when Thad arrived, the relief on his face was evident.

"I got your message," Thad said. "You're timing was good. I was about to start for Sacramento. What can I do for you?"

Benson regarded him carefully. Thad's prosperity was beginning to show. His dark frock coat was well tailored, his boots gleamed, and the silver buckle on his broad-brimmed flat-topped sombrero was thick and heavy.

Benson leaned back in his chair and grinned. "You're causing people a hell of a lot of trouble."

"Oh? In what way?"

"Well, son, it's none of my business, and probably I should bite my tongue, but I hate to stand by and see a whirlwind develop into a hurricane if I can do something about it."

Thad's brows rose, but he said nothing.

"I like you, and I like your wife. I met her at the Golden Eagle, as you know."

"I know," said Thad flatly. He gazed hard into Benson's face.

"Relax. I didn't know she was married. I do now. She's feeling pretty bad because she doesn't see you."

"You must have gotten pretty well acquainted with her." Thad's voice was hard.

"Oh, come on. Put down your gun. I don't want to be a busybody, but I'm going to take that chance because I like both of you. I think it's a damn shame that you're not together. You both want it."

Thad rose stiffly. "Is that all?"

Benson sighed. "Yes, that's all. And I can see I've gone about it wrong."

"Thanks for your interest," Thad said, turned on his heel, and departed.

Seething, as he walked down the street, it took awhile

before he realized that what he was feeling was jealous anger. Maybe Benson was right. Thad did not go to the stage office immediately but sat in his room for an hour, thinking. He wished he had not stalked off in a huff. "You both want it," Benson had said. How did he know that? Had Jo confided in him? The very thought made him angry, but he wished he had pursued the subject. What had she said? How had she said it? It was too late, Thad was sure, and he was beginning to reconcile himself to that fact. But was there still some hope?

Ever since his visit to San Jose and the Rancho Santa Elena, Thad had realized that Jo was still terribly important to him. Every time he thought of going to her, though, he drew back, because he was still afraid of failure. Another rejection, he knew, would be the last. It would end whatever hopes he had. He told himself day after day that he would go to her tomorrow, when he was more sure of himself. Tomorrow and tomorrow.

He finally rose and departed for the office of the Morgan Stage Company. En route, he told himself that, in view of what Benson had said, he *would* go to see Jo—tomorrow.

Jo's day was one of misery. She sat in her room during almost all of it, thinking of Thad, thinking of Clay and his hard eyes and angry determination of the night before. She thought also of the fact that she didn't have enough money to get back to Baltimore. Maybe Clay had insured that in the level of wages he paid her.

What would she do, if she were no longer employed at the Golden Eagle? She was not skilled as a seamstress or a cook. She might start a restaurant, but you needed money for that in San Francisco. As the days passed, it took more and more money. Working for a merchant or a tavern keeper also repelled her. There were not many jobs for women, and many of them labeled the woman as loose and approachable—as her job at the Golden Eagle almost had.

235

In the middle of the day, Jo went out on the street. Just as she came out, one of the shiny, glittering Concords of the Morgan Stage Company clattered by. Its six-horse team looked proud and fresh in their gleaming harness; the whip on the box cracked his lash picturesquely for the benefit of onlookers; and the coach was full of passengers to Stockton.

Thad *was* successful. What had Benson said? He was becoming a tycoon. Maybe that was why he had not come back to her. She had known of situations like that, where a man, dedicated to a woman, gradually forgot her when he became rich and was diverted to other interests. The thought angered her. Up to that moment, she had been thinking of going to him. The thought was difficult for her proud spirit. Never in her life had she admitted she was wrong. Never had she told him she was sorry for anything. She had always depended on him to take the blame, to make amends, to assume responsibility, to initiate the reconciliation process.

Now it appeared that was not going to happen. It was up to Jo to make the first move. For the first time in her life, she was beginning to admit to herself, albeit reluctantly and bitterly and unwillingly, that she could have, might have, been wrong. However, she was still utterly unwilling to bring herself to full surrender.

As Jo brooded, her anger rose, the same ready anger that always seethed and bubbled below the surface. Angrily she went back to her room. She would not go to Thad. If he did not come to her, to hell with him! Nor would she live like a beggar. She stood in the room looking out on the street. The afternoon fog was just beginning to drift in, and she knew that within the hour the city would be covered by a low, gray pall.

The hours were passing. She would have to go to the Golden Eagle. Clay would be there, waiting for an answer. There was still time for her to go to Thad, but she shook her head and silently rejected that. She could not demean herself, even to the husband who loved her, especially to him.

She thought a long time, as the fog covered the city, and the room grew dark. Then she rose and clenched her fists.

She would go to Clay and she would tell him yes. It was time for her to get ready for her job at the Golden Eagle.

It was half-past five. The city was gloomy, and the Japanese-lantern effect of the lighted tent-topped buildings was beginning to glow on the streets. In her room, Jo was dressed in her finery. She regarded herself in the blotched mirror and stiffened her resolve.

She had made up her mind. Her husband had deserted her. She would not go to him. She would not live as a beggar. There was only one answer.

Clay.

And yet, as she turned away from the mirror, a sense of misgiving overwhelmed her.

She did not want Clay. She wanted Thad.

She donned her cloak, and took a final look at herself in the mirror, made certain her jewelry was safely concealed in her purse, left the room, and headed for the stairs.

A man was ascending them, his face unrecognizable in the darkness. She pulled to one side to let him pass, but he did not. Instead, he halted and faced her.

"Jo," he said.

It was Clay. His face was sober. His eyes glinted, and the satanic brows were drawn together in a frown.

"Why are you here? I'm not late. I'm on my way to the Golden Eagle." The words tumbled from Jo's lips.

Looking up at her as she stood above him on the stairs, Clay took a deep, determined breath. "I came for your answer. If it's the wrong one, you won't be needed at the Golden Eagle."

"A stairway's no place to talk. Let's wait until the night's work is done," she replied.

"You're not listening," Clay retorted. "There's only

237

one answer that will get you to the restaurant again."

Jo suddenly felt frightened. She groped for words, for an approach that would soften that hard-eyed face below hers. "Clay, that's hardly the way to court a girl." She faltered, attempting to banter.

He refused to seize the bait. "Don't be ridiculous, Jo. This is no courtship. This is a business proposition. I've done you and your husband favors. Important ones. Now it's payoff time."

Jo wondered how she could ever have contemplated, even for a moment, surrendering to Clay. He was hard, inhuman, cruel. Not like Thad, who could not find words but who would not harm anyone, and who loved her, and who had been so terribly hurt by her stubborn insensitivity. She supposed it was too late. Thad was gone. Certainly, Clay was no adequate substitute.

"Well?" Clay said again in an insolent, demanding voice.

"No!" said Jo. "No! Compared with Thad, you're nothing! I wouldn't go with you to Russian Hill or anywhere!"

Clay's face whitened with rage. He was not accustomed to being denied. He advanced a step up the stairs, and she retreated.

"Ever since I've known you, you've accepted favors from me right and left. Gold for the passage from Panama to San Francisco. A plush position at the restaurant. Without it, you couldn't have paid your bils, let alone live in any style! But the last straw was when you killed me off with Benson. Come with me now to Russian Hill, or I'm cutting off my lifeline to you. Then where will you be? Thad isn't coming back. You know that."

A voice rose frm the foot of the stairs. "Where did you get that idea, that he isn't coming back?"

Both of them whirled and peered into the darkness below. A powerful man stood there, a man with gleaming boots and a gleaming silver watch chain that shone even in the dim light. The face was a blur, but the voice was Thad's.

Thad ascended the stairs. For the first time in his life, Clay was at a loss for words. "Jo," Thad said. His question came easily. For the first time, he was not at a loss for words. "Is this man bothering you?"

"Yes!" she said. "Yes, he is!"

Thad advanced until he was on the step below Clay's. His face was now seen clearly, and his eyes were firm and kind and his jaw square and hard.

"In that case," he said in a low voice, "he'd better leave!"

Again there was a silence. Clay had turned from Jo and was standing on the stairway between them. He stared at Thad and finally found his voice.

"After all I've done for both of you! I should have let you rot in Panama!"

Thad's huge hand reached forward and took hold of Clay's cravat and collar. "I'm not much good at arguing," Thad said. "Are you going downstairs, or do I have to push you?"

Choking, Clay clutched at the strong hand that had a firm grip on his collar and shouted in a voice that was rapidly being stifled, "Get your hands off me, you big ox! You deserted her. Why should I, or anyone, have pretended she is still your wife?"

Thad's hand tightened, and his voice grew lower and more threatening. "Nobody can say she's not my wife!" he declared. He pulled and lifted, and Clay's slighter body rose in the air, arced, and crashed on the lower stairs. Thad stood there as Clay picked himself up and debated whether or not to attack. He decided against it and, silently and seething with rage, bolted out of the door and onto the street.

Thad's voice had a directness and assuredness that Jo had never heard before. "You've just quit your job."

She stood there defiantly, facing him on the dimly-lit staircase until she said, "Don't think you can dictate to me, Thad Morgan!"

There was another pause, and he laughed. "I never thought I could, Jo. But now I'm doing it, and you've just quit your job."

He took her arm, and she accompanied him up the stairs.